BLOOD DEEP

Colin Stubbington

firecrest

CHIVERS PRESS
BATH

First published in Great Britain by Sphere Books Limited

First hardback edition 1983 by Chivers Press by arrangement with Sphere Books Limited

0 85997 529 0

Copyright © Colin Stubbington 1983

British Library Cataloguing in Publication Data

Stubbington, Colin
Blood deep.—(Firecrest books)
I. Title
823'.914[F]   PR6069.T/

ISBN 0–85997–529–0

Photoset, printed and bound
in Great Britain by
REDWOOD BURN LIMITED
Trowbridge, Wiltshire

Part One

July 1915

The July gale was short but severe, rucking the cold grey waters of the North Sea into a petulant fury that came sweeping across the fifty or so sea-miles from the Bligh Bank to the Aldeburgh Napes.

At ten fathoms, the effect of the gale was minimal; a mild rocking motion, enough to begin scouring away the sand that was banking round the whale-like object that had lain bottomed there these last six months.

Within the object itself, another factor assisted the gale: compressed air which, seeping through tight-shut valves, insidiously forced the water from the buoyancy tanks beyond. This slow filtration had been happening for some time now, so that the whale's weight and that of the water surrounding it were nearly equal.

And still the rocking motion of the gale kept up its argument, staining the restless water with drifting clouds of silt and mud. Bubble by bubble, the compressed air squeezed past its constraining valves, till at last, the whale shuddered, shifted, and then bumped along the sea-bed, sending a school of fish scudding before it. But, by early evening, its weight was no longer merely equal to that of the surrounding water, but lighter; and this time, the whale kept on rising, till at last, reluctantly, it broke surface, with the sea cascading from scoured and rusting topsides.

'Till the sea shall give up its dead . . .' an observer might have thought, had he seen the spectacle. But there was no observer, and then the whole picture was almost instantly blotted out by a squall which, coming like a black smear out of the south-east, hissed across the leaping wave tops.

Night fell . . .

Two dawns later, the whale came to rest in the shallows of the Sizewell Bank. Even stranded, its unmistakable shape still held a palpable air of menace; the sea had indeed

1

given up its dead . . .

Ashore, telephone bells began ringing to police and coastguard stations. Like a stone dropped into a still pool the stranded U-boat sent out widening rings—rings that rippled into unlikely backwaters, and set bobbing all manner of hidden interests.

The next morning, tugs appeared off the Sizewell Bank, moving cautiously in among the shoals separating them from the derelict. The tow was secured with difficulty, and the haul southwards to Harwich begun. Twice, the captive broke free before she was finally brought in past Landguard Point and persuaded into an unfrequented creek.

And then the experts came on board her. A day after the U-boat was finally opened up, a small group of these huddled round the smoky stove of a hut on the muddy foreshore.

Brandy flasks were circulating freely. Yesterday, when cutting-torch and chisel had finally won their way into the submarine, a green cloud of foetid, mephitic gases had burst from her and spread across the face of the creek. It had taken twenty-four hours before it was deemed safe for anyone to venture down into the submarine's interior.

Even before a rum-primed detail was sent down to remove the bodies of the U-boat's crew, a group of intelligence officers clambered down her conning-tower ladder. Despite surgical masks and the Lysol which had been sprayed into the U-boat's interior, the stench of death and dissolution was still intolerable.

Nor, a sharp-faced officer told himself, was it easy to maintain one's equanimity whilst leaning over the waxy, chlorine-blistered face of a corpse and groping in the poor devil's pockets for letters or wallet.

For relief, he turned to the U-boat's log—a log that was limp with condensation and green with mould. The last entry was dated exactly six months before. Presumably, the submarine must have bottomed for the night, and her crew had then suffocated as poisonous gases had seeped through the length of the boat. It had so nearly happened before . . .

2

Three hours later, the thin-faced officer stood in the hut on the creek's muddy foreshore. A diffident young sub-lieutenant pushed a letter towards him.

'This was on the submarine's C.O., sir. At first glance it would seem to be your pigeon . . .'

The older man took the letter, a paragraph near its middle catching his attention:

As for Wolf, he read, *he is on top of the world as you might well imagine. Instead of telling him to go away—as we all said they would—Top-Brass received him with open arms. Evidently, they'll be only too pleased to put his scheme into practice when the time's ripe. They've actually dignified his crazy idea with the title* Plan Atlantis. *The whole business has now become* TOP SECRET, *of course—so secret, that even Wolf's not supposed to know anything about it any more! He's far too junior! Anyway, when High Command does choose to let that particular cat out of the bag, it should catch the Allies where it hurts. I'm all for that, of course—but you can bet your last pfennig that it'll be top-brass that bags the glory and not poor old Wolf. Anyway, old fellow, for God's sake remember that all this is now under wraps and don't breathe a word . . .*

The letter tailed off into—this time—innocent gossip. Taking a notebook from his pocket, the lean-faced officer copied the letter out in full, then handed it back to the sub-lieutenant.

'Thank you, Mr Shellthorpe. As you say, the letter is most interesting. Is there a telephone anywhere here, do you know?'

'There's one in the next hut along the foreshore,' Shellthorpe advised.

'I'm deeply grateful to you.' The sharp-faced officer nodded and left the hut.

'Ah-ha!' someone said; 'whatever was in that letter of yours, Shellthorpe?'

'I'm not sure . . .'

'Well Casserlly is. I've only ever seen that expression on his face when he thinks there's something pretty big in the wind . . .'

3

But the wind's logic is often elusive and inscrutable. That letter found on the U-boat's dead captain left Casserlly with a puzzle that had all its pieces missing, bar one. A name. *Plan Atlantis* . . .

He spent a long afternoon in the library of the British Museum and emerged into the late afternoon sun with something akin to mental indigestion—and very little wiser.

Atlantis. Even the exact locale of that mythical continent was a matter of conjecture. But, Casserlly consoled himself, surely the fact that the Hun had chosen this name for an intended project told him *something*?

He carefully marshalled such small facts as he knew. Atlantis itself had disappeared beneath the sea. *U-31's* dead captain—and, presumably, the letter writer and the unknown Wolf—were all submarine officers, which reinforced the implication that *Plan Atlantis* had to do with undersea warfare.

Think, man! Casserlly goaded himself, until slowly, the letter's internal evidence began sorting itself into shape.

Firstly: *U-31's* dead captain had been a Kapitän-Leutnant Walter Keppler, with a wife named Hildegarde, and two small children, Hedda and Wolf.

Secondly: the letter-writer had used the familiar 'du'. Even more revealingly, he had addressed Keppler as 'Walter', and had referred to their mutal friend as 'Wolf'. This suggested that all three officers were very close friends indeed—and presumably of the same rank and similar seniority.

Casserlly paused and considered: what else was implied by this closeness of the three officers? That all three commanded their own submarines, perhaps; and that the unknown 'Wolf' as well as being something of a joke to his friends, must be something of a highflyer if he had been able to convince the German top-brass as to the soundness of his scheme . . .

Here, Casserlly brought the matter to the attention of his

4

own superiors—and discovered them less inclined than himself to take *Plan Atlantis* seriously. There were more urgent matters at hand. 1915 was proving a bleak year for the Allies, with one set-back after another, underlined by the continuing disasters in the Dardanelles. For a day or two, Casserlly doubted his own judgment—but then, his earlier intuition reaserted itself.

Amongst the many duties of Casserlly's Department, was that of re-interrogating newly-captured German officers. Interrogation, Casserlly had discovered, was an art in itself, and he had learnt a great deal since the beginning of the war.

A friendly approach and an appearance of knowing more than he in fact did, were both important parts of his stock in trade. Newly-captured prisoners of war reacted not-so very unlike newly-arrested criminals. The loss of freedom and the shock of capture were much the same.

In such a situation, a man felt relief at seeing a sympathetic face; his vigilance relaxed, and—as often as not—he talked.

Casserlly primed his subordinates as to the contents of Walter Keppler's letter, and himself interrogated any prisoners referred to him as being likely material. But he discovered little. In the latter months of 1915, U-boat activity in the Atlantic fell away; submarine sinkings were minimal and survivors fewer. *Plan Atlantis* remained a name and nothing more—its place, timing, and purpose, obscure.

Indeed, it was not until the following spring that Casserlly gained his first tenuous lead, when, in March, a sharp little battle in the North Sea between British and German destroyers provided more interrogation work than the Department had seen in months. The Navy had done its job well, and two German destroyers had been sent to the bottom.

Casserlly himself questioned the captain of the smaller of these, a guarded Kapitän-Leutnant Braun, still professionally sore at being bested after his promised light-cruiser support had failed to materialise.

Judicious sympathy soon loosened Braun's tongue; his

suspicions eased, until at last, with the air of the interrogation room blue with tobacco smoke, he and Casserlly were talking as one professional naval man to another.

Verdamnt! Braun growled. None of this would ever have happened if he'd stuck to submarines. Hiding his ignorance that the German had ever served in U-boats, Casserlly probed deeper, and the conversation was deviously brought round to the subject of Walter Keppler.

Surely, Casserlly hazarded, *U-31*'s disappearance must have cost a lot of head-shaking? Braun agreed that it had; eventually, it had been assumed that the submarine had been mined. If you asked him, the whole business had been preying on Willi von Mander's mind up to the time of his own final patrol. At least, that's what Wolf Kattschner had reckoned—and he should have known, being such a close friend of both. The 'Unholy Trinity' the three had always been known as . . .

'Ah, Kattschner,' Casserlly said; 'That's the very clever fellow, isn't it? The chap with all the bright ideas . . .'

Braun laughed: yes, clever—that summed Wolf up. The fellow always had a bee in his bonnet about something. He'd been kicked out to the Adriatic now to liaise with the Austrians—which served him right. Among Kattschner's many other lunacies he had once taken an extended period of unpaid leave in order to explore that part of the Med. Mind you, Braun explained, that hadn't been the Adriatic, now he came to think of it, but the Aegean . . .

A *fascinating* corner of the world, Casserlly agreed; *he'd* once spent a delightful cruise in the Dodecanese . . .

'The Cyclades was Wolf's stamping ground,' Braun said.

Perhaps he'd been indiscreet enough to show his triumph too openly, Casserlly afterwards accused himself—but, at this point, Braun had frowned, stubbed out his cigarette, and had refused to be drawn any further.

Still, Casserlly consoled himself, he could now make an educated guess as to the likeliest proving ground for Master Kattschner's little schemes. The name *Plan Atlantis* had been a pretty peice of deception. But, Casserlly asked himself: how much farther had he *really* got? Of *Plan*

Atlantis's purpose or likely timing, he still knew nothing.

Even so, he took his interrogation notes upstairs to the Department's Chief—that majestical officer known throughout the Service as the 'Panjandrum'. But Rear-Admiral Hawes remained determinedly unconvinced. Besides, he argued, if anything *did* blow up in those waters, the Aegean Squadron would be perfectly capable of dealing with it. Casserlly was dismissed. Outside the Panjandrum's door, he shook his head ruefully . . .

Still: there were other sources of information that he could tap—sources much nearer the likely epicentre of the coming storm . . .

Part Two

May–June 1916

At night, Athens stank of intrigue. It hung hotly on the windless darkness, palpable as the jasmine scent coming from the freshly-watered gardens lying on each side of the road leading out from the city.

Sandalled footsteps sounded on the shadowy roadway. The walker moved as quickly as he dared, intimidated by his sense of the night's watchfulness. Despite his care, he was by no means certain that he was unfollowed. Twice, he thought he had heard the stealthy sounds of footsteps following his own through the darkness. Forty minutes since, he had left Kolonaki; now, he was moving steadily upwards through the clutter of straggling suburbs that led to the outlying village of Kipseli.

The hurrying man had no great love for Athens. An islander himself, he felt stifled; an exile from the salt honesty of the sea. The Athens night had a thunderous clamminess that set his skin crawling; sweat tickled in his beard, and oozed stickily down the small of his spine.

He cursed softly but vividly—then grinned into his beard, remembering the boyhood mentor whose own language had so often smacked more of the sea than the seminary. Angered, Father Iannis had been wont to express himself with the fluent colour of the Piraeus waterfront. Remembrance of Father Iannis made the walker conscious of the black and clinging folds of the habit flapping against his legs, and the stove-pipe hat jammed down on his head.

Measuring his pace to his cassock, he strode on up through Kipseli—a sight so commonplace as to pass unnoticed; just one more priest, busy about some sacred duty . . .

All the same, he *was* noticed. A small child rushed at him out of the darkness, plucked at his sleeve, then kissed his hand. He muttered a blessing and moved on. Someone

8

called to the little girl, and she skipped off into the shadows.

Although it was nearly midnight, people still sat at their doorways; others thronged a roadside *taberna*, the lamplight drawing their faces in abrupt planes of light and dark. Enviously, he heard the chink of wine glasses, and his nose caught the pungent reek of Balkan tobacco.

As he passed the *taberna*, his ear caught noisy scraps of argument: 'The King ... Venizelos ... The election ... *Democracia*!'

He drew a despairing breath. *Politics*! The everlasting curse and preoccupation of his country always precariously poised between a turbulent *demos* and a foolish king.

Poor Greece ...

But, thankfully, the *taberna* wiseacres' argument kept them too busy to have eyes for the hurrying priest. Despite his earlier half-impression of being followed, he began to feel an increasing confidence.

Kipseli petered out at last; and then he found himself moving along a bare shoulder of hillside. With the sweat now ice-cold between his shoulder blades, he paused for a moment or two to get his bearings. Apart from the distant twanging of a *bouzouki* there was no sound from below him.

Drawing breath, he veered to his right where the steep lump of Tourko Vouno showed above him, black against the starshine. Lifting the skirts of his cassock, he set himself to climb, picking his way upward over ridged croppings of grey limestone. The scent of crushed thyme rose up from beneath his sandals. Once, stumbling, he plunged his hand into a clump of prickly pear. He swore, sucked at his thumb, then turned to stare back downhill into the darkness. Was that a faint trickle of falling stones coming from somewhere beneath him? He couldn't be sure ...

A flat tin-tan, tin-tonk of sound set his heart racing— then he grinned his relief. *Sheep-bells* ... He faced uphill and continued his climb.

After twenty more minutes, he reached the top. Before him, its thick darkness dusted by starlight, the top of Tourko Vouno was a saucer-shaped depression. He paused again. This was perhaps the trickiest part of his night's work. The top of Tourko Vouno was pock-marked by a series of squalid little holdings, each protected by at least a pair of savage, half-starved dogs. He only needed to set just one of these barking to wake the whole hill-top.

Narrowing his eyes against the darkness, he got his bearings. There, half-hidden to his left, the outline of the monastery roof showed as a patch of blackness against the skyline. That meant that the little chapel where his contact would be waiting lay almost directly to his right. Cautiously he moved on again, past one sleeping steadily and then another. A dog rattled at its chain, growled deep in its throat, and then thought better of it. The young man moved on till the domed bulk of the chapel loomed up before him, its whitewashed walls luminescent in the starlight.

Carefully, he skirted along its side, moving round to the little garden that lay behind it. A crumbling break in the wall showed him his entrance to a garden that was little more than a weedgrown courtyard. At its far end, lay the hut where the mad old anchoress who was the chapel's guardian lived.

The young man's nerve ends prickled; an arm's length away, the white blur of face gleamed in the darkness and a voice whispered: 'Father Iannis?'

'It takes three Iannis's to make one fool,' he replied, feeling absurd as he remembered the formula.

'Shall I call my brother "fool"?' the other voice replied, completing the ritual.

The young man moved forward: 'Have you got anything for me?'

'Something and nothing, I'm afraid. The jolly old Hun *is* up to something all right—*and* in the Cyclades. But *where*, exactly, and just what his little game is, I can't be certain...'

'Could it be a diversion, do you think?'

A shrug was implicit in the other's tones: 'God knows! But I don't think so. I should be able to give you the full score in a day or two. But I've got to watch my step. My new masters are beginning to smell a rat...'

'Be careful—'

10

But, even as the young man spoke, there was the faintest metallic click. Thunderous in the confined space of the courtyard, came the crashing burst of pistol shots and the darting stab of flame from a gun barrel.

The unseen contact gasped and fell. Slivers of stone from the courtyard wall whickered across the garden. Something gashed at the young man's cheek; a bullet plucked the sleeve of his habit.

He flung himself to the ground and rolled away into the shadows, groping frantically in the deep pocket of his cassock for the heavy Webley within. The weapon caught in the pocket's lining—then came free. He thumbed at the safety catch and aimed blindly into the darkness.

His fourth shot told. There was a yelp and his invisible enemy's weapon clattered across the flagstones. There was a scuffle of footsteps, a momentary blackening in that gap in the courtyard wall, and then his assailant was away across the hill-top, running a gauntlet of wildly barking dogs.

The old woman came out of her hut with a scream that was a prayer to the *Panaghia*. A shaft of light from the hut's open door accented the dead face of the young man's contact. A hole above one eye told its own story.

Then the young man, too, was running pell-mell down the mountainside, stumbling and falling, so that by the time he reached the outskirts of Athens, his every slow step was an agony. Although it was now long after midnight, the streets were still full of people, and he became conscious of curious eyes for his torn and dusty cassock and the brown smear of blood stiffening on his face.

'Po-po-po-po-po! A drunken priest, the sot, the womanising cuckold!' he heard someone shout and then the 'splot' as the fellow spat in the direction of his sandals. He sketched an ironic blessing and was rewarded with a string of blasphemies. He hurried away up a darkened sideroad, pursued by jeers and insults to his cloth.

Rain began to fall and somewhere, there was a far-off growl of thunder. At last he came to a high wall, overhung by the great leathery hands of fig-leaves on which the rain drummed loudly. A dozen more footsteps brought him to a

11

low door with a shuttered grille of wrought iron.

He rapped on the grille and it opened. Relieved and exhausted, he found himself in the sanctuary of the walled garden and was led towards the house from which he'd set out earlier in the evening.

In contrast to the young man's draggled appearance, the man waiting him in an upstairs room presented a picture of civilised urbanity; white tie, silk waistcoat and a shirt-front that, despite the heat, still managed to retain its stiffness.

Major Faulkenor raised an eyebrow at his visitor's appearance, greeting him in a voice that seemed a whole world away from that churchyard on Tourko Vouno. Faulkenor's tone was light, almost mocking, as though his guest had met with nothing worse than a slight mishap while out for a late-night stroll.

'My dear Michael! What *have* you been up to?'

The young man grimaced and accepted the whisky that was pushed towards him: 'There was someone waiting for us in the churchyard, sir. Orestes is dead . . .'

'The devil he is!' The lightness was wiped from Faulkenor's voice. 'Were you jumped before or after you'd made contact?'

'After—for what it's worth. Orestes just had time to tell me the Department's guesswork *is* correct. The enemy is up to something in the Cyclades. Though *when* or *what* that something is, Orestes hadn't been able to get at . . .'

'Damn!' Faulkenor said, toying with the lobe of one ear: 'London's not going to be very pleased about this . . .'

He turned away to pick up a telephone from his desk, and the young man sank wearily into a chair, surreptitiously remembering to render the Webley safe in his cassock pocket. He listened as Faulkenor began talking into the telephone, his voice once more light and urbane: 'Souris is back all right, Sandy . . . But it's bad news about Orestes . . . The fellow's gone west, I'm afraid . . .'

Michael Souris closed his eyes, trying to shut out his ugly little image of that dark hole above the closed eyes of the man simply known as 'Orestes'. Yet, to hear Faulkenor speaking, one might almost suppose that the fellow had rather let the side down by tiresomely cancelling a luncheon engagement...

Souris shook his head. He would *never* understand the English. Were they *really* as cold-blooded as they sounded?

* * *

Below the hospital, the hillside fell away in a sheer scarp. To Caradoc it seemed that, like a bird, he was soaring above the narrow estuary laid out below him. He pulled his dressing-gown closer about him. The morning still held a chill—a chill that would vanish just as soon as the sun lifted itself over the obtruding ridge of mountain behind the hospital. Then, it would be as it had been for days now— hot. Damned hot.

In the meantime, he told himself, washed and shaved as he already was, he still had a few more minutes in which to stare down at the little town of Porth Hafod, a jumble of slated roofs, jostling for breathing-space along the narrow shelf of land squeezed between the estuary and the tree-clad mountainside.

It all looked so very peaceful down below. A postman whistled on his round; a milkman's pony stopped and started at his own will. But Caradoc knew that the war had stretched its tentacles even into this remote corner of Wales. In a turn of the estuary down there lay a trot of minesweeping drifters and between the roofs of Capel Sion and the Berwyn Arms, he could see two of the destroyer *Random's* black-painted funnels—the same *Random* that had landed him and the handful of survivors from the 'mystery' ship, *Undine*, after she had been sunk in her engagement with two German U-boats off Hafod Head.

Caradoc bit at his lip. The previous evening, one of that precious handful had unexpectedly died—Bates, the steward: Bates, who with all *Undine's* officers dead or wounded had taken charge of her lifeboat...

Caradoc moved away from the window. Soon Sister Jones would be in to see why he wasn't dressed. It was time for him to put on the collection of uniform clothing sent up by *Random's* officers and which now, neatly pressed, was laid across the foot of his bed. Caradoc wondered whether

13

he dared risk a pipe while dressing. But—No!—Sister Jones had a nose like a fox-hound, and a tongue like a cat-o'-nine-tails. Like matrimony, she was not to be taken lightly . . .

Caradoc moved across to the bedroom mirror to put on his tie. One side of his face was still a mass of bruising from *Undine*'s action. Seen from the left, he told himself, he must look like a pretty fair substitute for the Piltdown Man . . .

The door flew open and Sister Jones stood in its threshold—five-foot three of angularities and starched linen. '*Duw*! There's a face to be showing a looking-glass that's done no harm to anyone. The vanity of the man!'

Caradoc touched his face: 'Still a bit of a mess, isn't it?'

'It always was, I'd say. You'll heal soon enough. Not like poor Mr Bates . . .'

'No . . . Not like Bates . . .'

'You men and your old wars. Like children you are—always fighting.'

'Not through choice . . .'

'No?' Sister Jones sounded unconvinced and Caradoc felt he hadn't the strength to argue the matter further. He straightened his tie and changed the subject: 'Has Captain Bennett given me his permission to see Kapitän-Leutnant Kirbschaus?'

Sister Jones sniffed: 'He has. Though *why* you should want to see *him*, I really can't think—'

'—Who's being childish now? Max Kirbschaus and I are old friends . . .'

'He's a *German*!'

'Only half of him . . .'

'That's enough to matter. Keep him on a diet of brimstone and cascara I would, if I had my way . . .'

Caradoc didn't waste time challenging her: Sister Jones's ferocity went no more than skin deep. Only yesterday, he'd seen her taking a bowl of roses from her own room and along the corridor to Max's. Caradoc moved away to make the same short journey. In a spirit of impudent defiance, he stuck his pipe in his mouth and was followed by a torrent of shrill disapproval. The sentry at Max's door snapped to attention, but winked slyly.

Caradoc opened the door and went in: a second sentry

was dismissed. Max was propped up in bed and Caradoc saw that his old friend was even thinner and more drawn than himself, and that his hair was now shot with white. The two men eyed each other uncertainly and without speaking. To hide his embarrassment, Caradoc glanced round the room. It was smaller and more spartanly furnished than his own, and its windows were heavily barred.

Max grinned: 'Sister Jones tells me this was where they used to lodge the local lunatics—amongst whom she evidently includes me.'

'Her bark's worse than her bite . . .'

'Thank God for that!—'

Caradoc laughed out loud, then wryly lifted his hands: 'Dammit, Max! There's heaps of questions I'd like to ask you—but, of course, I can't.'

'There's lots I'd like to ask you, too . . . But—name and rank—I'll tell you no more . . .'

'Have Bennett and his boys been at you?'

'They have . . . Clever chaps. They seem to know more about my business than I do. The nickname of my ship; the number of that submarine you torpedoed *and* the name of her captain. All details which they most politely invited me to confirm—'

'And which you with equal politeness declined . . .?'

'Quite . . .'

Caradoc pointed to the foot of Max's bed where a cage kept the bedclothes from weighing on his friend's injured leg: 'How are you coming along?'

'Well enough, all things considering. A few stitches and a fractured tailus bone—whatever *that* is . . .'

Yes, it was indeed 'well-enough', Caradoc told himself. He tried not to think of Max being pinned down amidst the twisted wreckage of his conning-tower and being dragged down by his sinking U-boat. Only a miracle had sent his old schoolfriend bobbing to the surface.

'What'll they do with you now, do you know?'

'A few more days here and then Thannington Hall—so your Captain Bennett says.'

'Thannington? Very swish. I almost wish I could join

15

you.'

'Why?'

'It's the Duke of Canterbury's place. There've been rude questions in Parliament about the idle luxury in which chaps like you are being kept...'

'Good! I could do with a bit of that sort of thing after the last few weeks.'

Max spoke lightly, but Caradoc caught the despairing undertones in his voice. How *hateful* to be a prisoner—even surrounded by the baroque splendours of Thannington Hall.

Max pointed to Caradoc's uniform: 'What about *you*, Ralph? No "survivor's-leave"? No flesh-pots of Town? Not back to duty already?'

'It seems so.'

'You joined the wrong navy—'

'*You* did, you mean!'

Suddenly embarrassed again, they took refuge in further inconsequentialities and then Caradoc made for the door. As he reached it, Max pulled himself up in the bed: 'You know, Ralph, I'm glad my fellows didn't shoot straighter...'

'Or mine—'

Caradoc closed the door behind him. Sister Jones blew sentiment away with a whiff of grapeshot. 'Tongue-pie you'll be getting if you've disturbed my patient!'

A spirit of mischief siezed Caradoc, and he made a sudden grab at Sister Jones's armour-plated waist. She gave an indignant squeal and fled. Caradoc turned to find himself face to face with the grinning figures of Heston-Wyatt, *Undine*'s Surgeon-Probationer, and Jayson, *Random*'s First-Lieutenant. The former's arm was still in a heavy sling from wounds he had received in the coaster's machine-gunned lifeboat.

'Will you have a word with our people before Jayson takes you away, sir?'

Caradoc's head pounded. Yes: he'd have a word. What else could he do? But what could he say to the tithe of men who, like himself, had survived *Undine*'s flaming wreck?

There were damned great dictionaries full of words—

and none of them any bloody use at all. Not for something like this . . .

*   *   *

An hour later, Caradoc stood beside *Random*'s captain, as the destroyer pushed her sharp bow out of Porth Hafod. The early June day was balmy and warm, and it became suddenly pleasurable to be free of responsibilities and to be nothing more nor less than a tripper.

But, for all the fineness of the weather, *Random*'s captain looked preoccupied. He and Jayson clucked their teeth and sadly shook their heads at each other a dozen times.

'A bad business, sir,' the First-Lieutenant ventured at last.

'We can't know for sure—not till we hear the *whole* story.'

'That's true, sir. But, all the same, *Invincible, Queen Mary* and *Ineluctable* going up—*Whoopf*:—just like that . . .'

'*Ineluctable*?' Caradoc asked.

Colston's tone was almost accusing: '*Don't say you haven't heard*?'

'Heard *what*, sir?'

Colston's head turned sharply: 'It seems that the Grand Fleet managed to catch Fritz outside his hidey-hole for once . . .'

'The Germans were brought to battle?'

'Yes—off Jutland. No one seems to know much about it as yet—only guesswork and rumour. But there *was* a hell of a mix-up in rotten visibility so it seems, and—' Colston frowned: 'Before Fritz left the scene, he handed out as much stick as he got. Beatty's battle-cruisers are supposed to have come off worst. Apparently they tried to hold the ring till Jellicoe could bring up his battlewagons . . .'

'And *Ineluctable*?'

'I only know what a fellow told me in Liverpool last night—and God knows where *he* got the story from. But he reckoned that *Ineluctable* just went up in smoke after taking a couple of hits on the midship turrets. The ship next in line steamed straight through where she'd been . . .'

'My God—'

17

Jayson's fist thumped the bridge rail: 'If only *Random* had been there!' He spoke as though the destroyer's presence would have settled the outcome of things beyond doubt.

'Yes . . . The destroyers had a stramash all of their own after nightfall,' Colston said wistfully; and then, noticing his guest's sudden pallor: 'I say, Caradoc—are you all right?'

Caradoc felt anything but all right; his head swam and pounded and the brightness had gone out of the day. Just two shells and a fine ship and a thousand good men gone . . .

Seeing Caradoc's sudden weakness, Colston was all concern; a steward was summoned to take *Random*'s guest below to the captain's own cabin.

When Caradoc had been led from the bridge, Colston gazed round the horizon for a few minutes deep in thought, and with his mouth pursed in an effort at remembrance.

'Caradoc . . .' he said at last, and pulled a wry face as he did so.

'Sir?' Jayson queried.

Colston jerked a thumb in the direction of the bridge ladder: 'It'd be a bit before your time, Number One—but that's the name of the chap who made a name for himself a few years back when he told Jacky Fisher that he could sink *Ineluctable* with a tin-opener . . .'

The First-Lieutenant whistled his disbelief: 'And he got away with *both* balls, sir?'

'Not really . . . He piled *Harbinger* up on the Binnacles a week or two later and they nobbled him for that . . .'

Jayson grimaced: 'Hard Cheddar. But so far as *Ineluctable* was concerned, it would seem he was right, wouldn't it, sir?'

'Yes . . .' *Random*'s captain shook his head pityingly: 'And just at this moment, Number One, I imagine our guest would give anything to have been proved wrong. Dead-wrong . . .'

*   *   *

Back in Queenstown once more, Caradoc made his way up the steep path to the C-in-C's residence. Jayson's cap sat like a pimple on his head and threatened at any minute to carry away in the teeth of a brisk south-easterly.

Admiral Bayly's niece at least seemed pleased to see him, kissing him lightly on his bruised cheek, and congratulating him on *Undine*'s victory. But, almost in the same instant, he was summoned into the presence of the admiral himself. The door closed behind Caradoc, and he faced Bayly uncertainly, prepared to accept such judgment as the admiral meted out.

Bayly looked stern—but, surely, that was the hint of a smile lurking behind the press of his lips? Then a hand reached out to pump at Caradoc's and he was pushed towards a chair, while the admiral made himself comfortable on the edge of his desk.

'Now, my boy—I want the *whole* story . . .'

Caradoc demurred: his report, he ventured. Bayly riffled at some papers. Reports, he grumbled, gave away *nothing*—or, at least, as conceived and concocted by most naval officers. The last captain capable of giving a good account of himself must have been Odysseus—

'—And look what a damned liar he *was!*' Caradoc said before he could stop himself.

Bayly smiled grimly: 'Still outspoken as ever, eh, Caradoc?'

'I—I'm sorry, sir . . .'

The admiral sighed: 'You must have some pity for us desk-bound warriors . . .'

Caradoc told his story. At its finish, Bayly tapped the pages of Caradoc's report: 'There's only one thing that puzzles me here. You say you thought you saw *three* columns of water rise beside that second U-boat?'

Caradoc lifted a hand to his bruised forehead: 'To be truthful, sir, I'm no longer very sure just what I saw. Perhaps by then, I was getting things confused with that old business of *Ineluctable*.'

'Ah, *Ineluctable* . . .' Bayly let the matter rest. He paused, then said: 'What would you like me to do for you now?'

Caradoc gaped at him in disbelief. Since *Harbinger*, he'd

grown used to being shuffled around like an unwanted parcel. Now, here was someone of Bayly's calibre asking him what *he* wanted to do . . .

The C-in-C spoke half to himself: 'There's *Fanciful*, of course. Much to his indignation, Shanklin, her present captain has been ordered into hospital. I can make you no promises, of course. But I *can* make my recommendations . . .'

Caradoc was thunderstruck. *Fanciful*! She was not as new as *Random*, of course—but she was still a destroyer.

Half-an-hour later, when Caradoc walked back down the hill towards Queenstown, it seemed that the south-easterly buffeted his ribs like an amiable friend. Below him, the harbour was full of shipping. But Caradoc had eyes for one vessel only—the long, lean hull of *Fanciful*, as lithe and dangerous-looking as a black panther . . .

*   *   *

But the prize was snatched from Caradoc even as he grasped at it. The next afternoon, he again found himself being interviewed by the admiral—an admiral who, this time, was angry, embarrassed and apologetic. By way of explanation, he handed Caradoc a slip of paper.

'I've had this signal about you, Caradoc. I've queried it, of course, but to no end. You're to report back to Jameshythe immediately.'

Jameshythe! The hated name was like a slap in the face; the final proof that in certain quarters, the name Caradoc still aroused enmity. Like a dud cheque, he was being returned to drawer . . .

Caradoc straightened up in front of Admiral Bayly's desk: 'I think I understand, sir . . .'

'That's a damned sight more than I do . . .'

As calmly and politely as he could, Caradoc took his leave of the admiral. As the door shut behind him, Bayly shook his head. Now just what the devil did someone in the Admiralty think he was playing at?

*   *   *

Three days later, Caradoc was back in Jameshythe. Despite the urgency with which he had been recalled, no one, it appeared, knew what to do with him. So far as Caradoc was concerned, he might simply have been 'returned to store!'

Days passed—'You might just as well proceed on leave, old chap . . .' he was told.

Angrily, he went. If this was the way *They* wanted things, *They* could fight the rest of their bloody war without him . . .

* * *

This sour mood dissipated in his slow journey across Kent. Once off Sheppey, the lush downland beyond absorbed him into itself, so that his sense of injustice ceased to rankle. Despite three changes of train, Caradoc found himself content, and the bitterness drained from him.

At one station, he admired the roses tended by an elderly porter; at the next he made friends with a somnolent marmalade cat; at the third, he merely sat in the sun and contemplatively smoked a pipe.

But, despite the sun, despite the easy drifts of pipe smoke, the war refused to be kept at bay for long. At each of the stations where he waited, long trains rumbled through, packed solid with a khaki mass of soldiery—a soldiery which, regardless of discomfort, appeared buoyant and cheerful, as though its journey was part of some great military Bank Holiday.

From the windows of one such train, a head was thrust out, and a stentorian voice bellowed: '*Are we down'earted?*' And then, perhaps a thousand voices bellowed their response to the questioner—the sound like the voice of England itself, vibrant on the June air. '*No-o!*' they answered their stentorian inquisitor; and then again, as their train entered the tunnel beyond the station: 'No-ooooo!'

So *this* was Kitchener's Army, was it, Caradoc told himself. And the trains? And the destination for which

21

those trains were bound? One didn't need a crystal ball to answer *that*, any more than one needed the whispers that insinuated themselves into every conversation these days: whispers that another 'Big Push' was imminent . . .

Caradoc chewed at his pipe stem. Full summer was the obvious time to blood the country's new and untried armies. A small chill seemed to sweep along the sunlit platform. Presumably the Boche had reached the same conclusion . . .

There was so much gossip, so much tittle-tattle. Surely by now, Fritz must know not only *where* the expected push would come, but *when* . . .

Caradoc's train pulled into the station with a clatter of loose connecting rods and a hiss of steam. As it puffed out of the station, he settled back in his seat, his thoughts drifting onwards to his destination: Wold. A brief telephone call the previous evening had assured him of his welcome at Ragged Robin Farm. Cousin Aidan and he had always got on well. Of Barbara, Aidan's wife, Caradoc knew less: a strikingly lovely girl, and town-bred, he had always thought it strange that she had chosen to become a farmer's wife.

Things must be very difficult for her now, with Aidan being with his regiment. But, better than they had been, perhaps. Last year, Aidan had been wounded at Loos and, since recovering, had been stationed at the Depot.

The train gave a whoop and descended into the darkness of an apparently endless tunnel. Bursting out into the sunlight at last, it slowed and came to a stop.

'*Thrennocke Wold! Thrennocke Wo-o-old!*'

'All right, William, I'll take the case myself,' Caradoc reassured the elderly porter, though handing him a shilling. Dazzled by the sun, he went out through the station building to the gravelled forecourt beyond. A trap waited for him, half-lost in a dappling splash of blue shadow. The figure of a woman in the trap raised a hand and waved: 'Cousin Ralph!' Half-closing his eyes against the glare, Caradoc recognised Barbara.

He heaved his case into the trap and clambered up himself. Barbara leant forward to kiss his cheek in greeting

22

and the trap moved out of the station yard into the lane beyond.

The air was sweet with the scent of newly-mown hay. Trees closed over the trap, and they bounced along the lane in a patchwork of light and shade. Caradoc glanced at Barbara and liked what he saw. It was difficult to recognise in her now the fashion-conscious woman he had first known. She was plumper than he remembered, so that beneath her simple, countrified dress, her body seemed a matter of ripe, graceful curves. She wore a starched white apron over this dress, and from beneath the hem of her skirt peeped the toes of a pair of heavy country boots. This ensemble was completed by an old-fashioned sun-bonnet. As much hood as bonnet, its gimp-like shape fell over her shoulders and shadowed her face.

Caradoc found its effect dangerously pleasing. Intoxicated by the smell of the hayfield past which the trap was moving, he found himself wondering just what it would feel like to lie in one of them with this woman beside him, while his hand gentled the tempting roundness of her breast, and then loosened the buttons of her bodice . . .

Barbara lifted her hand to her sun-bonnet. 'Aidan says I look like something out of the 'nineties. But it's very practical. *He* goes brown. I just freckle.'

Caradoc was grateful to be headed off from the tantalising direction of his thoughts: 'I think the bonnet's very fetching. You look the complete farmer's wife.'

'So I should! These days I'm the farmer, too!'

'Doesn't Aidan get home much?'

'He has done while he's had this training job. But that's almost over now. When this lot go to France, he'll go with them.'

'Again? He's quite got over that wound then?'

'So he says . . . But it's not true . . .'

Barbara fell silent and only began speaking again as they came in sight of Ragged Robin Farm. 'Aidan won't tell, but there's something pretty big in the wind, isn't there, Ralph?'

Caradoc nodded.

Barbara sighed: 'I thought so. For the last two months,

Aidan's only been able to snatch an odd hour or so away from the Depot. I suppose next week, or the one after that, maybe, he'll be off again to the front . . .'

Barbara's head was half-turned away, her face hidden behind the wing of her sun-bonnet. As the trap turned in through the gates of the farm, she said with dreadful finality: 'Aidan will be killed this time, Ralph. He knows it—I know it—just as surely as though it was already something in the past; something that has happened . . .'

Barbara suddenly turned towards Caradoc, and he saw the tears streaming down her cheeks: 'It's terrible to lie in bed at night alone with knowledge like that, Ralph . . . Terrible . . .'

The pony clattered to a halt in the farmyard: the June sun continued to blaze down from a flawless sky. But its heat was quite gone now. For a second time that day, Caradoc shivered . . .

*   *   *

The evening, Barbara and Caradoc sat together in the big farm kitchen. Brick-floored and black-beamed, it was the sort of room expressive of ancient generations—so much so, that consciousness of those generations was something almost palpable. At times, the present seemed a something of very small matter; a barely significant sentence scribbled on the palimpsest of the past.

A refectory table took up most of the centre of the kitchen. Supper was laid, but neither Caradoc nor Barbara made any move to eat. Outside, in the fading light, swifts flickered and screamed about the cowls of the hop-kilns. With a scrunch of gravel and a squeal of brakes, a car pulled into the farmyard.

'Aidan!'

Barbara rushed to the door. Caradoc stood as his cousin came into the kitchen. Like himself, Aidan had the family's aquiline nose and cool grey eyes. Now, Caradoc noted, that despite his cousin's tan, there was a luminosity under his drawn skin. Aidan kissed Barbara then grasped Caradoc's hand.

'Ralph, you old blighter, but it's good to see you!'

'And you, Aidan.'

His cousin laughed and ripped off his tunic, flinging it over the back of a chair. *'Now!* I've got a whole hour and a half to myself. Supper, a quick walk through the Orchard to Robin's Den, a bath—and then I must be on my way.'

'Must you?' Barbara sounded taut and constrained. Aidan stroked at the honey-coloured mass of her hair.

'I'm afraid I must, my dear. It's only because I've got such a jolly decent stick of a colonel that I'm here at all. I'm very lucky, all things considered—'

'Lucky...'

They sat down to table. Barbara said and ate little, but Aidan did so with such gusto that Caradoc found himself responding. On the surface, at least, Barbara's dark mood appeared to be passing: she seemed only too pleased to see that Aidan was laughing and talking like a schoolboy as he wolfed cold beef and pickles.

Supper over, Aidan and Caradoc took their promised walk. Barbara declined to join them, pleading a headache. Still talking, the two men strolled down through the orchard.

Aidan sighed: 'A mad world, my masters... Extraordinary, isn't it, Ralph? We inherit a world so beautiful that it can break your heart just to look at it. Then what do we do with that world? We blast it sick and silly with high explosives and choke it with poison gas...'

Caradoc found himself saying: 'At least the sea heals quickly—on the surface at least. A splash ... a swirl of discoloured water—and then everything's exactly as it was...'

'Lucky sea...'

They skirted the headlands of Robin's Den until they came back to the orchard. Caradoc suddenly asked: 'Aidan, when you came in this evening, you were wearing an ordinary Tommy's tunic ... Why?'

Aidan gave a short laugh: 'I've spent all day trying to teach some young subalterns how to lengthen the odds a little. Officers make awfully conspicuous targets, you know...'

'Are these New Army fellows very green?'

Aidan turned on his cousin sharply: 'Make no mistake about it, Ralph: once Kitchener's chaps have got the hang of things they'll be the best army this country's ever had—Cromwell's included. Kitchener's found us something infinitely precious. Something the like of which we've never seen before. And, God help us! If we waste these chaps, or throw their lives away wantonly, we'll never see their like again. They're the very soul of England . . .'

Together, they turned and retraced their way back through the long grass of the orchard. As they neared the farmhouse, Aidan asked: 'That German chap you brought down here a couple of times, Ralph—Max Kirbschaus. A jolly decent sort as I remember . . . D'you think there are many more like him on their side?'

'A fair proportion, I'd say . . .'

'Hmmm . . .' Aidan polished the bowl of his pipe against his cheek: 'It's a rum sort of business war, isn't it? I mean, I'm not sure whether the prospect of being knocked over by someone like old Max makes things better or worse—or just plain sillier . . .'

They reached the kitchen just as Barbara was lighting the first of the great brass oil-lamps. Aidan went upstairs to take his bath. Half-an-hour later, the big Vauxhall tourer roared out of the farm gates and into the sweet-scented night.

*   *   *

Caradoc leant over his scythe in a meadow sloping down to the railway. It had taken him most of the morning to cut a contemptibly thin strip of grass. Even so, the hiss of his scythe was pleasantly soothing and Caradoc felt almost at peace with his world.

Or, at least he would have done, had it not been for the constant movement of trains along the gleaming rails below him. Train after train, and each packed with the same inevitable khaki figures; figures which whistled, sang or cheered—and yet, in whose passing faces, he thought he detected a sort of hungry wistfulness.

26

Caradoc wiped the sweat from his brow and turned back to his work. The rhythm of scything was coming back to him now. As his blade hissed through the grass stems, the automatic habit of the thing began to absorb him, so that his mind was left free to wander.

Since that first night when he had returned, Aidan had only been back to the farm two or three times. Each time he had arrived, Caradoc had contrived to keep out of the way—but each time, he had been forestalled, either by Barbara or Aidan himself.

Caradoc watched them numbly. Dear God! No wonder they needed him as a sort of buttress; as a breakwater against which the deep seas of their grief could pound and expend themselves.

All the same, he felt a stab of guilt. In the last few days, watching Barbara busy about her work in kitchen and farm, he had come precariously near to falling in love with her. There was an increasing urge just to take her in his arms. An itch to—

Caradoc put a brake on his thoughts. They were a betrayal: of Barbara, of Aidan—and yes, of himself. They were most especially a betrayal now, when only this morning, Barbara had gone off to the Regimental Depot to see Aidan leave for France. She would be back in the late afternoon, and then he would borrow the Vauxhall and put himself out of temptation's way by going to see how Max Kirbschaus was settling in at Thannington Hall.

A waving handkerchief caught his eye, and Caradoc looked up to see a solitary figure leaning far, far out of a window at the rear of the latest passing train. He caught a quick glimpse of his cousin's aquiline nose, and a last flutter of the handkerchief, dipped as though in a salute of farewell. Then in a long echo, held between the steep chalk banks of the cutting, Caradoc heard his cousin's voice for the last time.

'Go-ood-bye-eeeeeeeeee!'

Part Three

Dog-Days

'Hrrrrrmmmmph!... Hurrrroooosh!' Major Prowst growled from beneath his bushy moustache. Max Kirbschaus nodded politely. At his first interview with Major Prowst on the day of his arrival at Thannington Hall, he had viewed the Camp Commandant with alarm.

Each one of those growls emerging from beneath Prowst's moustache—growls echoed by those coming from beneath the whiskery chops of the two large dogs of indeterminate breed sleeping under the Major's desk—had seemed pregnant with draconian if unintelligible threat.

In reality, as Max had since found, the Major was the kindest of men. But he was also astute. Thannington Hall might be a very comfortable spot in which to be lodged. But it was still a prisoner of war camp and the good major had every intention that his charges should remain IN...

But now, the Commandant was in full voice again.

'Hrrrmmmmph! Gerrrrrooo!' he began genially—from which Max elicited the information that he was about to be interrogated once more, and that a Mr Casserlly had arrived and was waiting to see him at this moment.

The two dogs glared unsympathetically up at Max over their moustaches: 'Now you're jolly well for it, my boy!' their look seemed to say.

But the Major shot a fierce scowl at them, bidding them mind their manners. Then he was soon in full spate again, his veinshot cheeks puffed out with an indignation that ruffled his whiskery upper lip like a gale through a hedge-top. The depths of the Commandant's annoyance caused a quite remarkable extension of his verbal contortions.

'This fellah Casserlly... Grrr! Looks like some sort o' intelligence wallah... Prrrph!... Sez he wants to ask yer some questions... Wouldn't tell *me* what sort o' questions... *Bloody impertinence...!*'

Prowst finished this speech by trumpeting into a half-

28

acre of handkerchief, inspecting the result with interest, as though hoping to find the offending Casserlly blasted into the depths of its yellow silk.

Max felt grateful for the Commandant's concern, uneasily guessing the reasons behind this latest attempt to question him. It was the same old story: *Gertrude*'s sinking of the barquentine *Magdalena*, and the atrocity story into which this had been deliberately whipped. Max felt he owed Prowst some explanation of what he was supposed to have done—but this was waved aside: '*Bloody* newspapers! *Bloody* twaddle! *Bloody lies!*'

The Major's dogs growled their accord. The Commandant stood: 'Better get things over... Watch Casserlly... Tricky bastard by the look of him... Stand no nonsense. I wouldn't... Hrrrrrrmmmmmph!'

Max followed Prowst out of his office and along a corridor. The Major's dogs, now biassed towards Max by their master's obvious favour, fell into step, feathering their sterns and snuffling through their moustaches. As Max limped along the passage, he felt a grateful affection for Prowst. A figure of fun he might be—but one with a fine instinct for fair play.

The Commandant flung open a door and announced in a truculent bellow: 'Kapitän-Leutnant Kirbschaus!'

As he did so, the dogs closed up to his heels, so that the room's solitary occupant was confronted by a phalanx of bristling moustaches. Max felt a momentary sympathy for the man called Casserlly. A combination of Prowst and his doggy familiars would surely be enough to shake the coolest confidence.

But, calm and detached, Mr Casserlly remained unruffled in face of the Commandant's obvious dislike. His eyes were distantly amused, like those of a good card player, confident of his hand.

The Major and his dogs withdrew—Prowst sending a blast of hot air down Max's neck as he whispered in a parade-ground bellow: 'Remembah what I told yer, Kirbschaus! *Watch* the boundah!'

The door slammed shut, and Max was left alone with Casserlly, who smiled gently: 'There's not much doubt which of us that warning was meant for, is there?'

Max made a non-committal answer. It was difficult to tell from Casserlly's tone just what his real reaction was to Prowst's unabashed rudeness.

In truth, Casserlly was convinced that this visit to Thannington Hall was neither more nor less than a fool's errand.

Magdalena . . . He reviewed the name with distaste. The man opposite him had sunk the old windjammer in circumstances that reflected every credit on his humanity— yet the story had been twisted into one of atrocity; a story that had been greedily seized on by newspapers avid for such nonsense. Now the aim was to make as much capital as possible by judicious exploitation of the whole episode.

Intelligence screamed at Casserlly that this would be a mistake. It was possible to be *too* clever. One false move now, and the opprobrium of the world's press would be directed at Britain rather than the enemy.

Still, Casserlly sighed; he had his orders. He reached into his briefcase and took out a sheaf of papers.

'You are Kapitän-Leutnant Kirbschaus?'

'Yes . . .'

'. . . Lately in command of His Imperial German Majesty's submarine, usually nicknamed *Gertrude* and part of the 9th Flotilla under the command of Captain Ernst Gebrecht?'

Max shook his head: 'I refuse to confirm or deny any of that . . .'

Casserlly tossed a couple of typewritten sheets of foolscap across the table: 'It's really a matter of academic interest only . . . No more . . .'

Max pushed the papers back across the table: 'Then why waste time, Mr Casserlly. We both know why you're really here . . .'

Casserlly experienced a sense of being outmanoeuvered: he had grown used to people trying to avoid giving him answers for as long as possible. Sensing his advantage, Max laid another card on the table: 'Supposing we start with a name, Mr Casserlly. Suppose we try . . . *Magdalena*?'

Casserlly unscrewed a fountain-pen and pushed

30

forward a sheet of paper: 'Perhaps you'd like to make a statement?'

Max's fist crashed down onto the table top as he snapped: 'No, I damned-well wouldn't! The only *proper* place to challenge such lies as your newspapers have seen fit to print about me is in a court of law—'

Casserlly's jaw dropped: 'My dear fellow, are you proposing to challenge us in *our* own courts?'

The mischief working in Max came bubbling to the surface: 'And *why* not, Mr Casserlly? I have been *grossly* libelled—and, enemy or not, as I understand it, English law is designed to protect the individual from such usage . . .'

Casserlly gaped. He had come to Thannington Hall secretly ashamed of his task and now here was the intended victim joyfully standing the whole business on its head. Suddenly helpless with amusement, Casserlly lay back in his chair and laughed. At last, he began tucking his papers back into his briefcase.

'Kapitän-Leutnant Kirbschaus, I really must warn you. Your submarine has been lost, with all your friends and the relevant log. In court, it would be your word alone against a subtle and unscrupulous prosecution—a prosecution that would have the backing of every one of those same damned newspapers that pilloried you in the first place—'

'—Then try me, and be damned!'

Casserlly sighed: 'Is there no one who could speak up for you?'

'Only the man who sank me—Ralph Caradoc. We were at school together . . .'

Casserlly found himself gaping again: 'The devil you were!'

Max cocked a malicious eyebrow: 'Didn't you know? Ralph Caradoc and I are very old friends . . .'

Casserlly silently promised his staff a very unpleasant hour on his return to the Department. Thanks to an incomplete brief, he had found himself less and less in command of this interview. He swallowed his pride; before he left this room, there was just one thing he wanted to know.

'Kapitän-Leutnant Kirbschaus,' he said; 'may I ask you a personal favour? As an old friend of Lieutenant-Commander Caradoc's, I wonder whether you could hazard a guess as to his present whereabouts?'

Max grinned: 'Is that an olive branch, sir?'

'A personal one—yes . . .'

'Well, sir, if Ralph is on leave, then I'd rather imagine he might be staying at his cousin's place—Ragged Robin Farm, down at Wold in Kent . . .'

Mr Casserlly made a note of the address and picked up his briefcase: 'I'm most deeply obliged to you, Kapitän-Leutnant . . .'

* * *

As his train carried him back to Paddington, Mr Casserlly pondered his afternoon's work. Apart from unearthing Caradoc's address, his journey had been a wasted one.

Academically, he considered Max Kirbschaus's threat to counter any moves made against him by using the law on his own behalf. It was a bold move—one whose audacity appealed to Mr Casserlly's arcane sense of humour. Whether or not the idea was feasible, he hadn't the least notion. Nor, probably, had Kirbschaus . . . All the same, it contained explosive possibilities for his Department. English Law was a tricky beast at the best of times. In the past, it had been invoked to protect the prisoner and the slave. So, why not now, in this case?

Mr Casserlly sighed. Making Max Kirbschaus into some sort of scapegoat was fraught with danger. At best, the Department might well be left looking ridiculous—and, at worst, something savage and barbaric before the bar of neutral opinion.

Besides: there were more important matters to get to grips with. This business of *Plan Atlantis* for example . . .

* * *

When Max limped back to his quarters, he found a little group of his fellow officers waiting him: two fellow naval

32

men, Johnen and Bekker; a cavalryman called von Munchen; and a disreputable little airman, Rudi Stoltz. The quartet sat on his bed while he told them how his interview with Casserlly had gone. Stoltz had an experienced nose for trouble and looked grave.

'That doesn't sound too good, sir . . .'

Von Munchen glared at Stoltz: *'You'd* know, of course . . .'

Equably aware of the Prussian's dislike for him, Stoltz smiled sweetly: 'When you've had trouble sitting on your tail as often as I have, you get a sixth sense for it . . .'

'Which is why you landed a brand-new Albatros on an R.F.C. airfield, I'll bet . . .' One of the naval officers murmured.

'Now *that* would be telling—' Stoltz said with a provocative wink.

'—And none of which is any help at all to old Max here,' the second naval officer, Bekker put in: 'You don't think they'd really dare put him on trial, do you?'

Von Munchen shook his head: 'The English are an odd lot when they get into one of their moods of righteous indignation. They'll twist that precious law of theirs inside out . . .'

The others looked grave. Apart from Max himself, von Munchen had the best working knowledge of any of them concerning England and the English.

'There you are then . . .' Stoltz said, for once in accord with von Munchen: 'That really only leaves us with one question, gentlemen: what the devil's to be done about it?'

Tentatively, Max put forward the notion that had jumped into his head while being interrogated by Casserlly: namely, challenging the British in their own courts . . .

'Magnifique—but hardly war,' von Munchen warned: 'Besides: they'd never let you . . .'

'It might just work,' Max insisted.

'And pigs might fly!' von Munchen scoffed: 'You know the British. Let them catch you when you're not looking and that's superior tactics. You do the same to *them*, and that vaunted sense of fair-play of theirs goes clean out of the window—'

'Not always...' Max insisted, divided in his loyalties.

'Well, speaking for myself, I wouldn't stick around to argue the point,' Stoltz said, pulling a face.

'Nor me,' von Munchen echoed.

Max lost patience: 'So—what do you propose I do? Make myself invisible and walk straight out past the guards and the barbed wire, whistling variations on *Die Wacht am Rhein*?'

'In *your* case,' Stoltz said softly: 'I'd do better than that. I'd forget the German half of myself for a while, and let the Englishman have a canter. With your particular advantages, I'd simply walk out of this place—*or ride*—and the guard on the gate'd salute me as I went...'

Stoltz had the room's whole attention now: disapproval of him was temporarily shelved as he outlined his plan for Max's escape. When he had finished, his audience gaped at him openmouthed.

The meeting was broken up by an orderly knocking on Max's door with a summons from the Commandant. 'Major Prowst's compliments, sir, but there's a naval gentleman to see you in his office...'

Max limped after his escort. What the devil was up *now*?

Prowst rose to greet him, his moustache frothing in a squall of mangled consonants: 'Ah! Kirbschaus—Friend o' yours ter see yer...'

A friend? Dazzled by the sun pouring in through the windows behind the Major's desk, Max at first failed to recognise the figure standing by the fireplace. But, if the face was for the moment a mere sun-splashed blur, that wide-legged, truculent stance was unmistakeable.

'Ralph!'

'Max, you old blighter!' Caradoc moved forward to shake hands. Major Prowst came out from behind his desk, looking like some preposterous walrus as he huffed and puffed through his moustache ends.

'Lots t'see to... C'n give yer an hour... Guard can stay outside... Make yerselves comfortable... Hurrrrooosh!'

The Commandant clamped his cap down onto his head

34

with the slap of a hand that would have brained a lesser man; then he and his dogs presented moustaches to each other, and the trio padded out through the open door.

Caradoc stared after him, slightly awed: 'What a terrifying old party . . .'

'He is that . . .'

'Keeps you in order, does he?'

'He not only keeps us in order, he keeps us *in*.'

Caradoc grinned: 'I've met old buffers like him before. They let on to being damned old fools—but they're as sharp as monkeys.'

Max blew out imaginary moustaches and loomed in fair approximation of Prowst's own tones: 'Hurrroosh! Don't do ter let on how clever y'are. Makes people *think* if yer do. *Bad* f'r 'em that . . .'

Caradoc laughed out loud: 'Not bad! That might have passed muster as the old pippin himself. I'd forgotten how good a mimic you always were . . .'

Max's heart bumped with excitement: So: he'd passed muster, had he? That was the first hurdle jumped . . .

Suddenly conscious of his reach-me-down collection of bits and pieces of borrowed uniform, Max felt ill-at-ease. Caradoc, elegant in new doe-skin, suggested a purposeful freedom. Comfortable as was his confinement here at Thannington Hall, yet it was still imprisonment; constriction. Much the same thought seemed to have struck Caradoc, for his friend suddenly pulled a face at the plaster nymphs disporting themselves on the ceiling and said: 'All very nice, no doubt—but it wouldn't be long before I'd want to be up and away . . .'

Max forced himself to say coolly: 'Oh, I think I shall be content to sit the rest of the war out here . . .'

He saw a shadow of disappointment cross his friend's face, and winked: 'Well . . . Perhaps not . . .'

They turned to other subjects, avoiding the deadground of their recent doings and chatting of old times; of schooldays and of the now long-ago holidays they had spent with each other's people in North Wales and Germany.

Max frowned in sudden recollection: 'That's odd—but

there was a chap here earlier in the afternoon who asked me where I might find you . . .'

Caradoc's eyebrows lifted: 'Someone asking for *me*?'

'Yes . . . A rather long-nosed type called Casserlly.'

Caradoc pulled a face: 'Casserlly! What did you tell him?'

'I hazarded a guess at your cousin Aidan's place— Ragged Robin Farm . . .'

'You're spot on as it happens. What did Casserlly say to that?'

'He said he was deeply obliged . . .'

'That sounds ominous . . .'

'You know Casserlly then?'

'We've had dealings. What did he want with you?'

'He came to tell me that your authorities still want to put me on trial for the sinking of the *Magdalena*.'

Caradoc exploded: 'But that's *preposterous*, Max! The whole story was a piece of newspaper "hate".'

'Oh, yes,' Max said bitterly: 'I know it. You know it. And, to give the devil his due, I think even Casserlly believes me. But *someone* wants my blood—'

'Why, God-dammit?' Caradoc began—but Major Prowst chose that moment to come back into the room. His dogs took up a comfortable spot beneath the window, while the Commandant delivered himself of a salvo of explosive pleasantries.

But Caradoc barely listened to these, preoccupied by the notion that Max might be brought to trial on a patently trumped-up charge. Ten minutes later, when he climbed into Aidan's Vauxhall and drove away, another thought struck him.

What on earth could Casserlly want with himself?

*   *   *

Caradoc's drive was a long one, but on near-empty roads he made good time. Evening became night—warm, clear, and with the moon at its full, so that the Vauxhall's lamps were almost unnecessary in its brilliant light.

Midnight saw him through the City, over the river, and speeding down the Old Kent Road. Beyond Bromley, he

36

was out into open countryside again, and with less than twenty miles between himself and Ragged Robin Farm. The moon was very big and full indeed. It hung over the white road like a cold, hypnotic eye . . .

The car lurched and skidded in a hailstorm of gravel, then, as Caradoc belatedly fought to retain control of its kicking wheel, canted crazily upwards onto the grassy bank beside the road. The Vauxhall came to a halt at last, still with two wheels high up the bank, but with no worse damage than to its paintwork.

For several minutes, Caradoc sat at the wheel, shaking and unable to move. He damned himself for a fool. Lord! he must have fallen asleep at the wheel . . .

He groped in his pocket for his pipe and lit it with trembling fingers, the sudden splash of the match flickering across the dashboard. Its image stayed on his retina, so that when a small thread of sparks began to shower down far away to the north-east, it was some seconds before his eyes registered them for what they were. But, even as he watched, the necklace of lights relentlessly fused themselves together, and flowered into a horrific gout of flame that tumbled slowly down from the night sky.

Only an airship could die with such monstrous magniloquence. Caradoc watched in horror as it fell to its destruction. He tried to judge the probable distance, but without a fixed point of reference, could only guess. Thirty or perhaps, forty miles he thought.

The terrible flare sank beyond the horizon, with a single great flash. The skyline grew dark again.

Sobered, and with his own near brush with death forgotten, Caradoc restarted the car, and very carefully drove the last fifteen miles home.

*   *   *

Mr Casserlly looked about him with chastened eyes. For mile on mile, it seemed, stretched a monotonous wasteland of fen and salting, interspersed with reed-grown meres. He shuddered, daunted by the marsh's poisonous desolation, its rumouring reeds and the huge emptiness of the sky above—a sky from which seeped a thin and penetrating rain.

Reluctantly Casserlly turned to face what he knew was behind him. For twenty or thirty acres, the wilderness lay stretched before him, a blackened depression of swamp from which every last trace of greenery had been turned to carbon by the inferno that had lately raged there. Even now, thin wisps of smoke still rose from the ground. Spread over this desolation, lay what was left of LZ.90's skeleton, most of it so molten by the hydrogen fire as to be distorted beyond recognition.

A vile stench hung over the whole marsh, the *lietmotifs* of which were only too hideously obvious—petrol and the roast-pork reek of broiled flesh . . .

Casserlly looked around him with distaste. There was this at least to be said for the sea: it buried its own dead . . . The tall figure of a Lieutenant-Commander with the wings of a pilot on his sleeve moved up to Casserlly's side.

'If you'd come this way, sir . . .'

Casserlly followed the airman beyond the circle of fire-blackened ground to where the fury of the holocaust had at last been expended. A creek, now full of charred rushes, had provided a natural fire-break, and the two men crossed this narrow waterway on a bridge of old railway sleepers. Then, the naval pilot set off down a muddy causeway between banks of reeds that reached above their heads.

They walked on for another sixty yards till their progress was halted by the challenge of an armed sentry. Now at last, Casserlly could see the reason for their long trek—a metallic something that after ploughing through a stand of willows, had half-buried itself in the side of a low dyke.

'The main gondola?'

The pilot nodded: 'Yes, sir . . . It must have broken away from the Zeppelin on the way down . . .'

Casserlly set himself to examining the gondola: every inch of paintwork had been blistered from its surface; crushed by the force with which it had struck the dyke, it had been compacted almost flat.

The naval pilot said softly: 'They're not all inside. I

reckon one or two of the poor bastards took the quick way down.'

The interior of the gondola was even worse than Casserlly's imagination had told him it would be. The airship's cox'n lay crucified on the shattered remnants of his wheel; the brains of a young leutnant oozed from his skull, and the captain's body had been driven far into what must once have been the airship's wireless. Almost nothing of the gondola's interior had been left intact: charts, log-books, papers lay strewn everywhere—and, over all, hung the reek of smoke and the blood which seemed to be splashed on every splintered surface.

His gorge rising, Casserlly managed to say to his guide: 'Do you see this sort of thing often?'

'Pretty often, sir . . .'

'God help you then . . .'

The pilot wiped a blood smear from his sleeve and said: 'I didn't bring you here without a purpose, sir. Look—' he bent himself even lower and crawled across to where what had once been the chart-table now lay crushed between the gondola's deckhead.

Casserlly looked puzzled, and the pilot shifted a chart to show what lay hidden beneath—a book with lead-bound covers that set Casserlly's hand reaching forward, his sickness forgotten. He opened the pages of his prize with fingers that were suddenly trembling. This was too good to be true. It was the sort of luck that every intelligence officer dreamed of; the joker in the pack; the gift of the high gods themselves.

'Is *that* what I think it is, sir?' The Lieutenant-Commander asked quietly.

'Oh, yes . . .' Casserlly answered with a calmness he was far from feeling. 'You've just come up with the German Navy's signal book . . .'

There was something else, too, that he did *not* mention— the sealed pages at the back of the book whose purpose was indicated by a single typewritten heading:

APPENDIX XXXVII: PLAN ATLANTIS.

                    *   *   *

Mr Casserlly's office was at the top of a tall, eighteenth-
century building in a cul-de-sac of St Mary at Rood. Its front
door—far below down several flights of steep stairs—bore
a discreet brass plate which said simply: 'The Balkan and
Levant Shipping Company'.

Ralph Caradoc sat in the office, staring at Mr Casserlly's
face with a certain mystification. Less than two hours
earlier, he had been working in the Long Meadow at
Ragged Robin Farm when a car had come skidding into the
yard and a hot and haughty young lieutenant had strode
down to the hayfield with the peremptory message that
Caradoc was required to return to London with him at
once. The young man's manner had been so abrupt that
Caradoc had been sorely tempted to kick his backside and
tell him to go to hell.

Now, he rather wished he had. The lieutenant had
driven up to Town with more dash than skill and his replies
to Caradoc's questions had been grunted monosyllables,
barely pitched this side of politeness. By the time Caradoc
was shown into Casserlly's Billingsgate office, his own
volatile temper was simmering.

Undine's end may have been an untidy business—but
surely he deserved something better than to be pushed
from pillar to post like an unwanted parcel? Yet here was
Casserlly staring at him with nostrils pinched as though
he'd been caught piddling against Nelson's Column...
Caradoc's face darkened as Casserlly began to speak.

'I understand that Admiral Bayly recommended you for
command of *Fanciful*?'

'Yes, sir...'

'A recommendation which their Lordships did not see fit
to endorse...'

'No, sir...'

'Significant, perhaps, that your name doesn't excite
confidence in certain quarters?'

There was no answering *that*... Caradoc sat and fumed
while Casserlly shuffled through some papers. After a

goodish pause his inquisitor asked: *'Why* did you take *Undine* away from her proper beat and up into the Irish Sea, Caradoc?'

Anger spurred Caradoc's answer: 'Because I was sick and tired of seeing the same charts on the table, day in and day out, sir!'

'And your feelings concerning *Ineluctabale*? Instinct? Intuition?'

'I . . . I don't know, sir.'

Cardoc looked up surprised to see a smile hovering along the thin line of Casserlly's lips; the papers were pushed into a folder and then his tormentor said: 'I have a job for you, Caradoc—if you'll take it. I'll warn you now; it's quite likely to be a thankless one in my opinion . . .'

Caradoc's decision was immediate: anything was better than spending the rest of the war at Jameshythe.

'I'll take it, sir . . .'

Casserlly pushed the folder towards him: 'Then you'd better read this, Caradoc. This is all we know about something called *Plan Atlantis* . . .'

*   *   *

An hour later, Caradoc sat in the quiet seclusion of his club. The Benbow was a peaceful unfashionable sort of place, just the thing for his present mood. Safe in its old-fashioned sanctuary, Caradoc sat in the window-seat of a dark panelled room, looking down on the leafy tops of a row of London planes, while his mind tried to come to grips with what he'd heard and read that afternoon.

Plan Atlantis . . . Even the evidence for the existence of such a plan was sketchy enough in all conscience: a letter found in a derelict U-boat; a too-talkative German prisoner; the report of a Greek spy; the ciphers discovered in the wreck of that airship he'd watched blaze down a night or so ago.

As an ancient club servant set down a decanter by his side, Caradoc digested a few hard facts at his disposal. What with one thing and another, Allied stock was not exactly high in the Eastern Mediterranean at this moment.

The Greek King was pro-German, though Venizelos and most of the people were pro-Allied. Even so, if the Central Powers looked like coming out on top, the Greeks might consider it expedient to throw in their lot with Germany, surrounded as they were by traditional enemies—which would make the line of communications to the Suez Canal hazardous in the extreme. Certainly, the Navy had few ships to spare.

Casserlly had been careful to define Caradoc's role: 'We can't afford another reverse in those waters. Such information as we have, suggests that *Plan Atlantis* is almost certainly scheduled to take place in the Cyclades. It is *also* the Allied intention later this summer to apply a little pressure on the Greeks by sending a combined fleet into Piraeus and Salamis. What we must know is whether *Plan Atlantis* would present that fleet with a totally unacceptable risk . . .'

'But, surely, the Aegean Squadron is best placed to sniff out the likelihood of such a threat, sir?'

'In normal circumstances I'd agree with you, Caradoc. But, in this case, I'm not sure. Instinct tells me that the poacher's ferret might be more use than a pack of clumsy if well-intentioned hounds . . .'

'Another *Undine*, sir?'

'Something even smaller, I'm afraid—an armed schooner.'

Now, as he sipped at his glass and stared down at the plane trees beneath the window, Caradoc wryly wondered just what his new command would offer by way of armament. By the sound of things, a crystal ball and a divining rod might well be handiest . . .

He lit his pipe and watched the shadows lengthening along the street below him. It scarcely seemed possible that it was only a few short hours since his peremptory summons from Long Meadow by Lieutenant Roebuck. Ragged Robin Farm seemed a thousand miles away. Perhaps it was just as well that Casserlly's summons had come. In the last few days, he had been within a toucher of making an unforgivable fool of himself with Barbara—and it was no good him trying to disguise the fact.

No more use than him trying to hide from himself the certainty that he was head over heels in love with her . . .

*   *   *

Petty Officer 'Kitty' Wells struggled to swim upwards and break clear of the deep seas of sleep that were sucking him down. A worried face peered up at him—a face belonging to a stocky figure holding up a steaming mug of tea.

'Bad dreams, Kitty?'

Wells pulled a face in answer and the stocky man jerked a thumb in the direction of the hammock: 'Never knowed anyone push a guard'n'steerage 'mick as long as you . . .'

Wells shrugged and yawned: 'I spent half the night tied up to Custom House Steps. The Bloke sent young Westicott ashore on some errand or other . . .'

'And you nipped ashore for a crafty wet in Vassallo's, I suppose . . .'

'I might have done . . .'

'And to see 'is daughter, Carmelina.'

'That'd be telling . . .'

'Just so long as no little bird's gone whisperin' in the Jaunty's ear—which reminds me: our 'Erbert told me to pass the word for you, so I wouldn't 'ang about.'

'Christ!' Wells dropped down from his hammock with a bump: 'What does Carver want?'

'Depends what you've got on your conscience . . .'

'Job's comforter!' Wells stowed his hammock, the seven marling hitches falling into place with swift, practised turns.

Five minutes later, he stood in the Regulating Office, slightly breathless, both with hurry and the pangs of an uneasy conscience. It didn't pay to get athwart Herbert Carver's hawse . . . Avoiding the Master-At-Arm's eye, Wells fixed his own on the line of Gangway Books on their shelf above Carver's head: Jaunty Carver had an all-seeing eye that would have done credit to the Recording Angel . . .

Wells nearly sighed his relief aloud as Carver began: 'That request of yours for a draft . . . It's come

43

through . . .'

'Thank you, Master.'

Carver shook his head reproachfully: 'Don't thank me. God knows what you want it for . . .'

Wells didn't answer; his reasons were a bit obscure, even to himself. When the word had come down that a petty-officer with experience in coastal sail was required for duties elsewhere, he had jumped at the chance.

The Master-at-Arms tut-tutted his disapproval: 'You've a promisin' career ahead of you, Wells—if you watch your step . . .' Carver followed the line of Wells' eyes and added: '*And*, y'could do worse than to take a long gawp at them books while you're at it. Where you're going, the whole caboodle'll most likely be on *your* slop-chit. *Your* responsibility . . .'

'When do I go, Master?'

'They want you by yesterday forenoon at the latest—so you'll have to smack it about. You know the drill . . .'

'But *what* ship?'

'Don't ask *me*! Could be HMS-ruddy-*Pinafore* for all I know—' Carver waved a hand at Wells in dismissal

So! For once, Carver had proved less than all-seeing, Wells crowed to himself as he reached the door of the Regulating Office. But, the Master-at-Arms it seemed had one last shot to fire:

'Oh, and Kitty, my son—steer clear of Vassallo's. His liquour'd blind an army mule. As for Carmelina—' The Jaunty's cold eyes gleamed sardonically: 'It'd be a shame if that nose o' yours was to drop off one day . . .'

Seconds later, a scarlet-faced Wells was safely beyond the Regulating Office door. Herbert Carver had maintained his reputation for omniscience to the end . . .

*　　*　　*

Caradoc stared at the countryside passing his carriage window. He was consumed by a sense of guilt. These last few days, he had treated Ragged Robin Farm as a sort of hotel, returning late each evening to gulp down supper and sleep for a few hours before dashing off again.

Barbara had accepted his comings and goings in silence, and had helped him pack the previous afternoon when he had made his final sortie up to town. He had stayed overnight at his club, feeling a sense of reprieve, of acquittal even. One more night with Barbara so close and he'd have—

The locomotive at the head of the train gave a hollow whoop as it disappeared into the darkness of Thrennocke Tunnel. Grateful for the darkness, Caradoc shuddered. Lord! How near he'd come to making an unspeakable fool of himself. Whatever his feelings for Barbara, he had no right to give them rein. *Besides:* what did those feelings amount to? Love? Or a grubby, uncouth itch that had a lewder name?

The train burst out of the tunnel into dazzling June sunlight—just as it had a few short days ago at the start of his leave. But this time—thankfully—the train did not stop at Wold, but rattled through the dozing halt with another yelp of its whistle. A haycock-dotted meadow appeared at the window and close by the lineside fence stood the figure of a woman. There was the familiar flash of a blue dress and the white gleam of a sunbonnet.

Suddenly, Caradoc found himself up at the open window and waving ... waving. Then, as the engine gave a last whoop of its whistle, the harebell-dotted sides of the cutting rose up beside the rushing train, and Barbara was gone from sight...

*   *   *

Although well-aware of the threatened trial hanging over Max Kirbschaus's head, it was not without misgivings that Colonel Froebel acceded to the escape plan that Stoltz and Max put up to him. As the camp's senior German officer, Froebel's first reaction was astonishment and a barely-checked impulse to tell the two men to go away and not waste his time.

The plan was simplicity in itself. Dressed as a British naval commander and in Prowst's own car, it was Max's intention to leave Thannington openly by driving out through the camp's main gates and then taking a train to London...

'*Preposterous!*' was the colonel's first reaction—but, as Stoltz repeated the plan, Froebel became less sure. For all its audacity, the scheme had been well thought out. Its success largely hung on the way certain individuals were known to react—and these individuals had been meticulously observed. As Stoltz pointed out, a prisoner of war had plenty of time for that sort of thing.

Slowly, Froebel's expression changed from one of disbelief to red-faced approval: 'When could you be ready to try?'

'To-day week, sir.'

Since then, Max had found himself thrust more and more into Stoltz's company. Rather against his will (or was it because of von Munchen's barely-veiled disapproval?), Max became increasingly taken with the fellow. Stoltz was an engaging little man with a fund of improbable stories. And, despite the fact that he was outranked by the remaining four members of the escape committee, including Max himself, it was the airman who took charge of the whole business.

It was Stoltz who had pointed out the advantage of Max's Englishness; Stoltz who had decided that, with his still game ankle, Max must travel by car and train. The man's staff-work was extraordinary. It was Stoltz who organised the watches on the camp's guard-room, on Major Prowst, on his orderlies and drivers and on the others whose whereabouts and behaviour it might be necessary to anticipate.

It was Stoltz who set an engineer officer into devising a set of picklocks; Stoltz who called in the uniforms of every naval officer in the place, selecting the best and putting them on one side for alteration; Stoltz who then, after subjecting Max to the sort of measuring only given by a master tailor, began unpicking these garments and recutting them into a uniform that, so far as Max could tell, might have been the very best that Gieves could provide...

At his final fitting, Max stood before a full-length mirror

46

and gaped. *This* was how he might have looked had he taken his mother's nationality and not his father's. He was no longer Kapitän-Leutnant Kirbschaus, but Commander Kirbhouse, DSO, DSC, RN, he thought, noting the ribbons that Stoltz had sewn onto the chest of his monkey-jacket. Max stared at his reflection in wonderment.

Impulsively, he turned to Stoltz: 'My dear chap, how can I even begin to thank you?'

Stoltz grinned: 'By putting in a good word for me at my court martial . . .'

'Your *court martial*?'

'You know, sir, I really think that you're the only man in the place who gives me the benefit of the doubt about that damned Albatros . . .'

Max looked puzzled: 'I've never even considered the matter.'

Stoltz's grin froze at its corners: 'Others aren't so considerate . . . Besides: never mind the Albatros. I've a worse flaw than that. I'm a Jew . . .'

Max shrugged: 'That's something else I've never even given a thought about, Rudi . . .'

Stoltz's mischievous smile became itself again: 'Which is why you've *yourself* to thank that you're standing there in that uniform . . .' He winked impudently and caressed the sleeve of Max's jacket between his fingers: 'A lovely bit of *schmutter*, sir . . .'

*　　　*　　　*

That same evening, all five members of the escape committee, plus Colonel Froebel, sat in Max's room. Along the corridor, other officers kept watch for prowling guards. Knowing themselves safe, the escape committee went over its plans for one last time with Colonel Froebel acting as inquisitor while von Munchen outlined the precise plan of campaign.

'At 07.50, sir, Major Prowst finishes breakfast; then, he visits the lavatory till eight, when he comes out and takes his morning walk . . .'

'Eight o'clock, exactly?' Froebel asked.

'Eight o'clock on the dot, sir,' von Munchen confirmed. 'The Commandant then whistles up those two damned great mongrels of his and goes for what he calls his constitutional... Out through the front doors, five minutes on the terrace, then down along the drive till he meets that circular road running round the park. By 08.20 he's about half-way along this, which means he's directly behind the house, *and* at the spot furthest from the guard-room gates...'

'Hmmm...' The colonel grunted.

Johnen and Bekker took up the tale: 'At 8.00, sir,' Bekker said; 'The guard is changed on the gate. That means that although they've got the book of who's come in, *they won't have actually seen those people themselves*. Nor will the guard-sergeant have had time to check the book...'

'So that no one will be certain whether Prowst has had an early morning visitor or not?'

'Precisely, sir...'

Johnen put in: 'As soon as the Commandant is safely off the terrace, Bekker and I will divert the attention of the sentry outside his door.'

'How?'

Bekker blushed: 'The-er guard will be Private Flower, sir... He's... um... susceptible to sailors...'

'Great God in heaven! And in the meantime?'

Stoltz said coolly: 'I shall be unlocking the door to Major Prowst's quarters, sir...' He held up the engineer officer's picklocks. 'Once inside the Commandant's office, I shall unbolt the door that leads to the library where Kapitän-Leutnant Kirbschaus will be waiting...'

'In British uniform?'

'Yes, sir. He will come into the Commandant's office where he will make a telephone call down to the duty-driver's room...'

'And *how* will you do that?'

'Stoltz means that I shall do it, sir,' Max said: 'I can do a very fair imitation of Major Prowst...'

'Y'don't look too happy about it?'

'It doesn't seem *quite cricket* somehow, sir...'

The room's other occupants grinned at Max's scruples:

the use—and in English—of that particular idiom was typical of the man.

To cover the embarrassment of the moment, Froebel asked: 'Who's Prowst's duty-driver tomorrow morning?'

'Private Pipkin, sir . . .'

This time everyone smiled. They all knew Pipkin—that completely simple-minded man with fallen arches and two left feet who, despite these handicaps, lived in a dreamworld of playing professional football for Accrington Stanley.

Stoltz said slowly: 'Apart from Pipkin, there's one more factor in our favour—Prowst's impatience. He simply can't bear to be kept waiting. If he's in a hurry, his drivers are supposed to blow a special sort of tantara on the horn, and the guards open the gate to let him through . . .'

The colonel looked sceptical: 'Ah! But that's for Prowst himself. What about a visitor?'

'We don't see why it shouldn't work, sir—particularly if the visitor is a brass-hat being driven in Prowst's own car by Prowst's own driver. It seems worth a gamble anyway . . .'

'—Especially at that hour of the morning,' Johnen said with a grin: 'The word is that Prowst's not altogether human till about nine o'clock most days . . . No sentry's going to risk a complaint being made by an obviously important visitor.'

'No-o . . .' Colonel Froebel said, grinning sheepishly, and aware that there was *another* middle-aged officer who was given a wide berth till well on in the morning: 'Right now . . . Assuming that Kirbschaus here gets through the gates safely—what then?'

'Private Pipkin will have been instructed that he's to get the Major's visitor to the Town Station at the double, sir . . . There's a non-stop train to London at eight forty-five . . .'

'And whatever else Pipkin's faults may be, he's supposed to be a damned good driver . . .'

The colonel thought for a few moments, then came to a decision. He tapped his fingers on the arm of his chair and said: 'The whole scheme's quite mad of course, gentlemen.

All the same, *I think we'll go ahead as planned . . .'*

*   *   *

When the others had left Max's room, Colonel Froebel remained. He continued to tap his fingers on the arm of his chair and then said: 'I've still got reservations about this whole mad-cap business, Kirbschaus. But, apart from that absurd threat to put you on trial, there's one other consideration that has persuaded me to let you go ahead.'

'Something important, sir?' Max asked.

'That's something you might be better qualified to judge.'

'*Me*, sir?'

'Have you come across a fellow in the West wing—name of Braun? Lost an argument with some British destroyer?'

'I've spoken to him once or twice, sir.'

'Hmmm . . . The poor devil's got a bit of a bad conscience at the moment. He confessed to me that he'd talked a bit too freely when he was interrogated. He said he'd let on to knowing someone called Kattschner—'

'Wolf Kattschner?'

'That's right. Braun said the interrogation officer was very interested in Kattschner's trips to the Cyclades. The interrogating officer's name was Casserlly . . . Does that ring a bell?'

'It does . . .'

The colonel put up a warning hand: 'I don't want to know àny more. But it does seem to me that our side has something up its sleeve—and that the British have at least *some* notion what that something is . . .'

When Froebel had left his room, Max did some rapid thinking. Yes: he knew both what that *something* was and its code-name. Wolf Kattschner was a clever fellow—but he did far too much talking. And Casserlly? Was it simply coincidence that he had urgently wanted to know Ralph Caradoc's whereabouts? Max's intuition said no.

He went to bed with but one thought in mind: tomorrow's escape attempt *must* be a success . . .

*　　*　　*

Arriving in Taranto, Caradoc found himself hurried on board a destroyer that was singled up and impatient to depart. Even as he went up over the brow and saluted, the last wires splashed away. A threshing of screws; a vibration thrilling her slim hull—and then the destroyer was clear of the quay and cutting a white wake through that Mediterranean blueness which always came as such a returning surprise to northern eyes.

'Whither away?' Caradoc asked himself in sudden exultation: 'Why! to Malta and the fabulous Aegean!'

*　　*　　*

Max Kirbschaus slept fitfully, and greeted the dawn with relief. He slipped from his bed and began to wash and shave. At six, Stoltz came into his room and with deftly gentle hands, stripped the plaster from Max's ankle. Beneath the plaster, the flesh was still blue-black with bruising, and Max winced as Stoltz tightly strapped his leg from foot to knee.

'Let's just hope that you don't have to take to your feet, sir.'

'I'm hardly likely to try walking across the North Sea . . .'

'Ah, you Gentiles—where's your faith?' Stoltz taunted him.

Max dressed himself in front of the mirror, watching the birth of that other self of his—the Englishman that might have been.

Stoltz called Max over to the table and pointed out further accessories: 'There's your case with the rest of your gear . . . Remember: you're a pukka sahib, so you wouldn't be seen dead carrying it yourself. Here's a walking-stick. You'd carry one anyway—but you're also a wounded hero. With a bit of luck, no one'll get round to asking which side's. Gloves. Wrist-watch, *and* the Colonel's gold-cigarette case which he says he'd be grateful if you'd return after the war. And-ah!—I nearly forgot . . .

51

My wallet—'

'—But it's *stuffed* with English money, Rudi!'

'Don't worry, I didn't come by any of it honestly.'

'You'll end up in jug one of these days.'

'I probably shall if that frozen-faced bastard von Munchen gets his way.' Stoltz paused and listened as a distant clock struck the half-hour: 'Seven-thirty. Roll Call. I'd better get myself down to the terrace.'

When Stoltz had left him, Max stripped off his jacket and slipped a dressing-gown over his shoulders. He moved across to the window, opened it and leant out. Below him, the terrace was crowded with officers, straggling in three unmilitary-looking ranks across its width. Because of his injured leg, Max had been given permission to answer his name from his bedroom window. This morning's Roll Call, taken by a pernickety little subaltern, went slowly and Max inwardly cursed as precious minutes ticked away. But at last the Roll Call was over and the untidy parade broke up.

Stoltz bounced back into Max's room, breathless after having taken the stairs four at a time. He watched as Max put on monkey-jacket and oak-leaved cap, then gave him a final critical survey.

'You'll do, sir. Now ... time to go, I think. We'd better be getting along to the library.'

Stoltz moved to the door and tapped at it with his knuckles. There was the welcome sound of two, sharp affirmative knocks. Coast clear! Stoltz and Max stole from the room. Johnen took Max's case and the trio crept round a seldom-used passage leading to the library. When they reached this, Stoltz went to work with a picklock, jerking up a triumphant thumb as his door swung open.

'Now, don't forget, sir, bolt the door and wait.'

Obediently Max closed the door and bolted it, hearing his companions' footsteps hurrying down the corridor outside.

He reached up and took down a bound copy of Punch from one of the library shelves, then settled himself to wait. Now that things were under way, he felt perfectly calm.

* * *

Stoltz and Johnen returned the front way to Major Prowst's quarters. Someone sitting on a window-seat and ostensibly reading, jerked three fingers in their direction. Ah! Stoltz told himself; that means the old boy has been out on the terrace for three minutes.

The two men slowed their pace as they neared the Commandant's door, not wanting to interrupt Bekker while he was doing his stuff with Private Flower. They watched from behind a pillar as the young officer wheedled Flower away from his post. Money for old rope, Stoltz told himself—the whole camp knew about Flower.

Five metres... Ten ... and then Flower and his quarry were away out of sight and round a corner and Stoltz's picklock was probing at the latch of Prowst's door. A small movement—a squeak of momentary stiffness and then the lock opened with a soft click. Quick as a cat, Stoltz was round the door and into Prowst's office. The reek of the major's morning pipe was so strong on the air that Stoltz had to suppress a sneeze as he tip-toe'd across to the French windows.

Cautiously he looked outside—then drew back sharply. *Damnation!* Prowst and those bloody dogs of his were still on the terrace, airing their moustaches...

'Move, you old bugger, *move!*' Stoltz begged.

At last the Commandant made his leisurely way off the terrace. One of the dogs looked back with a suspicious eye at the open windows of his master's room; made a step or two towards the French windows—but was then brusquely called to heel.

'Come *along*, Bouncer, yer demned old fool!'

Stoltz breathed a sigh of relief. He moved swiftly across the room and slipped back the bolts of the library door, started to open it and found Max coolly reading a long outdated volume of Punch.

'Come on!'

Max put the Punch tidily back onto its shelf and followed Stoltz into Prowst's room. Outwardly calm, his heart began bumping. Everything now stood or fell by the credibility of his performance in the next couple of minutes. Stoltz pointed to Prowst's desk.

'There's the internal telephone, sir.'

Max moved forward, mentally crossing his fingers, picked up the telephone and twirled the little handle by its side. The line buzzed, jangled and then cleared as the receiver was lifted at the other end. Taking a deep breath, and then in imagination filtering his words through a moustache like a hedgerow, Max bellowed: 'Pipkin! Is that you?'

*   *   *

Accrington Stanley were all over Blackburn Rovers in the Final of the F.A. Cup, and Private Pipkin was on the point of getting his hat-trick when the telephone jangled in the duty-driver's room. The anticipatory ring of the crowd's cheers sent Pipkin skywards—the jangling of the field telephone dragged him sharply back to earth.

'Dead-Shot' Pipkin, the Idol of Accrington, was immediately shrunk to the spavined figure of Private Enoch Pipkin, butt of the 8th Palatines—that tremulous creature who very nearly dropped the telephone as he held it to his ear and recognised the familiar blast of his master's voice. With his right puttee making an untidy tangle as it slid down his calf, Pipkin stamped to attention on the bare boards of the floor.

'Yes, sah! I-am-standin'- to-attention-and- salutin'-you, sah!' Pipkin bleated.

'Salutin', me arse...' Prowst grumbled in his most authentic, pre-9.00 a.m. tones—and Pipkin trembled anew.

'Now get this into yer thick head—' Prowst woofed—and Pipkin desperately struggled to take in the string of orders that rumbled in the telephone receiver.

'Got an important visitor in me office. Naval fellah. Got to catch the eight-forty-five into Town. Bloody hot water for *someone* if he don't. No excuse. Don't waste time at the gate. Jilde's the order of the day. Better use me special signal—'

'But, sir!' Pipkin squeaked: 'Your orders about that—'

'*God-damn-and-blast-my-bloody-orders*!' Prowst thundered pleasantly, whilst Pipkin removed the telephone to arm's length in order to save his ear drum: 'Just get yer ruddy arse up here at the double—what?'

A further blast of invective came down from above, and the line went dead.

*   *   *

As Max put the telephone down, he turned to find Stoltz looking at him in open-mouthed admiration: 'I'd have sworn that was the old bastard himself . . .'

'Let's hope friend Pipkin does . . .'

'The poor devil's feet won't touch the ground all the way up here . . .'

Stoltz fetched Max's case from the library and placed it just inside the door of Prowst's office: 'Right . . . Now I'd better vanish.' He shook Max's hand: 'Good luck, sir! And don't forget: keep Pipkin hopping about—Don't give him time to think . . .'

'I understand . . .'

Stoltz winked and disappeared through the library door. Max counted up to twenty and flung the Commandant's office door wide open. Private Flower was back in place outside, red-faced and in mortal dread of the charges that Bekker—with the support of three witnesses—had threatened to prefer to Major Prowst. At the sight of Max appearing unexpectedly from behind him, Flower half-dropped his rifle and slapped clumsily at its butt.

Max prodded the offender with his walking-stick: 'Was that intended as a salute or an insult, my man?'

Flower was saved from his predicament by the sight of Pipkin scrambling towards the doorway, struggling to hold up the unravelling coils of his puttees. Max looked at Pipkin's dishevelled figure in disbelief. God in Heaven! Was he expected to trust himself to *that* in Prowst's great brute of a Napier?

'Are you Major Prowst's driver?'

'Yessah!' Pipkin struggled to keep control of his voice—a voice which, in moments of crisis, treacherously descanted

55

from octave to octave: 'Thissway, sah.'

Pipkin set off down the passage at a determined canter.

'*My case*, man.'

Pipkin turned, refused to meet Max's eye and, following the pointing ferrule of his stick, picked up the case from where it stood just inside the Commandant's office, conscious only of an enormous relief that Prowst was nowhere in sight.

The Napier stood at the foot of a broad flight of steps leading down from Thannington Hall's Palladian facade. The car's long, barrel-shaped bonnet concealed a six-and-a-half litre engine, and behind this, its seats were two bucket-like objects completely exposed to the elements.

As Pipkin strapped his case behind these seats, Max affected an impatient tapping of his stick and a prolonged inspection of his watch.

'Come along, man—come along!'

Max allowed himself to be helped up into one of those appalling buckets and then Pipkin went round to the front of the car and heaved at the starting handle. The Napier backfired like an elephant breaking wind and juddered violently. Pipkin scrambled into place beside Max and the car shot away down the drive in a hail of gravel.

Max looked pointedly at his watch again: 'We have just sixteen minutes, Pipkin.'

'Leave it to me, sah!' Pipkin's foot pressed down on the accelerator and the Napier thrummed down the road with increasing speed. A bend, a tree-covered bank—and then the guard-room was in view.

Win or lose in the next twenty seconds.

Max leant forward so that one gold-braided arm was clearly in view as it rested against the windscreen.

'Major Prowst's special signal, Pipkin!'

'Sah!' Pipkin's hand closed over the bulp of the horn.

Pah-pah-pah-pip-pip-paaaaaaaaaaaaaaah!

The guard came tumbling from the guard-room, a purple-faced sergeant bellowing orders. What was it going to be, Max asked himself—a hail of bullets—Or?

The gate barrier swung upwards, and the guard crashed into the 'Present' with a fine slapping of rifle magazine tha could be heard above the roar of the Napier's engine. Max put a lazy hand to his cap peak in answer. As the car went through the gateway, Pipkin's foot pressed down even further on the accelerator pedal and the brute fairly leapt forward, jamming Max back against his seat.

There was still time for the guard to realise his mistake. The muscles in Max's back knotted as he waited for the smack of bullets in his flesh—shots that probably he would never hear.

But no shots came. The drumming of the Napier's exhaust rose to a frenzy against the hedgerows, and in less than a minute, the guard-room was out of sight and left far behind.

*   *   *

Pipkin made the Town station with several minutes to spare. Max let his manner unfreeze a trifle. He took half-a-sovereign from his pocket.

'Thank you, my man. You are an excellent driver.'

'Tha should see my play football, sir.'

'I daresay.' Max pressed the half-sovereign into Pipkin's hand: 'Major Prowst asked me to tell you that you're to leave the car at Benskin's Garage, and that you may then take the rest of the day for yourself before picking up the car at six. Do you understand me?'

Pipkin gaped: 'T'car to Benskin's, and the rest o' the day to mesen' Ee! Ah'm reet grateful, sir.'

Pipkin jumped down and unstrapped Max's case. It was *always* a pleasure to work for real gentlemen.

*   *   *

By an oversight, the only telephone lines connecting Thannington Hall with the outside world ran not from the guard-room, but from the house itself. A hundred yards from the hall, the wires ran through a concealing clump of trees. Given an officer with a pair of wire-cutting pliers, and a considerable pre-war reputation as a climber, it was the work of a few minutes to make sure that Thannington

57

Hall was cut off from the outside world.

Paradoxically, this precaution proved to be unnecessary. The guard-sergeant, appalled by his picquet's drill, spent the better part of the morning putting his squaddies through the 'present' while the Camp visitors' book stayed unchecked on the guard-room table.

For four critical hours, Max's absence remained unsuspected and undiscovered.

*　　　*　　　*

Max leant back in the corner of his first-class carriage and watched the Berkshire scenery fly by. It touched him to remember how, at the sight of his limp, the whole of the Thannington Town Station staff, down to the underporter's cat, had formed a guard of honour to his carriage. Max's smile faded. If his appearance had already come to light, there was every chance that he'd find a very different sort of reception waiting him at Paddington.

He lit a cigarette from Colonel Froebel's gold-case; he'd cross *that* particular bridge if and when he ever came to it. In the meantime, he could relish a pleasant hour of freedom.

But there was no guard waiting him at Paddington. Instead, as he limped across that part of the concourse known as 'The Lawn', he found himself gravely answering the salutes of leavebound ratings and was then handed into a taxi by a porter whose command was only just this side of the obsequious.

'Where to, Guv'nor?'

'Liverpool Street Station, please.'

The taxi pulled away. But, halfway across London, Max' heady sense of freedom got the better of him and became dangerous imp of mischief. He longed for a drink—a drink taken as one free man in the company of others. Half-way along Piccadilly, the sight of a familiar hotel decided him. The *Bicester*—The *Bicester* with that discreet little upstair bar long-known to generations of naval men as th Gunroom. Ralph Caradoc had introduced him to the place many years ago. On impulse, Max leant forward an stopped the taxi.

'I'll be about twenty minutes, cabby.'

'Right-oh, sir.'

Max entered the hotel and found his way upstairs to the Gunroom, pushing his way into the remembered bar with its panelled walls almost obscured by prints of ancient battles and naval heroes. Even though it was now barely noon, the room was already thronged.

Max allowed himself two gins, then turned to go. Suddenly, he was overwhelmingly conscious that in coming here, he had taken the stupidest of risks. He was surrounded by total strangers—yet there, between himself and the door was one face that was vaguely familiar; a face that was avidly watching his own.

With an effort of recall, Max put a name to the face, dragging it out of a seventeen-year limbo of memory. *Felpersham*. The same Felpersham who had then been a weedy urchin in dirty Eton collar and striped trousers during his last term at Admiral's Walk.

Max cursed the bravado that had brought him here to the Gunroom. As he made his apparently casual way to the door, he did his best to keep recognition out of his face. But, Felpersham too, it seemed, had the sort of memory with a faculty for leaping seventeen years. As Max passed him, Felpersham, with the wavy rings of an R.N.V.R. officer on his sleeve, moved into his path.

'I say, sir . . . Max Kirbschaus, isn't it?'

With his voice outwardly cold at being thus accosted, Max said: 'Yes . .' Inwardly, he was thinking: 'Ah, now! Wait for it . . . the accusation . . . The denunciation.'

Felpersham breathed heavily, and with difficulty, focussed his eyes on Max's. Even at this hour, it was evident he had been drinking deeply. Suddenly he reached out a hand and pumped at Max's.

'I jolly well thought so!' He prodded clumsily at the medal ribbons on Max's chest: 'A bally good show, if I might say so, sir. I always said you were one of us really.'

Max opened his mouth to answer, but Felpersham was already gone, blindly stumbling away towards the bar.

Fool! Max damned himself as he returned to his taxi. It

59

was bad enough that he had so nearly given himself away. But *far* worse that he had nearly scuppered his chance of getting home with the information that the British knew of the existence of *Plan Atlantis*.

*   *   *

In the sunlight of early evening, Max finally stood on the quayside at Maldon. But this was a very different man to the urbane commander of morning and afternoon.

In salt-water stained clothing and with his few remaining possessions wrapped in a tattered bundle, this new Max cut a sad figure as he limped along the quay. The limp was real, for by now, his broken ankle throbbed and ached within its constricting bandage. One more step, he thought and he would simply fall down. Gritting his teeth, Max struggled forward against the pain now striking up through the whole length of his leg and into his groin.

Keep moving, man! he willed himself, for within fifty yards of him lay the promise of sanctuary and home—a promise shaped by the familiar lines of the Danish coaster, *Ingrid Anders*. Lars Anders, the youngest of old Erik Anders' splendid sons, was the master of *Ingrid Anders*. He and Max had known each other all their lives and old Fritz Kirbschaus had been Lars's Godfather.

All the same, Max thought, it was one hell of an imposition he was about to lay on this friendship. Still: it had to be tried; Lars could always say 'No'. Hefting up his tattered bundle, Max limped across the quay towards the *Ingrid Anders*'s gangway.

She was wearing the Peter at her foremast, and therefore about to sail.

*   *   *

Fifteen hundred miles away, and three nights later, another officer boarded ship in an equally unorthodox manner.

Part Four

The Wheeling Islands

With its engine throttled back till its sound was a subdued poppling, the pinnace wallowed uneasily in the troughs of the long swells pushing southwards three miles off Valetta. The night was hot but moonless; the sky half-covered by a patchy overcast whose ragged gaps showed constellations as clearly defined as in the pages of a nautical almanac.

But neither the midshipman in command of the pinnace, nor the passengers standing by him in the boat's sternsheets, had eyes for such things. Even this close to Malta one could never be *quite* sure what vessel might not suddenly loom out of the darkness; and a challenge could well be answered by the beat of powerful engines and a burst of fire—which was why the crew of the pinnace's little three-pounder was closed-up ready.

Only a few weeks before, a minefield had been laid—by a 'neutral' Greek, it was alleged—a minefield which had put paid to the old battleship *Russell* and the armed yacht *Erin*. Yes: it paid to keep one's eyes skinned.

Besides—the midshipman glanced towards the shadowy figures of his passengers; he had a rendezvous to keep—the Bloke'd jolly-well have his guts for garters if he failed.

Even so, the snotty couldn't help wondering why there should be this need for so much hurry and secrecy. He looked towards his passengers again. The younger he ignored as belonging to a mere 'wart', another snotty like himself and therefore of no account. The older man looked something different. The pinnace's youthful commander had got a brief squint at him in a torch beam as he'd come on board: thirtyish at a guess, and with a taut, tough, amiable face with a no-nonsense look about it.

It was those same taut looks that were filling the disregarded 'wart' with apprehension. Mr Pembury's confidence had reached its nadir in the last six months. Falling foul of the Senior Sub-Lieutenant in the Flagship's gunroom, Pembury had been beaten with a monotonous frequency that had left him bewildered and mutinous. In the last few days, a moment's incautious handling of his picquet-boat had removed *Devastation*'s starboard accommodation ladder—an error for which he had been beaten again. Fourteen months before a similar incaution at Gallipoli had earned Pembury the D.S.C.

Sensing the youngster's growing inclination to attack Sub-Lieutenant Rixon with his own walking-stick, *Devastation*'s Commander had judged that Pembury's removal would be beneficial to all parties. Pembury was, of course, too young to see the kindness in this. He could only see himself as having been booted out of *Devastation* as a failure.

The look-out in the pinnace's bow called softly: 'Engines ahead, sir.'

A signal lamp flashed and was answered.

'Boat ahoy.'

The pinnace's midshipman drew in breath and, signifying that he had the approaching vessel's captain on board, answered the hail with a single word: '*Bryony!*'

The uneasiness of the pinnace's motion ceased as she surged forward to round to against the schooner *Bryony*'s side. Pembury moved towards the pinnace's gunwale, and his fellow midshipman whispered savagely: 'Wait for your captain, *ass!*'

Caradoc stood poised on the gunwale. No matter how many times he had previously done it, this was something he detested—this leap from boat to ship in the darkness, with the ever-present threat of humiliation or worse waiting an error of judgement.

Rising and falling in the thick darkness, the schooner's low waist seemed formidably high. The pinnace lifted and Caradoc leapt, scrabbling for a frantic moment at the schooner's rail, before being urgently hauled over the side by the seat of his pants. He crashed down onto the deck beneath. Before he could rise, Pembury tumbled down on top of him, knocking every last vestige of breath from his body.

Winded as he was, Caradoc suddenly found himself

helpless with laughter. His situation at least had a bizarre sort of style. What a way to take command!—without salutes, and without ceremonial; like a drunken A.B. making a pier-head jump.

*   *   *

Now, after two days of damnable rain, the weather had cleared. The morning was clean-washed and cool, though later it would be hot. In England now, people were going to church and the early morning air would carry on its breath the scent of frying bacon.

Aidan glanced along the trench. In the limpid light, the men who waited with him seemed like the painted figures in some mediaeval figure. Their bowl-shaped helmets and impedimenta might have belonged to an army of crusaders. Only the blunt-nosed Lee-Enfields destroyed the illusion of timelessness, and betrayed the picture as belonging to the present—as did the unearthly din raging above the trench where shells wailed and screeched as the long barrage reached towards its climax. Guns thumped and snarled; the earth heaved as though its very foundations were being sapped and shaken. To the crash of field gun and howitzer, the mortars added their own peculiar cough and plop.

A curious lassitude held Aidan; a detachment that left him remote and unmoved. Quite certain that within the next hour he would be dead, he felt cut off from all emotion except a gentle melancholy.

He thought of Barbara and tried to picture her—but her face refused to shape itself in his mind. Sadness stole over Aidan as he thought of Barbara opening the inevitable telegram that must reach her in a few days' time. *The War Office regrets to inform you.* His sadness was not for himself . . .

A runner interrupted Aidan's wool-gathering. 'Colonel Boughton's compliments, sir, and I'm to tell you that he'll be going over with "A" Company as planned.'

Aidan nodded at the man: 'Thank the colonel, and wish him "Good luck" from me, will you, Foster?'

'Very good, sir.' The runner saluted and was gone.

So: the colonel was ignoring Divisional Headquarters, was he?—and the order instructing all battalion commanders that they were to retire to a place of safety in the coming attack. Trust Boughton . . .

Aidan looked up as a figure slopped through the muddy trench towards him: Sergeant Robinson.

'Not long now, sir.'

'No . . . The colonel had things out with DHQ, then?'

'Yes, sir. *And* got a flea in his ear.'

'What did he say to that?'

'Plenty.'

Above the heads of the men crouching in the trench, the bombardment was reaching to an intolerable climax. From somewhere away to the right, there was a crump as a shell fell short, exploding in the packed British lines. A choking cloud of evil-tasting smoke gusted along the trench, and then the heart-stopping cry: '*Stretcher-bearers!*'

Aidan glanced at his watch. Seven twenty-five. Ladders had long been set up against the trench wall. Now men began moving towards them. Five more minutes to zero, Aidan thought—and never a five minutes in the whole of eternity that had felt either so short or so long. He glanced at Robinson and nodded.

'Fix bayonets!'

There was a clatter along the trench as the long swordlike bayonets were clipped home above the muzzles of a hundred rifles. The men appeared grey and fatalistic; each withdrawn into himself. Few spoke. Nods rather than words were the coinage of the good luck wishes exchanged between friends. An elusive tang of rain-soaked earth and drenched weeds drifted into the trench from no-man's land. A pair of heedless swallows, appearing suddenly from nowhere, jinked along the parapet. Envying the birds their freedom, men watched them go with hungry eyes.

Aidan's detachment left him. He was possessed by a sense of pity such as he had never before known in his life. He looked at the faces of the men round him with something akin to love. How many of them would still be alive by nightfall? Farm-labourers, factory hands, counter-jumpers, the Jacks of a hundred trades—they were the best that England could give.

Aidan took a flask from his pocket and passed it to Sergeant Robinson. The sergeant drank, then made to hand the flask back, but Aidan shook his head. He had no need of whisky.

'Pass it along the line.'

Other bottles and flasks appeared from nowhere, and the scent of rum was hot on the reeking air. Helmeted heads tilted; mouths drank. Aidan found himself thinking of the Rector who, back home in the village church at Wold, would even now be lifting the Communion Chalice in the act of Consecration:

This is my blood of the New Testament, which was shed for you and for many.

Was the thought blasphemous? Aidan couldn't think so. There would be so much blood shed to-day; so many Gethsemanes; so many little Calvaries that would not seem little to the men who must endure them.

But the time was gone for further musing. The hands of Aidan's watch stood at seven thirty, and the barrage suddenly lifted, leaving the whole front possessed by an unnatural silence.

'God bless you all.'

Aidan found himself climbing a ladder, and in moments was up over the parapet of the trench and out into the low, blinding sunlight of early morning. Without looking back, he pressed on, passing through entanglements of wire in front of the battalion's own trenches, and then onwards into no-man's land beyond. He moved steadily; the men behind him were too laiden to run. Seeing no target for the rifle he carried, Aidan tucked it comfortably under his arm, like a man out for a morning's shooting.

From somewhere in front of him, an insistent yet undangerous tock-tocking sound began. The enemy machine-guns. The air began to sigh and moan with the whisper of passing bullets.

Away to his left, Aidan could see where 'A' Company were making their way towards the German lines. The ground over which they had to pass had been particularly badly cut up by the long bombardment, and he could see the dumpy figure of Colonel Boughton as he led the way over the morass, pointing out the best lines of approach with his walking stick. The tubby little figure with its unwarlike stick might have been absurd, but somehow wasn't.

And now, as well as the machine-guns, the enemy's artillery was beginning to range on the khaki tide straggling across no-man's land. The earth burst upwards in brief chrysanthemum flowers; flowers in which men were blasted to quivering gobbets of meat. 'A' Company seemed to check and hesitate—a movement that was no more than a shiver, like the wind passing through a field of wheat. Then, at a jaunty uplift of the Colonel's stick, 'A' Company's dwindling remnants went on, with heads bowed against the machine-gun bullets as though butting into a squall of sleet.

Aidan heard himself cry out as he saw the Colonel go down onto his knees, feebly waving away the forbidden assistance and struggling to his feet once more and staggering onwards. But Aidan's relief was shortlived. Hit and hit again, Colonel Boughton finally fell face downwards in the mud.

Aidan found himself sobbing. 'A' Company was failing even to reach its dead colonel. Man by man it was melting away into the nothingness of death. Now, perhaps, only a score remained alive and on their feet, vainly searching for shelter where there was none.

For the first time, Aidan turned to look back at the men following him. These, too, had been pitifully winnowed. Even as he glanced back, Aidan saw Sergeant Robinson's trim figure dissolve into a bloody mass of rags and bone—rags and bone which writhed and shrieked their torment.

Oh, Christ! Where was detachment *now*?

Aidan moved on. Loos had been bad—but this? This reached into nightmare realms where the unthinkable was the commonplace. He stumbled blindly forward till he reached the enemy wire.

It was uncut, of course—they had been fools to delude themselves otherwise. Bullets whined and yearned at him, but he remained unhit. Hopelessly, Aidan groped his way along the wire, fumbling for the breach he knew had not been made . . .

And then, at last, something sent the rifle spinning from out of his hand. A something else bit at his steel helmet and cut through it. Aidan felt his body arch as he was lifted high and backwards—and then, he was falling, falling into the darkness of eternity and death.

Oh, Barbara.

*   *   *

'The first turn of the screw cancels all debts . . .'

Ralph Caradoc woke with a start as the phrase slipped down into his unconscious. Now, suddenly awake, he had not the least idea where he was. The narrow box-like shape of the space in which he lay, suggested a coffin. But it was a very comfortable coffin and it was only by an effort of will, that Caradoc resisted the temptation to sink back into sleep.

Gathering his wits, he sat up in his bunk, listening to the murmuring of a wooden vessel under sail. A brilliant splash of sunlight dropped in through the open skylight—and, Lord! it was hot!

There was a knock at the cabin door, and *Bryony*'s first-lieutenant came into the cabin.

'A fine morning, sir.'

Caradoc was coldly angry: 'I thought I gave orders that I was to be called at dawn?'

The first-lieutenant looked surprised: 'But you *were*, sir. You came on deck for a quarter of an hour or so, then told me to carry on.'

'I did?'

'I can assure you, sir—'

Caradoc frowned, struggling to remember the first-lieutenant's name. Souris? Yes, that was it. Dark-eyed, raven-haired, olive-skinned . . . A Greek by his looks and name. The Lord alone knew what a Greek was doing masquerading as an R.N.V.R. officer.

His tone curt with dismissal, Caradoc said: 'I'll dress and

be up on deck in a few minutes, Souris.'

The smile faded from Souris's face as he turned towards the cabin door: 'Very good, sir.' Inwardly he was seething. Caradoc seemed everything he most disliked about the British: stiff-necked; unimaginative and graceless.

When his first-lieutenant had returned on deck, Caradoc looked at the clothes laid out for him across a chair: cotton-trousers, shirt, and an old pair of laceless sand-shoes. Well, he told himself reaching for this disreputable clothing, if he *must* play pirates again, then the eastern end of the Mediterranean was as good a place as any in which to do it—and a damned sight more comfortable than the Western Approaches in winter.

Suddenly, guiltily, he remembered just why he had woken with such a start. He had been dreaming of Barbara—a Barbara for whom otherwise, he had scarcely spared a thought since leaving England. Caradoc winced: the events of his dream were only too clear to him now. Barbara and he had been naked in each other's arms. As to the rest . . .

Hastily, he finished dressing and went on deck.

*   *   *

Half an hour later, and with Souris for guide, Caradoc was finishing his inspection of his new command. No more than seventy-five feet from taffrail to her flaring beakhead, *Bryony*'s total length was almost doubled by the thrust of her sharp bowsprit and her fifty feet of mainboom, half of which jutted far beyond her stern.

The exaggerated dimensions of these spars startled Caradoc. He had been led to expect a humble trading schooner: *Bryony* more nearly resembled a 'J' Class yacht. She was masted to match bowsprit and mainboom, with two towering columns of cedar rising seventy feet above her deck—masts that, wickedly raked, gave her an authentically piratical appearance.

A 'Syrian schooner', Souris called her, and every dramatic line of hull and masts betrayed her quality: disreputable and louche though it might be, yet still of an unmistakable breeding.

Already Caradoc knew that she had speed. With the wind an aeolian humming in her shrouds and the purple-blue water churned into a creaming wake under her heel, *Bryony* was making nearly ten knots, despite the drag of the screw through her quarter.

Caradoc stared aloft. That great leg-o'-mutton mainsail alone must amount to what? Nearly three-and-a-half *thousand* square feet of canvas. Its ally on the foremast couldn't be much less. And the main-staysail, and those three splendid triangles stretched on her arching bowsprit?

Caradoc felt a sense of disquiet. The biggest thing he had ever handled under sail had been a cutter—thirty-two feet of comparatively sedate and forgiving beaminess, a whole world away from this spirited, tearing thoroughbred.

He felt something near panic. It was all very well telling himself that the principles of sailing remained the same whatever the ship. True that might be—but you still had to know where to begin. Caradoc thought with longing of the gleaming Thornycroft engine down below. Engines were *biddable*. You called down a voice pipe, or reached for the handle of a telegraph—and you were obeyed.

Then, too, as a naval auxiliary, *Bryony* barely existed. A collapsible deck house just abaft the foremast hid a venerable three-pounder of unfamiliar pattern. Aft, a canvas shroud concealed a one-pounder pom-pom of temperamental reputation. Lord! Caradoc told himself, *Bryony* would find herself in trouble against a determinedly handled picket-boat.

Out of countenance, he mooched aft. Stiff-legged with annoyance, he all-but slid down *Bryony*'s sloping deck into her lee scuppers. He grumbled and swore, and the men on deck exchanged glances and became extravagently busy.

Well, let 'em! Caradoc told himself morosely. After the men he had known in *Undine*, the faces around him seemed characterless and empty.

Caradoc looked up to find himself being quizzically eyed by the lanky figure of a man who had just emerged on deck. He was a disreputable figure, with a five-day growth of beard and outlandishly dressed in fez, collarless embroidered shirt, and drooping Turkish trousers supported by a crimson cummer-bund. Caradoc stared. Despite the fellow's exotic appearance, there was something familiar about him. Caradoc searched his memory, then gaped:

'Good God! *Harbinger* . . . Ordinary Seaman Wells.'

'*Petty Officer* Wells these days, sir.'

'You must have mended your ways.'

Wells grinned: 'P'raps it's just that I don't seem to get found out quite so often these days, sir.'

'You'd better not get found out at all with me!'

'I'll remember that, sir.'

Caradoc pointed to Wells's drooping pants: 'What's the idea of looking like something from the chorus of Chu Chin Chow?'

'Y'mean the trousers, sir? Crap-traps the lads call 'em. Look!'

Wells chuckled and pointed, so that for the first time, Caradoc noticed that all the men working on *Bryony*'s deck were similarly trousered. He swore inwardly. Christ! What did someone think this was—some sort of pantomine?

'And just *whose* idea was that, Wells?' he asked coldly.

'Number One's, sir. Apparently he used to trade up and down the islands and the Levant with a crew of Syrians.'

'Did he now.' Caradoc glared for'ard at Souris's distant figure bent low over the bowsprit gammoning. Then, without another word to Wells, Caradoc turned and retreated aft to the sanctuary of his cabin.

Damn Souris! Damn and blast the fellow! He seemed to have thought of *everything*.

*　　*　　*

Noon. Thank God that for all her exotic looks and his own eccentric rig, *Bryony* was still one of H.M. ships, Wells told himself as he retired with his tot to the tiny cuddy which he shared with the schooner's morose E.R.A., McNab. The fact that the E.R.A. was presently below, tinkering with the Thornycroft, filled Wells with relief.

McNab had a 'T' against his name in *Bryony*'s books—the

'T' standing for temperance. But there was nothing at all temperate about the E.R.A. who belonged to some horrible sect back home in his native hills; a sect which regarded the whole world (and particularly the drinking part of it) as being in league with the devil and therefore damned—a point of view which McNab loudly expressed every tot-time.

Thankful to be alone, therefore, Wells propped himself in the corner of his bunk and sipped his *neaters*. He needed to think; for since his brief meeting with Caradoc an hour or so back, he'd begun to question his own wisdom in leaving a comfortable number.

Caradoc seemed changed from the days Wells remembered in *Harbinger*. He had always been taut, but the asperity that had shown itself this morning, the eagerness to find fault, had been something altogether new. And, as for that barely-disguised mistrust and dislike of his own first-lieutenant. Wells took a long pull at his tot as an unpleasant possibility came into his mind. Perhaps what he had witnessed had been an ominous portent of one of those inexplicable antipathies that sometimes happened between two men.

Wells finished his rum. God help everyone if that was the case. In a vessel as small as *Bryony* that would spell real trouble.

McNab ducked into the little caboosh, wiping his hands on a wad of cotton waste, his jutting nose sniffing disapproval of the hot smell of rum hanging on the close air. The E.R.A.'s mouth opened preparatory to beginning his usual sermon, but Wells was in no mood for such cant.

'Man!—' McNab began, but got no further. He found himself alone in the caboosh and with his mouth firmly stopped by the cotton waste with which he had been cleaning his hands.

*   *   *

Bryony ghosted through the short Mediterranean twilight like some grey, silent moth. Somewhat self-consciously taking the watch, Mr Pembury called the helmsman's wandering attention back to the job at hand. The seaman sucked briefly at a hollow tooth, then dutifully twitched at the spokes of the wheel.

In a moment or two more, the breeze would die away altogether and what bothered Pembury was how he should announce this fact to his captain. Awareness of Caradoc's ill mood had permeated the schooner and Pembury had no ambition to draw attention to himself. With Caradoc in the frame of temper he'd been all day—and, for all Pembury knew, that temper might be typical of the man—he felt that there wasn't much to choose between calling his captain, or being asked to put his head in a lion's mouth. If anything, the latter seemed the safer option.

Pembury sighed. Was the *whole* Navy made up of bastards? Or was it just that he had the unhappy knack of running into them these days?

A numb resignation swept over the midshipman as he saw the great mainsail above his head shiver and drop into useless swags of canvas. The ill moment could be put off no longer. Pembury took a deep breath and nodded to a waiting member of the watch.

'Call the captain, please, Ferris.'

'Aye, aye, sir.'

No more enthusiastic about this duty than the midshipman, the angular Ferris ducked down into the open hatchway, and Pembury awaited his captain's arrival on deck with fatalistic gloom. He couldn't put his finger on anything he'd done wrong since taking the watch—but doubtless there was *something* for which he'd be blamed: *something* which—as usual!—he'd be accused of making a bloody hash of.

* * *

Michael Souris studiously avoided his captain's eye while Takis, the cook-steward, anxiously hovered over the table with a silver tureen. When the soup had been served and the steward had gone, Souris began eating in silence, until he heard Caradoc give a grunt that might have either been a stifled chuckle, or the starting gun for another burst of

72

annoyance.

Souris remained silent: to say anything at all might lay him open to that anger which, all day had seemed to emanate from Caradoc like the crackle of static electricity. But then, Souris heard Caradoc laughing—the same clear, unequivocal laughter with which his captain had greeted his own precipitate arrival on *Bryony*'s deck the previous evening. Startled, the first-lieutenant looked up, his eyes searching Caradoc's face for any sign that the laughter was false. But—No!—Caradoc appeared to be enjoying some joke hugely; a joke, which it appeared, was largely at his own expense.

'Sir?' Souris queried.

An un-English gesture of Caradoc's hands embraced the whole saloon; the whole ship: 'I was just wondering what my old term officer would say if he could see me now.'

Common politeness dictated that Souris's 'Really, sir?' should sound like an invitation to explain.

Caradoc went on: 'I used to enjoy a dubious reputation under sail on the Dart—particulary after I rammed the ferry in a cutter. Finally, I was banished to the cricket field, under pain of execution if I ever went near the river again without permission and a qualified keeper.'

Souris gaped at Caradoc, too astonished for amusement. It seemed an unlikely sort of confession. But, it was also, he was quick to perceive, a veiled expression of self-doubt; a roundabout apology even. Against his will, Souris found himself warming to Caradoc, particularly when he went on: 'So! For the peace of my old term officer's soul, you'll have to regard yourself as being appointed official bear-leader till I get the weight of things.'

The atmosphere in the saloon palpably thawed. In the gimballed lamp's gently swinging light, the first lieutenant studied Caradoc's face as they ate and talked. It was a deeply tired face, too, Souris noticed, fine-drawn as though marked by some harsh experience. Yet, that same fine-drawn look only added to the face's undeniable authority—an authority put there by breeding and the sea and yet which looked inwards on itself, as though unwilling to take itself for granted.

By the end of dinner, Souris found himself talking freely, recounting adventures which he'd met with trading up and down the Levant. Some of those adventures had run close against the knuckle of the law and Caradoc said with a deceptive inconsequentiality: 'An ancestor of mine was hanged for piracy.'

Souris capped this: '*Two* of mine were.'

Ferris arrived at the saloon door with Mr Pembury's message that the wind had dropped, and Caradoc and Souris went on deck. For a few brief moments, Pembury was relieved to note the absence of tension in the air as he received orders for the watch to take in sail and the Thornycroft to be started. Yet, soon, despite the warmth of the night, the throb of the powerful engine, and the schooner's easy motion as she moved through the dark sea, Pembury's doubts returned.

Surely it was time that somebody blamed him for *something* . . .

* * *

The dozen men who made up *Bryony*'s fo'c'sle spoke with the accents of as many fishing and coasting ports the length and breadth of Britain. But, they had this in common; that they were each and everyone of them 'stick-and-string' sailors—men whose peacetime livelihoods had been precariously won under canvas and at the vagaries of wind and tide.

It was for this reason that each of them had been combed from the Fleet in Malta. In peacetime, they had been reservists, gambling a period of training against the certainty of a bounty. They regarded the Navy with a certain ambivalence, with awe, sometimes; but more often with a scoffing irritation.

Off watch, their talk was clannish—reminiscent, salty, ribald, knowledgeable and prejudiced. Who knew the sea as *they* did? Caradoc's arrival on board gave them scope for a new distrust—a disapproval which it was left to the Yorkshireman, Earnshaw, to express.

'Tha-at Caradoc,' he said, jetting a stream of tobacco juice into a distant spit-kid: 'Ah'll tell thes what *he* is, an' all. He's nobbut a bloody steam-kettle sailor!'

Brixham trawler chewed at his pipe-stem: 'My old dad used ter say as there were three useless things yew could have aboard ship, m'dear: an umbrella, a wheelbarrow—and a naval officer.'

The watch below guffawed. Next door in his little caboosh, Wells clenched his fists. What did that bloody lot beyond the bulkhead know anyway, dragged off their mud-flats, or from winding creeks that somehow symbolised their narrowness of outlook?

They hadn't spent a long night on *Harbinger's* bridge, when, with his own world lying shattered beneath his feet, Caradoc had contrived to keep the destroyer's few survivors in good spirits.

The mounting grumble of voices from the fo'c'sle went far to making up Wells's mind for him, but it was a sneering whine of: 'If yer ask me, mates, the owner's no more a seaman than I'm an Admiral of the Fleet!' that finally brought the petty officer out of his bunk. That sort of talking needed nipping in the bud right away! With a badly stubbed toe giving an edge of pain to his anger, Wells burst into the fo'c'sle: 'Pipe down!'

Five of the fo'c'sle's occupants settled for caution: the sixth, anonymous as he thought in the darkness of his bunk, sniggered: 'Who'll make us—you?'

Well's reaction was swift. He'd identified the sneerer for certain now—Fadger, who called himself a bawleyman, but was more likely some sort of Gravesend waterfront lounger and bully. Wells was across the fo'c'sle and leaning over his victim with terrifying suddeness.

'You never will make no Admiral of the Fleet, Fadger—but you'll do as Captain of the Heads!'

'It's me watch below!'

'Git moving, sonny!' With a twist of his sinewy wrist, Wells jerked Fadger from his bunk and down onto the deck with a jarring thump and crash.

Fadger swore and lashed out with a bare foot at Wells's crutch and an agonised spasm of pain shot through the petty officer's body. Fadger yowled in triumph, but the yowl turned to one of baffled rage as Wells had him by the scruff of the neck and with one arm twisted in an agonising lock. Half-kicking, half-pushing him, Wells propelled Fadger towards the open door of the heads. Without further ceremony, the bawleyman was sent sprawling into the tiny, stinking, hutch, and the door jammed shut behind him.

'Should feel like an home from home to you in there, Fadger.'

Wells turned and limped his way back to the fo'c'sle.

'Anyone else anything to say?' he enquired.

But not so much as a snore answered him. Satisfied, Wells returned to his cot. *His slop-chit*? *His responsibility*?

There were more ways of instilling discipline than ever appeared in the pages of King's Regulations and Admiralty Instructions.

*　　*　　*

The north-west wind sprang up again with the dawn—a fluky zephyr at first, but gradually hardening during the forenoon, so that *Bryony* surged westwards with her log reeling off a steady nine knots.

Caradoc came on deck early. Hands behind back, he stood by the helmsman for a few minutes before reluctantly returning below. Souris joined him in his cabin and together they spread out a chart on the Cyclades on Caradoc's desk top.

'Why do they call 'em "the Wheeling Isles", Number One?'

'Because they're like the spokes round the island of Delos, sir. *Besides*: that's the sort of effect they always seem to have on you when you come to them afresh—as though someone's shifted them around while you've been away.'

Caradoc peered down at the chart in perplexity: 'The sailing directions say there are nineteen islands. I've counted 'em on the chart half-a dozen times and come up with a different answer every time. But, numbers apart, the same question always remains—where do we begin?'

Souris pulled a face: 'I've been asking myself the same

question for days, sir.'

Caradoc's fingers tapped at the chart: 'We can count out Milos, I think—the French have got a base there. Syra is too populous. Kea has only one good harbour, and not much else to offer in the way of deep water anchorages.'

'Well. That's eliminated three, sir.'

'*Three*! And, even then, we can't be *certain*.' Caradoc swallowed his pride: '*You're* the local man, Souris—what do you think?'

Souris pondered: 'That's just my problem, sir. It's not that I *can't* think of likely places—I can—all too many of them. We've got something like three thousand square miles of water and hundreds of miles of coastline to choose from—much of it *possible*—and with very little we can safely ignore.'

'Especially when we don't even know what we're looking for.'

'Quite, sir.'

The two men remained silent for some moments, contemplating the chart. Caradoc laughed ruefully: 'Well . . . I was warned that we'd be looking for a needle in a haystack.'

'There's a time-limit, too, isn't there, sir?'

'You know about the intention to put a fleet into Salamis?'

'Yes, sir.'

'Then we've two or three months. No more.'

Souris's head jerked upwards in the emphatic Greek negative: 'Then the whole thing's impossible, sir—unless we have the most stupendous luck.'

Caradoc put a match to his pipe and laughed wryly: 'It looks as though we'll have to carry on blind for the while, Number One. We'll make our number at Milos according to orders—and then think again. In the meantime—' His eyes returned to the chart: 'You'd better give me some idea where the Aegean Squadron is supposed to have hidden our petrol.'

*   *   *

On the sixth day, the wind unseasonably backed to the south eastwards and strengthened. By late afternoon, a full gale was blowing and the Mediterranean blue had changed to a mean greyness that the North Sea might have envied. With her stern buffeted by a succession of short, punching seas, *Bryony* ran before the gale under shortened canvas and dropped anchor off Pylos.

By the next dawn, the gale had almost blown itself out, and the wind had veered round to the north-west again. *Bryony* had not been the only vessel forced to run for shelter. During the night she had been joined by several small fishing boats. Half-a-mile westwards, a large schooner was already making sail.

Michael Souris watched her departure with unfriendly eyes: 'Now I wonder just what she's up to?'

'An old acquaintance, Number One?' Caradoc asked.

'An old enemy, sir,' the first lieutenant said: 'She's owned by the Koritsases of Famagousta. They're into any dirty game you like to mention. I wonder what they're up to now?'

'Why?'

Souris handed his binoculars to his captain: 'Someone's spent a great deal of money on the old *Ikaria* recently, sir— *and* gone to a great deal of trouble to alter her appearance. Why?'

'A lot of people are making a great deal of money out of this war, Number One.'

'It's how the Koritsases might be making theirs that worries me, sir.'

'But Cyprus is a British possession.'

'That didn't stop the Koritsases having a lot of pre-war interests with the Hamburg-Athenia Shipping Consortium.'

'Oh?—'

Caradoc waited for his First Lieutenant to say more, but instead, Souris's face shaped itself into taut, unforgiving lines, as though he was looking back onto some particularly unpleasant memory; and, when he spoke, it was only to ask permission to start getting under way.

Michael Souris thought with longing of pre-war days when he had sailed these same waters, bothered only by the occasional Bill of Landing and when his relationship with the local customs had always been eased by a handful of drachmas. They had been good days—days when, with the whole of the Middle sea as his oyster, he had pottered between its sleepier ports like some latter-day Odysseus. *Now*—even in a vessel as small and as far-removed from Naval orthodoxy as *Bryony*—there always seemed to be a small mountain of paperwork requiring the First Lieutenant's attention.

Souris groaned and turned his attention to the conduct sheet of one Able-Seaman Hughes, who, since mobilization in 1914, had evidently thought of his war as being *against* the Royal Navy.

Leave breaking, fighting, drunkenness, urinating on the mess-decks—it was all there on Hughes's crime-sheet. Yet Hughes's looks belied his reputation: a small, slight, even diffident figure, his sins were less the product of an inate bloody-mindedness than by a now quite desperate sense of isolation. A North Walian, with barely a hundred words of English, Hughes's efforts to make himself understood, had resulted in him becoming a figure of fun.

A confused yet proud little man, Hughes had kicked over the traces. His next stop should have been cells—but, collusion between a kindly Divisional Officer and a wise Commander had kept him from these and instead, Hughes had found himself drafted to *Bryony*.

Though Souris was only vaguely aware of it, Hughes had already come very near to regaining his self-respect. Each evening at dusk, Caradoc exercised *Bryony*'s puny armament against discarded crates and boxes. Practice with the three-pounder had been indifferent, but—and Hughes's stature grew two inches at the memory!—that of the pom-pom had been anything but second rate. Crate after crate had been shattered into matchwood by the probing fire of the Hotchkiss, until the previous evening, when the guns had at last been secured, a laughing

Caradoc had christened Hughes in the time-honoured Welsh way by tacking his name and trade together.

Hughes-Pom-Pom.

Hughes had felt the resurgence of an almost forgotten pride—the sort of pride that didn't need a dozen pints and a scrap with a sixteen-stone stoker to give it substance. *Ach y fi!* He was finished with that old nonsense.

He was Hughes-Pom-Pom—and his own man again.

*   *   *

In Milos, a tall officer in the uniform of the French Naval Air Service came on board. He introduced himself as Raymond Yves. As Caradoc led the Frenchman below, he saw that Yves moved with the disjointed awkwardness of a clockwork toy badly in need of oiling. Negotiating the steep companion ladder, the airman slipped and all but fell. Caradoc put out a hand to steady him, and Yves smiled with painful gratitude.

'It is a pity that God did not do that for me in the first place.'

'Were you shot down?'

'No, M'sieu—my Bleriot fall to pieces—Pffff!—before ze war. That was quite as . . . *effective*.'

Two hours later, Caradoc found himself seated in the rear cockpit of a small sea-plane on the far side of the harbour. The sun of a Greek afternoon beat down on his helmeted head; rivers of sweat poured down his body and two small ponds of his own grease grew in the bottom corners of his goggles. In front of Caradoc and almost blocking out his view for'ard, sat the over-tall figure of Yves, the upper part of his body absurdly high in its seat, as though the aircraft were too small for him.

A mechanic climbed onto the plane's floats and hurled a stream of unintelligible French in Yves's direction. The pilot's thumb jerked upwards in emphatic affirmative and the propellor was swung. The plane's engine snarled—and, almost before Caradoc knew quite what was happening, the Nieuport was racing full tilt across the indigo waters of the harbour, bumping and juddering as

80

though they were made of ridged concrete. Caradoc gritted his teeth and prayed that the aircraft would hold together.

But then, surprisingly, the spine-numbing jarring ceased, and the sea-plane was in the air. Caradoc looked down astonished at the whitewashed, diminished blocks of churches and houses. There, dancing gently beneath the aircraft's port wing was *Bryony* herself—a toy ship, waiting insertion into her rightful bottle.

The wide bay looked different too. From this height, the sea's dark indigo had become transmuted into a dozen different translucent purples, blues and greens, marking the deeps and shallows of the anchorage.

Caradoc set himself to look and learn. From up here, he could actually see down *into* the water to the loom of the hidden reefs and banks of weed. The wreck of an old tramp was clearly visible and another that might have been the hull of a destroyer.

Yves turned the aircraft eastwards. Milos was left behind them. Two lumpy islands appeared away northwards, painted in the sage-green and grey which Caradoc soon came to realise was the predominant colour of Greece when seen from the air. The plane droned on. One by one, the arid and mountainous islands of Pholegandros, Sikinos and Ios slipped beneath the plane.

Caradoc felt quite relaxed now. A man had a god's-eye view from up here. Nothing escaped him. A pair of destroyers steamed southwards on urgent business; a light-cruiser and a further trio of escorts moved to meet them. What damned fools they had all been not to think of aircraft in the first place!

But now, Yves was swinging the plane round in a wide, banking turn that would bring them back on to the reciprocal course to the one they had been flying. Ios, Sikinos and Pholegandros were passed in reverse order.

Caradoc did a few sums in his head. Time. Distance. Range. With the old freighter that served as a sea-plane carrier for Yves' flight, there was no corner of the Cyclades that lay beyond reckoning. To Yves and his pilots, the whole archipelago lay open like a book—difficult and obscure though its print might be.

But, already the great harbour of Milos was opening up beneath the Nieuport again. After making a wide circuit round the bay to lose height, Yves dropped the sea-plane down towards the blue waters beneath. Miniature houses, churches and ships all rapidly grew into something resembling their own size, stopped their lazy dance beneath the aircraft's wings, and began flashing past at an increasing pace. Then the floats hit the water and once again came that spine-jarring sensation of travelling over rigid concrete. But this roughness died away as the plane slowed and finally came to rest, curtseying gently on the slightest of lops.

Half-an-hour later, Caradoc was back on board *Bryony*, where he was met by a concerned-looking Souris who handed him a flimsy scrap of paper: 'This came in for you from the French wireless-station an hour ago, sir. I rather think it's bad news.'

Caradoc unfolded the paper. Its message appeared to be the transcript of a telegram. Although its message only consisted of half-a-dozen words, he had to read them twice before understanding came:

AIDAN REPORTED MISSING BELIEVED KILLED, BARBARA.

*   *   *

Bryony lay hove-to a dozen miles off Sifnos, the small night breezes warm and carrying on their breath the faint mingled scents of lemon trees, tamarisk and thyme. The night *seemed* peaceful enough, but Caradoc was sharply conscious of the unseen figures of the schooner's crew surrounding him in the darkness. Wells at the wheel; the crews of three-pounder and pom-pom closed up and ready as they had been this last hour since their escort had mislaid them.

The look-out for'ard spotted their errant guardian first: 'Trawler away on the port bow, sir!'

A hardening area of darkness shaped itself into the unmistakable silhouette of a trawler. A lamp morsed briefly, petulantly—and was answered from *Bryony*'s deck. The schooner rolled gently with a subdued murmur of timbers, like the sigh of a tired man easing cramped limbs.

The trawler's signal lamp flashed again. Earnshaw, *Bryony*'s signalman, sounded indignant: 'Eh! T'cheeky booger wants t'know where *we* got to.'

'Tell him "Looking for him!"' Caradoc snapped, then changed his mind: 'No . . . Belay that. Just acknowledge.'

After an exchange of farewells, the trawler turned away towards Milos and quickly dissolved into the darkness. The Thornycroft growled and a chuckle began under *Bryony*'s forefoot as though she too was eager to be about her business.

Caradoc moved aft to where Wells stood at the wheel: 'Steer north-east by east, Wells.'

'Nor'-east by east it is, sir.'

Bryony's search was at last beginning.

Part Five

The Wheeling Islands

Beginning and beginning, Caradoc told himself as day after day unravelled itself in unvarying and fruitless monotony. It was only after the first week, when *Bryony* had backed and filled amongst the sheltered bays of Sifnos that he at last began to get a true perspective of the impossibility of the schooner's task.

Even with her auxiliary engine, *Bryony* was still too slow to have time for anything more than the most superficial of searches along the littoral of each island—islands that, for all their apparent smallness on the chart, each represented a formidable task in itself. Even with Souris as pilot and guide—a Souris who seemed to know every corner of the islands—the possibility of success seemed to grow remoter with each passing day. At best, all the schooner could do was make a token patrol of each island—a circumnavigation that did little more than scratch the surface of things.

Standing with his legs comfortably astraddle in the cobalt shadow of *Bryony*'s mainsail, Caradoc tried to concentrate his mind on the job at hand. Despite its growing unreality, the urgency of the business nagged at him like an aching tooth. *Plan Atlantis*? What *was* it? And just how long had he to come up with the right answer?

Half-closing his eyes against the forenoon glare, Caradoc looked along the deck. Souris and Wells had their heads together, deep in discussion about some aspect of shipboard management, the gestures of both Greek and Englishman shaping eloquent gestures in the air.

Caradoc knew he had struck lucky with them both. Humorous and philosophical, they seemed to have enforced their personalities on *Bryony*'s fo'c'sle to some purpose—a fo'c'sle which, Caradoc knew, had been disposed to exert a bloody-minded independence

Still: everyone seemed cheerful enough now, Caradoc

told himself. Idly, he wondered just what part Wells had played in this and grinned. Perhaps it was better *not* to ask.

Now, the men almost seemed to be relishing the make-believe world that went with their pantomime dress and were enjoying *Bryony*'s slow progress through the islands. To them, this was time out; sailing as the Good Lord had intended it should be—and a whole world away from the precarious business of snatching a living round their own hazardous shores.

Eight bells signalled mid-day and with them came the heartening cry of 'Up-Spirits!' As if in confirmation of Caradoc's thoughts, a seaman straightened up from his work, and, after a long look round the glistering blue waters, announced to no one in particular: 'Lor'! Fiddler's Green, this is.'

Caradoc filled his pipe. He was glad someone was happy.

*   *   *

Despite his own doubts as to the feasability of *Bryony*'s search, Petty Officer Wells, too, felt contentment. He was doing a job he knew and doing it well.

That he'd had to take drastic measures to sort out *Bryony*'s crowd for'ard, worried him not at all. On the contrary, it gave him a certain confidence in them: at least they'd got *spirit*. A Chatham rating himself, Wells had long-since become used to ship's companies with a bit of mettle.

As for *Bryony* herself, Wells viewed her with unalloyed love. The schooner's graceful lines satisfied something very deep within him—something that a more sophisticated man might just have called his soul.

*   *   *

Only one man felt out of tune with the growing sense of well-being on board the schooner—Fadger, the bawley-man; that same Fadger whom Wells had promoted Captain of *Bryony*'s noisome heads. To Fadger's bitterness, his rough handling had gained him little sympathy. On the contrary, the fo'c'sle had seemed to enjoy the incident hugely and Fadger had found himself the butt of an unprintable and ribald humour.

Indeed, fo'c'sle opinion was that Fadger had sat up and begged for trouble—and therefore had no complaint because Wells had obliged him. Bred in a rough, unsentimental school, the fo'c'sle crowd saw nothing unreasonable in the way Fadger had been licked into line. They knew the score. Such methods were drastic, but without malice and the lesson seldom needed repeating.

But Fadger was different. In judging him to be less seaman than waterfront lounger, Wells had not been far from the mark. In civilian life, Fadger had fancied himself as being a very fly boy indeed—and, as such, he remembered his treatment at Wells's hands with a festering savagery.

'I'll get that mucker one day—you'll see!' he announced to the fo'c'sle—and the fo'c'sle reacted with humiliating scorn. 'You'll *what*?' It laughed, recalling Fadger's performance in the heads: '*You'll what? You*?—'

Remembering that contemptuous '*You*?' the poisonous little nub at the centre of Fadger's being ached like an abscess. *He'd show those disbelieving sods . . . He'd square that bastard Wells . . .*

*   *   *

If *Undine*'s wireless room had been diminutive, then *Bryony*'s resembled nothing so much as a rabbit hutch—a hutch which had been built round its occupant, a large pink man with wrinkling button-nose, buck teeth and the surname of Warren, who had inevitably been christened Bunny from his first day on board.

To-night, as Caradoc appeared at the wireless-room door, Warren twitched nervously and whispered: 'The French seem very perturbed about something, sir.'

Inwardly cursing the telegraphist for the fact that this information hadn't been passed up to him earlier, Caradoc snapped. 'Perturbed? What about, Warren?'

The rabbit twitched a nervous nose: 'One of the aircraft from Milos is missing, sir. One of our reconnaissance flight so far as I could make out.'

'Somewhere in this direction?'

'No, sir. Down to the south, I think. The French didn't give an exact position—just a general area.'

'Then there's nothing we can do to help.'

'No, sir.'

Unjustly, Caradoc found himself almost loathing Warren's rabbity softness. He went up on deck, pondering the missing Frenchmen's chances. Pretty small in his opinion. *Plan Atlantis* had already claimed its first victims.

* * *

Two evenings later, *Bryony* lay at anchor in three fathoms of water, north-east of Kithnos. The *Meltemi* had been in boisterous mood that afternoon, but had died away with the setting sun, leaving the schooner rising and falling to its residual swell.

Bryony's dinghy lay alongside with Wells, the cadaverous East-Anglian called Ferris, Hughes-Pom-Pom, and another Welshman, Evans, ready at the oars, waiting for Caradoc and Souris to clamber over the schooner's rail. Souris frequently landed alone on mysterious errands; but, whenever he could, Caradoc liked to get ashore in his first-lieutenant's company, defying convention and leaving Pembury in command. When Caradoc went ashore with Souris, the two men dined at the likeliest-looking *taberna*.

While the first-lieutenant asked what questions he could and the pair of them kept their eyes open.

Working in pairs, the four outlandishly dressed ratings did much the same. None of the four spoke Greek, but they could *watch*.

Caradoc and Souris dropped down into the dinghy and were rowed ashore. Loutron looked a pretty dead-and-alive place, Caradoc thought as he clambered out of the dinghy under the gaze of a row of moustachio'd fishermen who reminded him of Major Prowst.

Together, captain and first-lieutenant made their way

towards the village. The only *taberna* in sight was an unkempt affair, with no more than four tables set in a barren rectangle of ground where a trio of dispirited goats nibbled at a pile of potato peelings.

'Hobson's choice,' Caradoc growled.

'Maxim's or starve,' Souris agreed.

They sat down at a table as far away as possible from the goats and ordered their meal. Wine came—and, glass in hand, Caradoc set himself to watch. It was something he was becoming very good at lately.

Further along the village street, Wells and Ferris kept a watchful eye on the passers-by taking the evening air. The stares of the passing Greeks were frank in their curiosity and Wells had come to realise that this was their way. It would be the eye that *didn't* stare at him now that would rouse his suspicion.

Wells was gratified to notice the interest that his own appearance seemed to excite in the young and nubile womanhood that passed beneath his gaze. His rapidly growing beard, fez and pantaloons seemed to draw any number of looks from dark, langorous eyes. Nothing averse, Wells ogled back. They were handsome little parties. Thank Gawd his missus couldn't see him now! Abdul the Damned with his harem of thousands.

Cor! Now *there* was a thought.

*   *   *

Early the next afternoon, *Bryony* ghosted in towards Kavea Bay on a tremulous feather of breeze that fitfully came and went, frequently leaving the schooner becalmed above the gathering flawlessness of her own reflection. Then, when all likelihood of further airs seemed out of the question, her canvas slowly filled again and she slid onwards, shivering her mirrored image into fragments.

This afternoon, Caradoc had ordered a 'make-and-mend', so that apart from himself, a barely troubled helmsman and a pair of drooping-eyed look-outs, everyone was either asleep below, or flaked out on the baking deck in the windless shadow of an awning. But there would be plenty of activity at nightfall, Caradoc reflected: Souris had a contact to meet ashore and *Bryony*'s nearly-empty fuel tanks must be replenished.

As the schooner crept imperceptibly shorewards, Caradoc screwed up his eyes against the brazen glare of the sun and stared inland. Blistering in the afternoon heat, Kea gave the lie to the Aegean's legendary clarity. The baking air danced and quivered, so that even had the eye-pieces of his binoculars not filled with sweat the moment he put them to his eyes, then their use would still have been nullified by the vibrating landscape.

Even the high, angular mountain ridge forming Kea's backbone appeared insubstantial in the quivering air; and the deep valleys scoring this backbone, seemed as far off and remote as the craters of the moon. Lower down than these, dark clumps of oak forest were apparently rooted in gulfs of opaque and fathomless shadow.

Seen from this distance, Kea became an island of ethereal beauty, as unreal and ephemeral as a dream. Once ashore, as Caradoc was well aware, things would be very different. A burnt-out landscape, scoured to a bitter bone; an all-pervading reek of donkey-dung; and the sense of a poor, proud people damned by too much history and too much sun.

The crackle of an aircraft engine broke into his reverie, and somewhat belatedly, one of the look-outs roused himself to shout: 'Aircraft to starboard, sir!'

Yves.

'Will he land, do you think, sir?' Souris asked, coming up on deck with a towel draped hastily round his loins.

Caradoc shook his head: 'I shouldn't think so. There's no wind and no lop on the water. He wouldn't be able to unstick again.'

As if in confirmation of Caradoc's opinion, the seaplane's wings fluttered and something fell away from its fuselage—a something with a long pennant behind it that streamed out as it dropped towards the sea. A small splash marked where the object had fallen and then a widening circle of rings as it bobbed to the surface.

The dinghy moved away from *Bryony*'s side and out

across the sun-dazzled waters. Raymond Yves brought his Nieuport round once more, making sure that his message was being recovered. Then, when at last Pembury waved the package aloft, the seaplane's wings waggled in acknowledgement, before it turned away southwards and in minutes was no more than a faint and diminishing drone on the still air.

*   *   *

At sunset, *Bryony* lay below the spur of mountainside with its domed chapel that marked Michael Souris's meeting-place with his contact. Caradoc turned to him. 'Are you sure of your directions?'

Souris nodded and grinned: 'Not that I need them.' He pointed to the line of oakwoods lying beneath the mountain spur: 'I was chased through that lot once by an irate father.'

'What had you done?'

'Nothing . . . He arrived too soon.'

For a second time that day, the dinghy was pulled alongside. A second boat was launched—a curious folding affair that looked too frail to float. Together, the two boats disappeared into the gathering dusk.

Caradoc set himself to watch and wait. Apart from himself, a couple of ratings and Warren, the remainder of *Bryony*'s people were ashore. Caradoc lit his pipe; the two seamen yarned quietly on the fore-hatch: Warren quietly roasted below in the oven of his wireless-hutch.

As a distraction, Caradoc turned his mind to the message that Yves had brought that afternoon. It had been the usual negative. Despite flying several patrols each day, Yves's flight had seen nothing to arouse suspicion. Further, no trace had been found of that missing aircraft. Engine-trouble, Yves had hazarded: the aircraft of his flight were all reaching a critical state.

For'ard, the talk of the two ratings had now reached the absorbing topic of pubs the pair had known. Caradoc eavesdropped: seldom had he found himself so acutely aware of the ultimate penalty of command—it's ancient price called isolation.

*   *   *

At the end of a long ten minutes pull, *Bryony*'s boats grounded softly on a sandy beach. After a few last whispered instructions to Pembury, Souris moved off alone along the shore. When the first-lieutenant had been swallowed up by the darkness, Pembury detailed a man to remain with the boats. Then, with his eyes becoming ever more accustomed to the darkness, Pembury stared inland to check his bearings. Ah! Good. There was the hummock of the mountain above him, and the breastlike dome of that little church. Now that he knew where he was, Pembury whispered his party into order.

'What are we lookin' for, sir?' someone asked.

'There's the ruin of an old windmill tower on the ridge to the right of that church,' Pembury said, pointing upwards to the starlit silhouette: 'Right! Petty Officer Wells—you take the rear.'

'Aye, aye, sir.'

The party moved off in single file across the beach, stumbling in the dry, clinging sand. Beyond the beach, they came into the dark shadow of the oakwoods. Someone tripped and cursed. Beyond the belt of trees, there was a rough trackway that had to be crossed. Their feet slipped in something soft and sticky. A ripe scent of donkey tainted the air.

Underfoot, the now steeply-rising ground was little more than a scree of loose and slippery shale, across which, it was difficult to move in silence. Despite his youth and fitness, Pembury soon found himself gasping for breath and with sweat soaking his shirt. But, for all this, a sense of adventure gripped him.

A pair of basilisk eyes glared at the midshipman out of the darkness and he barely suppressed a yell of panic. Someone stumbled into him from behind and the landing-party bumped to a halt.

'Maaaaaaaaaaaaaa!' bleated a contemptuous goat before sidling away into the shadows. His sense of adventure

91

somewhat chastened, Pembury led his men on up the mountainside.

*   *   *

A mile away, Michael Souris moved quietly up the mountainside. Despite his preoccupation, he chuckled inwardly, remembering that the last time he had come this way, it had been with Ariadne Theopoulou's father hot on his tail. Bang! had gone one barrel of the old man's shotgung, then—Bang! the other, and the shot had rattled through the scrub of bushes behind him.

Still bubbling with inward amusement, Souris paused to get his bearings and find the precise path where that little piece of bother had begun. He moved on twenty yards, then found what he was looking for—a narrow, stepped trackway leading abruptly upwards.

The first-lieutenant's sense of euphoria faded. In spite of the night's stillness, only broken by the soft stirring of leaves and the strident churring of the unsleeping cicadas, he began to feel uneasy. The darkness had a brooding, watchful quality—just as it had the night he'd moved up this same path to meet Ariadne Theopoulou.

He stopped again, sniffing suspiciously at the wind, his keen nose catching a smell that should not have been there—Tobacco!

Taken by surprise, Souris made an incautious movement, and his foot sent a small trickle of stones skittering down the pathway. There was a triumphant yell from above, then the muzzle-flash and report of a gun, followed by a second. Souris cried out in pain, fell; and then, his body battered and pulverised, found himself rolling faster and faster down the rocky slopes of the hill.

*   *   *

'That was one complication I *wasn't* looking for, sir,' Souris admitted painfully, while Caradoc tweezered the last of the shot-gun pellets from his shoulder: 'How was I to know that old man Theopoulos would still want my blood after three years? He knows *Bryony*, of course . . . He must have watched us as we came in, and spotted me as I went ashore. Thank God the old bastard isn't a Cretan . . .'

'Why?' Caradoc asked.

'He'd have shot straighter . . .'

Caradoc did his best to keep his face straight; Souris was punctured in pride as well as body. The whole story was already common knowledge to everyone on board, of course. The schooner's very timbers seemed to tremble with an echo of ribald laughter. It was all very bad for discipline. But, as Caradoc was perfectly aware, the story of Souris's midnight adventures had set the seal on his popularity so far as the fo'c'sle was concerned.

Laughter and Naval rectitude struggled within Caradoc as Ferris's determined stage-whisper floated down through the cabin sky-light.

'*Marry the wench!*'

*   *   *

Day in, day out, the schooner continued her ceaseless patrolling, poking into near-derelict harbours that looked as though they hadn't seen anything bigger than a caique in years.

In retrospect, Caradoc now found that he could scarcely remember any single one of them in detail. *Bryony*'s anchor had dropped down through the gin-clear waters of so many. Nor, Caradoc found, had he any clearer memory of the islands where these harbours had been found: forlorn Ghroura, with its brooding air of ancient melancholy, a place of exile and captivity; worldly, sceptical Andros, where—or so Souris maintained—during a recent earthquake, the islanders had foregathered on the beach to shake their fists at the Almighty; Tinos, separated from Andros by the narrowest of straits, and yet whose folk were as devout as their neighbours were determinedly agnostic. During the same earthquake that had raised the ire of the Andriotes, all Tinos had been down on its knees—or so Souris said.

Caradoc went up on deck for a breath of evening air.

Bryony was passing through the long, three-mile wide strait separating Paros from Naxos. The sun dropped down over Paros like a golden disc, and on Naxos away to port, the island's successive waves of blue mountain were deeply etched with shadow.

For'ard, Wells was yarning with Earnshaw and Ferris. Quiet as their voices were, the sound carried clearly on the still evening air. With many a wink and much cocking of his head, Earnshaw was spinning a preposterous tale of landing dutiable cargoes under the very noses of the Customs in his native Staithes.

'You aren't goin' to stand there and tell us you got away with it?'

'I am, tha knaws.'

'In that case,' Wells said, after pausing to find an expression that matched his feeling: 'All I can say is, Yorkie, that you must have the luck of the Nine Blind Bastards.'

The very unexpectedness of the phrase caught Caradoc's imagination. It was just the turn of fortune that *Bryony* needed now. The sort of lucky stroke that broke the Bank at Monte Carlo—the Luck of the Nine Blind Bastards.

*   *   *

In Bryony's enclosed little world, and with the monotony of her days under the Greek sun, Fadger's rodent mind found nothing to occupy it but the memory of humiliation at Wells's hands.

The fact that the rest of the fo'c'sle hands had long since lost their earlier mistrust of Wells earned Fadger's derision. He had spoken this contempt too loudly—and Earnshaw had split his lip for him, a fact that gave Fadger one more reason for hating Wells, so devious and twisted now had his thinking become.

But, devious and twisted or not, Fadger was at last becoming dangerous. There were always plenty of black nights at sea, nights in the dark of the moon—and any one of them now, he'd square accounts with that bleeder Wells.

A blow and a splash in the darkness—and that would be that.

94

*   *   *

Reporting on his latest rendezvous ashore, Michael Souris shuffled the charts on Caradoc's desk till he came up with the one of Delos. His eye ran over it for a moment, then he pointed: 'Panos, my informant, claims he saw a U-boat *there*.'

Caradoc bent forward, following the line of Souris's finger to where it pointed at the Dili Strait, separating Delos and Rhenea Island. Half an inch above Souris's finger-nail, and like too small a cork in the neck of a bottle, the steep little island of Remati divided the channel in two. Caradoc looked doubtful: the eastern side of the strait was quite impossible for a submarine—but its western counterpart looked a little more promising, though even that shoaled to a bare five fathoms in its shallowest part at a point where the channel was no more than a mere half-cable wide.

'Did Panos say he saw periscopes, or was the submarine surfaced?'

'He said surfaced, sir.'

'Hmmm. That's *just* feasible. Even so, it must have been a damned small submarine.'

'Panos said it was, sir. No more than forty metres long.'

'That's something just under one hundred and twenty feet, isn't it?'

'Yes, sir.'

'Did your informant say whether the submarine had a gun?'

'He said not, sir.'

'That'd make the brute one of their little coastal minelayers then. Handy craft.'

'What about the question of range, sir?'

Caradoc shrugged: 'With a base in the Cyclades, even a radius of four hundred miles'd give Fritz plenty of scope for action.'

'But still limited.'

'Not necessarily. Not given a submarine—or *sub-marines*—with modified bunkerage, and a tender or two—

coasters about our own size, say. *Besides* even with a radius of only four hundred miles, the whole of the Aegean is within effective compass. Salamis and Piraeus would be a mere few hours cruising away. Suppose our people *do* put a Fleet there. Suppose Panos *is* telling the truth, and that the Germans have a base here and submarine waiting ready. Comes *Der Tag*, and all Brother Boche will have to do is lay his eggs, and then quietly toddle off home, with the sound of distant bangs making sweet music in his ears. Result: one more nasty dent in Allied prestige in this part of the world—and well-merited iron-crosses all round.'

Souris remained doubtful: 'The Dili Strait. That means back-tracking on ourselves, sir. We spent three days pottering round Mykonos, and another two at Delos.'

'We could still have missed *something*.'

'Panos has a bad reputation as a liar, sir.'

'The Department employs him—'

'And, maybe, the enemy's counterpart of the Department for all we know, sir.'

Caradoc came to a decision: 'We'll just have to risk that ... Pass the word down below for that Scots misery, McNab, will you, Number One.'

'Aye, aye, sir.'

Ten minutes later, the Thornycroft coughed into life. Peering seawards from the darkened shoreline, the man called Panos watched as the schooner's dim form shaped a course northwards, and congratulated himself on the success of his guile. It was fun playing the ends against the middle—profitable, too. Drachmas, pounds, marks—they were all money, and-therefore-one and the same thing to him, no matter who paid; no matter who lived or died.

*   *   *

Late the next afternoon, *Bryony* lay in Fourni Bay. Dazzling in the high sun, Delos stretched away eastwards, reaching up to the conical peak of Mount Cynthos sharp against the skyline.

Since arriving just before dawn, *Bryony* had dutifully searched the coastline for signs of enemy activity, but without success. The schooner's water was running low, and Souris took a party away in the dinghy to find a hidden spring he knew of. He returned half an hour later to supervise the filling of the water-tanks, and Caradoc went ashore in his place.

Caradoc felt the need to think and stretch his legs; he had over-ruled Souris's judgement of Panos and had been proved *wrong*. He was angry with himself, and his body demanded the spur of physical activity.

Before he had moved two hundred yards inland, Caradoc's shirt was wringing wet. A white path stretched upwards in front of his feet; cicadas churred incessantly; lizards flickered away in front of him—sudden-sharp stabs of brilliant colour that instantly froze into stillness, with only a trembling of tiny throats to betray their presence.

Time seemed of small account. At last, Caradoc came across the island's famous lions. Puissant and preternaturally fine-gutted, they stared with blind-eyed disdain towards horizons far beyond those of the crystal Aegean. Hieratic and withdrawn, they gazed beyond gods and beyond eternity, lost in contemplation of an endless now.

Caradoc found the lions' detachment unnerving and moved away down a path shadowed by a scrub of low bushes. Flies buzzed about his head and settled stickily on his sweaty forehead, ignoring his brushing hand. Caradoc took his pipe from his pocket. He'd soon shift those beggars!

He found the welcome shade of a couple of stunted olive trees, and with one foot poised on the remains of a low wall, stopped and lit his pipe.

'Hi—*you* there!' A voice admonished him: 'I did not spend the better part of two years uncovering that splendid example of ancient masonry for you to go and destroy it with your wretched feet. Kindly step *down*, sir!'

Caradoc found himself staring down into the face of an enraged gnome. The gnome was purple-face with anger, and the sun glinted off his pince-nez in sharp little daggers of light. Caradoc moved his foot hurriedly. The old boy *might* look nearly as ancient as that bit of wall—but he also looked dangerous.

The gnome's wrath, however, seemed to be subsiding. He sniffed at the air for a moment or two, and then asked in a voice that was almost wheedling.

'I say, m'boy, you wouldn't be able to spare a pipeful of that excellent baccy you're smoking, would you?'

It seemed as reasonable a peace overture as any. Caradoc handed his pouch over without a word. The gnome pushed an eager nose down into its contents and sniffed:

'Fribourg and Treyer's Navy Cut?'

'Yes, sir.'

'Elysium, dear boy—*Elysium*!'

The old man delved into the capacious pocket of his shorts and produced a pipe that reminded Caradoc of the funnel of an ocean liner. Tobacco was stuffed into this like hay into a furnace. A match fizzled, the tobacco flared—and the olive trees briefly disappeared in a pall of blue smoke. The gnome was wracked by a fit of coughing—a fit so convulsive that is seemed he must either choke or fall to pieces. It was two minutes before he had the matter under control; then his face assumed a look of beatific contentment, like that of a baby with a well-filled bottle. In between puffs, he observed: 'The Greeks are a poor but estimable people, m'boy. But their tobacco is a depressing reminder of how vital a part the donkey and the goat both play in their economy. What do they call you, young man?'

'Caradoc, sir. Ralph Caradoc.'

'Are you the captain of that little schooner down below?'

'I'm her *master*, yes sir.'

'Master? I'd have said you had more the look of a *naval* man, meself. Still. That's none of my damned business. I'm Crampton—Professor Crampton.'

'The archaeologist?'

'Thassright.'

Caradoc allowed himself to be led further along the path until they reached a tent whose flaps gave a welcome splash of cobalt shade, in which was set a table and a couple of wicker chairs. Professor Crampton disappeared into his tent and came out again with a bottle of whisky and two glasses.

He poured two stiff pegs, and Caradoc relaxed while the old man launched himself into a spate of talk; the tittle-tattle of over half a century of excavations and explorations; talk of ancient disappointments, and on triumphs turning on the random discovery of some apparently trivial yet vital clue.

After a time, Caradoc found the elderly burble pleasantly soporific. Indeed, the old man's talk rarely seemed to impinge on the twentieth century at all. Like the lions of Delos themselves, Professor Crampton seemed inclined to treat centuries and millenia as being of small account. Caradoc's earlier introspective mood returned, and he only came back to himself as he heard Crampton say: 'Of course, my boy—this present war of yours. It's nothing new. It's really only the Peloponnesian War writ large—that's all. The same death of reason. You're all brave fools, my boy—and that's the best that can be said for you.

'This twentieth century of yours. At my age, it is something I do not even wish to consider. The broken stones of the past are sad—but it's a sadness that is dulled and therefore manageable. But the broken stones of *your* present? Ah, my boy—the tears and blood which stain *them* are still wet.'

The old man dived back into his tent and returned, cradling in his hands, the bronze figurine of a girl. The little statue was no more than a few inches high, and Caradoc took it from the old man, marvelling at its exquisite modelling. The bronze was so clean and sharp in its casting that it might have been made yesterday; and yet, in his hands, Caradoc felt the fret and press of centuries: 'How old is this, sir?'

'As fresh as tomorrow—or, as old as the hills. Who *cares*. Artistry like that is for ever. Man's cry to the gods that he is immortal too, and not always a savage.'

Caradoc ran his finger up the subtle line of the bronze girl's arm: 'Where did you find this, sir?'

'*I* didn't find it. The chap who did was a young fellow who used to come here in a yacht before the war. *He* was a naval officer. A German one. He found that little bronze in Santorini—that's down to the south, y'know. Yes: young

Kattschner told me he tripped over a rock, and there this young lady was.' Crampton sighed: 'Now *where*'s that pleasant young fellow these days, I wonder? He was a most likeable chap—knowledgeable, too. He had one or two most interestin' theories. He reckoned old Plato had got his measurements all wrong when translatin' Strabo—'

Caradoc found his attention wandering away. The dry rattle of the old man's voice began to rival the monotony of the cicadas. But ... but ... *that name*? Kattschner? Suddenly, Caradoc came back to the present as though he'd been kicked in the behind.

'Ye-es ...' Crampton said, pushing his pince-nez up onto the bridge of his nose: 'It was my young friend's theory that the lost continent of *Atlantis* was not a continent at all, but an island—an island set not in the Atlantic, but *here*, in the Cyclades.'

Caradoc's tongue felt too big for his mouth as he asked: 'Would you happen to remember just which island, sir?'

'Think I'm goin' ga-ga or something, m'boy?' Crampton snapped with a return of his earlier asperity: 'Of course I remember. It was the same island that figurine you're holding came from. Santorini. Yes ... I really must say that I always found young Kattschner's thesis *extremely* well-argued. He convinced *me* ...'

Caradoc stood: 'If you'll excuse me, sir—'

Crampton sounded disappointed. 'What? Goin' so soon? I'd half hoped for another pipe of your most estimable tobacco ...'

Caradoc mustered what patience he could while the old man laboriously refilled his blunderbuss of a briar, then hurried back down to the beach.

Plato? ... Strabo? ... That was all Greek to him. But a German officer who had known the Cyclades well, and who had a convincing theory that Santorini was Atlantis? That was something *very* different. And—*Kattschner*?— Caradoc cursed himself for a fool. Of course the name was familiar. It had occurred over and over again in those reports which Casserlly had shown him.

Sweat soaked and out of breath, Caradoc reached the beach at a run, careless of dignity. A hundred yards away, he could see Ferris and the dinghy's crew waiting him, lolling in a patch of shade beneath an outcrop of rock.

The boat's crew gaped towards its captain in amazement. Don't say the skipper'd got an irate Greek father on *his* tail, too.

Awfficers.

*   *   *

Max eased his cramped body along the bottomboards of the boat, careful not to disturb Erik Anders who, injured and unconscious, lay with his head in the protective crook offered by Max's arm. The middle of the North Sea, at night, was a damned cold place to be even at midsummer. Max's body felt cold and wet beyond all further enduring.

A dozen inches of icy, scummy water swished round the bottom of the boat with its every sluggish movement. The previous day, the boat's five more or less uninjured survivors had spent the morning plugging what holes they could find, and the afternoon baling. But the sea had found this work out, and soon the boat would be gunwale deep again—a waterlogged piece of flotsam waiting to be drowned at the sea's will.

Max twisted his body along the bottomboards again, to tuck the soaking blanket further round Erik Anders's body. For his own part, an increasing apathy was sapping his will to survive. He was spent now, and with nothing more to offer. It was all over and finished with him, he felt—bar the actual dying.

He drifted away into an uneasy doze: was it three or four nights ago now that the *Ingrid Anders* had been sunk?

The torpedo had hit her shortly after midnight—a cold, sharp midnight with a rising sea, and a wind from the east that was like a newly-honed razor. The torpedo had been fired without warning, and regardless of the illuminated *Dannebrogs* on the coaster's side. In two minutes, the *Ingrid Anders* had rolled over and sunk, leaving no more than a widening smooth of oil in which a handful of men threshed wildly, an upturned lifeboat, and a few, shattered crates.

Max had come to himself, treading water, and with the

101

burden of Anders's body in his arms. Voices had cried out and screamed in the darkness—voices that were sometimes all-too ominously choked in mid-cry. The top of a crate had floated near, and Max had managed to get Anders's body on top of it, and twisted his own wrist through a rope handle.

In the cold light of dawn, old Olaf Pedersen, the coaster's giant of a bosun, swam round collecting the night's few survivors. There were six altogether—including the *Ingrid Anders*'s still unconscious captain.

It took the five comparatively fit men all that first morning to right the capsized boat, which promptly settled down to its gunwales. Together Max and Pedersen managed to get Anders into the boat and wrap him with their coats and the one blanket they could muster. They could keep the injured man warm, if not dry.

Then, with the three seamen who were the other survivors, Max and Pedersen set about a systematic search of the boat. They found very little. The capsize had emptied the boat both of its store of food and its water. Nearly everything else had vanished too; flares and compass, most of the oars, the rudder and the boat's mast and sail. All the sea had left them was a pair of oars and a small triangle of sail-canvas. Apart from these, they had terrifyingly few other aids to help them reach safety: a pair of balers found jammed under a thwart; Max's watch which would serve in lieu of a compass should they see the sun; the seamens' knives, and three or four fathoms of mackerel line from the capacious depths of Pedersen's pocket.

Max addressed himself to helping old Pedersen make what sail the boat could, stepping an oar in the tabernacle and then setting that absurd little triangle of canvas.

'I reckon you'll be the only one to have much notion of navigation, sir,' the bosun grunted—though he jerked a thumb at the trysail and added: 'Not that there'll be much working to windward with that pocket handkerchief.'

Even before the end of that first day, thirst had become their enemy—a thirst which began as a matter of chapped, dry lips and swollen tongues, and which later became an agonised ache for water.

The much-frequented North Sea appeared swept of shipping. Besides, in three days, and with the slow dying of the wind, the horizon had closed in to something not much more than a mile.

Occasional glimpses of the sun and some mental calculations that were really little better than guesses, told Max that they could hardly be much more than a dozen miles from where *Ingrid Anders* had been torpedoed. But he kept this information to himself. There was discouragement enough in the boat already without him adding this bleak and pessimistic morsel.

Then, yesterday afternoon, and at old Pedersen's insistence, they had made a systematic survey of the boat, stuffing its now visibly working seams with scraps of torn clothing. The bailers and the boat's semi-rotary pump had been brought into action again. They had pumped and baled till they were on the edge of oblivion—and then they had pumped again.

The boat had at last slowly emptied—but a remaining sluggishness had told them two things: that its buoyancy tanks had been holed, and that structurally, it had been strained past much further enduring. *If it should really come on to blow.*

Max woke from his doze to find Pedersen leaning over him: 'Dawn, sir.'

Max managed to mumble: 'I'll take a spell at the steering oar.'

Pedersen didn't answer, but stared down at Erik Anders. Suddenly, he stopped and thrust a hand in beneath the cocooning blanket and laid it on the unconscious man's heart. The bosun's body momentarily stiffened, and then he turned to stare at Max with the hopeless eyes of a lost dog.

'He's gone, sir.'

'No!' Max too bent over Anders's still body, feeling for his wrist, and meeting flesh and bone as cold as marble and from which all tremor of life had drained.

Pedersen straightened: 'He was a good captain ... A good man...'

Max nodded dumbly, remembering his own boyhood

103

weeks spent at the Anders's Vejle home, and where old Pedersen (Yes! He had been old Pedersen even then) had taught Erik and himself to sail in a dumpy little proam that looked like a barrel sawn in half.

Max pulled the water-stained blanket up to cover the dead man's face. It was the last kindness he could do Anders, the boyhood companion who had risked a great deal in helping him to escape. But this particular risk had not been one of the foreseeable ones—that he would be killed by the friends of the man he was trying to help.

Bleakly, Max looked towards the three Danish seamen huddled together in the bows of the boat, their faces almost void of expression. If anything at all was to be read in them, then it was the sailor's oldest lesson of all; that the sea sometimes gave, but that more often, it took away . . .

Fifty yards away, unnoticed, despite a prodigious snorting of vents and ruffle of grey waters, a submarine surfaced.

'Boat, there! *Boat, ahoy!*'

It was a full half minute further before the officer on the submarine's conning-tower could attract the attention of the five survivors. When he did so, they stared towards the submarine in apathy. The officer had spoken in German—so what could they expect now?—a hail of machine-gun bullets?

'How many of there are you?'

'Five.'

'Have you food and water? A compass?'

'No.'

There was a long moment of consideration on the U-boat's conning-tower; then: 'I can fit you in somewhere . . . Stand by . . .'

The submarine nudged in closer until it was alongside the lifeboat. Ratings ran out along its deck, lines were flung down—lines which the survivors in the boat barely had strength to secure.

The voice on the bridge was now urgent: 'Come on now! Look alive there!'

The look-outs were sharply reminded that their damned duty was to watch the horizon and not to gawp down into the boat. The German sailors, too, shouted their hurry. Finding that Max could not walk, a pair of burly seamen half-lifted, half-dragged him up onto the U-boat's forecastle. Roughly, but not unkindly, they bundled him up the conning-tower ladder to where the U-boat's captain was still urging his men to smack it about.

'I'm sorry. But if that one's dead, then leave him . . .'

Max looked up at his rescuer. It was a small world: Fritz Joachim, his own late first-lieutenant's boon companion—and now evidently promoted to a command of his own.

But now, the U-boat ratings were helping the Danish seamen down through the conning-tower hatch, with Joachim plainly on tenterhooks to be submerged and under way again. Pedersen stood beside Max for a moment, staring down towards the lifeboat which had now been cast loose and was drifting away, taking with it Erik Anders's lifeless body. In a voice that was like an echo of some past existence, the bosun said: 'No man lives till evening whom the fates doom at dawning.'

Max found himself being pushed down the conning-tower ladder, and was unable to stifle a grunt of pain as he fell the last few feet with a rating and then Joachim came crashing down on top of him.

Joachim snapped a rapid string of orders, and the submarine was dived to periscope depth and resumed her homeward journey. With this safely accomplished, Joachim now had some time to give attention to his prisoners. He turned, and gaped in astonishment as he caught sight of Max:

'Great God in Heaven! Max Kirbschaus! Where the devil did you spring from, sir?'

Max's head was swimming now, and a curious dancing mist was closing in on him as he managed to whisper:

'From England . . . I managed to escape . . .'

'Get Kapitän-Leutnant Kirbschaus to my bunk!'

As someone put a supporting arm under his shoulders, Max managed to gasp: 'I'm sorry about Karl Hass, Joachim. He was a damned good fellow—'

But, astonishingly, Joachim's face was alight with laughter: 'But, of course, sir—you wouldn't know . . . How could you? Karl is *safe*. He got *Gertrude* home . . .'

*   *   *

For years, Fate had stalked Raymond Yves like a lover, patiently biding its appointed time . . .

Below his Nieuport's wing-tip floated the great caldera of Santorini. Even in the Aegean sunlight, the island somehow contrived to look sinister, Yves thought—like a coiled and venomous snake, passive for the moment, and at rest, but still deadly. At the caldera's centre, the volcanic island called Neo Kaimeni sent up a column of sulphurous smoke.

To counter the sombre effect of Santorini, Yves banked the sea-plane away to the south-east where, a dozen kilometres away, lay the tiny islets of Khristiani, Askania, and, smallest of all, little Eskati Island which was little more than a cropping of rock. Set in line, the islands were merely three small summits of a ridge of submerged mountains, and to Yves, the bare sage-and-grey of the two larger ones seemed like a microcosm of Greece itself, set in a sea-scape of Empyrean blueness.

With stick and rudder in opposition to take off speed by side-slipping, he brought the plane down so low over Khristiani that to get round the island's three-hundred metre summit, he had to drop one wing and bank round it, with a handful of surprised-looking goats staring down at him from above as he skimmed by.

Coming round the shoulder of the island, Yves found himself above the slight, rock-bound concavity that was the only possible anchorage Khristiani could offer. Indeed, to his surprise, he saw that there was a schooner lying there now—a schooner that with her raking masts and extravagant bowsprit, he at first mistook for *Bryony*.

But, almost in the same instant, he recognised that the anchored vessel was not Caradoc's—though someone was doing their damnedest to reinforce that impression. In that one swift moment as he passed above the schooner, Yves had seen something else too; a something which, even though hidden by shadow where it lay between the schooner's side and the steep-to wall of cliff beside it, was quite unmistakably grey and cigar-shaped . . .

Yves wrenched the Nieuport round to return for a second look. Doubt shaped itself as the schooner grew larger with every passing second and friendly hands were waved at him from its decks. Then, when he was irrevocably committed to his approach, he saw the apparently solid sides of a deckhouse slide down, exposing the barrels of a pair of double-mounted parabellums.

The Nieuport staggered as bullets lashed into its wings and engine-cowling. Hot oil spewed back into Yves' face; he felt savage and numbing blows in chest and shoulder. Blindly, he wrenched at the stick, and the sea-plane flicked away exposing its belly to the parabellums. With smoke pouring back from its engine in a long, greasy plume, the stricken Nieuport flattened out above the surface of the sea, and flickered away like a wounded snipe.

Barely conscious now, Yves struggled to keep the sea-plane flying. With its shadow racing along just before it on the surface of the sea, he knew he had succeeded in rounding Khristiani and was heading back in the direction of Milos. But, minute by minute, shadow and sea-plane drew even closer together, until at last they kissed and met, and the sea broke over the Nieuport in an iron wall of water.

Inside a minute, it was as though the disturbance had never happened. Not so much as a single piece of wreckage floated to the surface to show that such a man as Raymond Yves had ever existed . . .

Part Six

August. The Burning Islands

Caradoc reached for his pipe—then returned it to his pocket with a grimace of distaste. In the last two days, he had had ample time to regret the grateful impulse that had made him send the last of his Fribourg and Treyer Navy Cut ashore to Professor Crampton. *Bryony*'s own store of issue tobacco had long been finished, and like the rest of the schooner's company, Caradoc was forced to make shift with whatever could be got ashore—stuff which tainted his well-loved pipe and which flared in its bowl like hay . . .

Souris had been amused by his captain's gullibility.

'But, sir!' He had expostulated: 'Everyone knows old Crampton in the Cyclades. The man's quite—what do you call it in English?—ga-ga.'

'He said he wasn't.'

'Well, he would have to, wouldn't he?'

'But, dammit, Michael—Crampton's *famous*. I'm no archaeologist, but even *I've* heard of him.'

Souris shrugged: 'He may have been famous once, sir— but he's gained a fair reputation for dottiness since.'

'Oh.' Caradoc was deflated: a fine sort of fool he'd look, working on the say-so of someone like that. And yet, he told himself mutinously, Crampton hadn't struck him as being mad. Odd and eccentric, yes—but nothing worse.

Besides, Caradoc reminded himself, there were the undeniable facts that Crampton *had* met a German officer called Kattschner before the war; that Kattschner's name *had* featured prominently in Casserlly's intelligence reports, and that Kattschner himself held an intriguing and arguable theory that Atlantis and Santorini were one and the same place.

Even after Caradoc explained these reasons to Souris, the first-lieutenant still looked doubtful as the order was given to proceed south: 'That Atlantis idea could be a blind or a bluff, sir.'

'We'll have to risk that.'

Now, after two days of drifting southwards in light airs, Caradoc was not so sure. The previous evening, Warren had intercepted a German wireless message—a signal which after an hour's struggling with his copy of the German codes, Caradoc had deciphered as *Atlantis: Alcibiades; Alcestes*. The German Admiralty had obligingly appended a neat list of meanings for these codewords— words, which while giving nothing else away, ordered in terse and seamanlike language:

Atlantis: Proceed with manoeuvre forthwith.

Now, doubt returned to nag at Caradoc. Suppose he *was* taking *Bryony* in the wrong direction? Once more, he reached into his pocket for his pipe and chewed on its cold and comfortless stem . . .

*   *   *

'The wind's freshening, sir.'

'Not before bloody time.'

Caradoc regretted his ill-humour, and pulled a wry face at Souris. Captain and first-lieutenant exchanged significant glances. Above the nearing cats'-paws, the sky was darkening to an ominous purple colour. In an hour or so, *Bryony* would be getting all the wind she could handle—and with something to spare. Responding to the hardening breeze, the schooner surged forward, with that old familiar chuckle beginning under her forefoot.

In three quarters of an hour, they had raised Santorini, seen from the schooner's decks as a ridge of low peaks; a ridge lower at its centre than at its extremities. For Caradoc's benefit, Souris pointed out the landmarks. That low cape to port was Cape Kolomvos, and those two lofty mountain tops inland were Megalo Vouno and Mount St Elias. That slaty gleam of water at the island's centre was the north entrance to the caldera, and those grey, unremarkable hillocks were the volcanic islets of Neo and Palaia Kaimeni.

Caradoc pointed to the column of dirty looking smoke rising from Neo Kaimeni: 'It looks as though your volcano's eaten something that disagreed with it . . .'

He stared towards the column of smoke; a column which, as the wind reached it, was flattened out into a greasy blanket, which reminded him of a destroyer laying smoke.

Souris was about to say something when he suddenly stiffened as a flicker of white sail away to port caught his attention, creeping out from the land a mile or so beyond Cape Kolomvos. Without a word of explanation, the first-lieutenant darted away from Caradoc's side, and with his binoculars slung round his neck, swarmed up the port shrouds. The urgency of his manner communicated itself to the men down on deck. Caradoc saw Wells move to the schooner's wheel.

Caradoc used his own binoculars in an attempt to discover just what it was about the stranger that was so agitating Souris. The distant vessel looked commonplace to him—a schooner not unlike *Bryony* herself, and therefore commonplace enough amongst these islands.

But now, Souris came down the shrouds with even more urgency than he had climbed them, sliding down with a speed that boded ill for his hands. But, rope-burned or not, the first-lieutenant was triumphant; his dark eyes gleamed with mingled anger and excitement as he shouted:

'Do you see her? Do you see her?'

'She's a schooner like *Bryony*.'

For one moment, Caradoc thought Souris would shake him in his excitement. 'That's the whole point, sir! Not just *like Bryony*—she's meant to *be Bryony*!'

'Are you sure of that?'

'I'd stake my soul on it. Sir—do you remember that schooner we saw at Navarino when we put in for shelter? Well—' Souris's finger jabbed towards the horizon: 'That's her—the *Iskaria*. Those damned Koritsases. They've got her under Bermudan instead of gaff-rig. They extended her jib-boom till it's twice its old length—and they've done a paint job on her counter to try and make it look like a transom.'

That did it. A few months ago, Caradoc had gone to a great deal of trouble himself, disguising a ship's appearance. That the *Iskaria* had gone to similar pains, told him just one thing: that she was up to no good.

'Man the sheets! Wells!'

'Sir?'

'Steer south-east.'

Wells swung at the spokes of the wheel: 'Sou'-east it is, sir.'

The great boom rolled majestically across as *Bryony* came round on her new course; the fore-sail was whisker-poled out to port and goose-winged, she began running down in pursuit of her imitator.

Caradoc stared at her through his binoculars. The *Iskaria* appeared not to have sighted *Bryony* as yet, though she too had altered course, coming up into the wind, and then, with the wind broad abeam, reaching in towards Santorini again. With a long seven or eight miles separating the two schooners, the longer she remained ignorant of pursuit the better. Caradoc felt an atavistic surge of excitement. There was a primitive intoxication about running down one's quarry under sail. Now, at last, he understood something of what his long line of naval forebears must have felt in chase of Spaniard or Frenchman.

Apparently still ignorant that she was being pursued, the *Iskaria* had disappeared behind Cape Kolomvos again. *Bryony* had already gained a mile on her—perhaps, even, a shade more. Whatever business they were engaged on in *Iskaria* evidently kept them far too preoccupied to be keeping even the most elementary look-out.

'Smoke on the port quarter, sir!'

Caradoc whipped round with his binoculars already up at his eyes. The smoke was a flat smear across the surface of the sea, not unlike that he had seen blowing from Neo Kaimeni. He adjusted the focus of the binoculars, and a trio of destroyers burst through the smoke and shaped themselves in the lenses. Sterns down, and with the great vee's of their bow-waves lifting like gull's wings far back along their hulls, the trio was moving at tremendous speed.

'What the devil do *they* want?'

Souris answered: 'The Aegean Squadron's destroyers often rendezvous off Cape Kolomvos, sir.'

'It's taken something more than a rendezvous to put the wind up their tails like that, Number One. It looks to me as though they share our interest in our friend.'

A look of annoyance darkened Souris's face—a look echoed by Mr Pembury's schoolboy wail of dismay: 'But *we* saw her first!'

Souris was more calculating: 'It'll be a close run thing which of us comes up with *Iskaria* first, sir.'

'Neck and neck I should think—*and* with that little lot, too.' Caradoc pointed to where, away to the north-west, the line of the horizon was blackened and blotted out by a swiftly moving line of ugly-looking cloud.

A new thought struck him. Were those three destroyers aware of their quarry's identity? Or were they assuming that the schooner they were racing to intercept was *Bryony* herself? Caradoc stared from the destroyers to the *Iskaria* then back again.

And *still* it seemed that the disguised schooner was equally unaware of either *Bryony* or the rapidly closing destroyers. Caradoc glanced aft again. There was that damned storm to be taken into the reckoning now, too, coming down on them with the speed of a train.

But now, at last, *Iskaria* suddenly shot up into the wind with a tremendous flurry of headsails. Now, *surely*, Caradoc told himself, she must see her pursuers?

But, no... For a long moment, *Iskaria* hung in irons before slowly paying off onto a reach that took her in towards Santorini once more. What the devil was she up to?

Caradoc heard Wells grumble from behind the wheel: 'Just look at her! Up'n down, up'n down—just like a Pompey whore parading in front of the Angel on paynight.'

Souris too was clearly puzzled: 'If you were to ask me, I'd say *Iskaria* was *inviting* pursuit.'

The same thought struck Caradoc: 'Earnshaw! Stand by to signal.'

Cape Kolomvos was broad on *Bryony*'s beam now, no more than a long cableslength distant, and with the shallowly radius'd curve of the bay opening to a long straight line of featureless coastline. Caradoc screwed up his eyes in an effort at calculation. *Iskaria* couldn't be much more than a mile distant now. And now, too, at last, it seemed they had been sighted, for *Iskaria* shot up into the wind, came round through it, and then, goosewinged like themselves, ran from her pursuers.

Souris was contemptuous: '*Bryony*'s got the beating of her *any* day.'

But, whether *Bryony* had the beating of *Iskaria* or not, now seemed academic, for it was clear the destroyers must reach their common quarry first. But, now confronted by a pair of *Bryony*s, doubt seemed to set in amongst the destroyers—a doubt that was evidenced by the leading destroyer's peremptory challenge.

'Make our number, Earnshaw,' Caradoc ordered.

Perched on the main-hatch, Earnshaw's signal flags wagged briskly. That suspicion remained, showed in the increasingly flurried exchange of signals that followed.

An unidentified voice growled: 'Them buggers are just dyin' to land a four-inch brick on us.'

Fast losing patience himself, Caradoc was inclined to agree: 'Earnshaw! Make Psalms Twenty-six, Nine.'

'Aye, aye, sir.'

Suspicion died. A quarter of a mile to port, the destroyers sped past in an arrow straight line, the turbulent whiteness of their combined wakes making a line seemingly drawn to the darkening horizon. Looking at Caradoc, Michael Souris noted his mouth quirked with what might have been anger, amusement, or both.

'Psalms, Twenty-six, Nine, sir?'

The quirk became a definite grin: 'Gather not my soul with sinners, nor my life with bloody men.'

The leading destroyer now challenged *Bryony*'s imposter—a challenge that, unanswered, resulted in the bang of a gun from the destroyer's foredeck, and the splash of a shell a hundred yards beyond the fleeing vessel.

The wind was so strong now, that the smoke from the gun was torn to shreds and dispersed in an instant; the report coming as a flat and muffled 'Kerrr-whoooof!'

New sounds now were forcing their recognition on

attentions hitherto wholly taken up by the excitement of the chase. A rising discordancy of notes was being sung in *Bryony*'s rigging, and the pursuing storm raced across the face of the sea with a loudening hiss.

Everyone in *Bryony* was aware of the approaching danger, yet held by the drama of seeing the strange schooner brought to book. Calculating and experienced eyes glanced astern and then up at the straining pyramids of *Bryony*'s canvas. It was now a matter of bare minutes before that little lot aft was on them—precious minutes in which to get in sail before the schooner's sticks were ripped clean out of her. Caradoc came to an immediate decision. He opened his mouth to give the order to hand sail—but, even as he did so, *Bryony* buried her nose deep into a steepening sea, stopping short as though she had run into a solid wall.

As she did so, a high, wild yell from Hughes Pom-Pom brought a terrifying new threat into immediate account.

'Nine to port, sir, wasn't it—And one to starboard!'

Christ! Caradoc dived to one rail, Souris to the other. *Bryony*'s creaming bow-wave caught something which rose lazily to the surface, with the storm light glinting on its wetly shining surface. Menacing as the bared fangs of a cobra, the horns of the mine hung in the air for a moment as though blindly searching for their prey. For a second as long as an eternity, it seemed to Caradoc that the mine must surely be dragged into *Bryony*'s side below him by the rushing turbulence of water. But then, caught by an outward eddy, the thing rolled drunkenly away to bob grotesquely in the schooner's wake.

A third mine broke surface two cables lengths away on *Bryony*'s port bow. Caradoc punched at Earnshaw's shoulder: 'Warn the destroyers, Earnshaw!'

The Yorkshireman fairly danced on the hatch-covers in his efforts to get the destroyers' attention. But they, it seemed, had no eyes for anything but the counterfeit *Bryony*, still vainly running from her swifter pursuers. A second warning shot was fired, and then a third.

Earnshaw looked round hopelessly: 'No acknowledgement, sir!'

'Keep on trying.'

Bryony's view of the destroyers was now a quarter one. Belatedly, the rearmost destroyer sheered abruptly away to port, heeling over almost onto her beam-ends as she did so, and with the red-and-white chequered flag, 'U', breaking out from her signal halyards as she repeated *Bryony*'s signal: *You are standing into danger!*

But her sisters rushed straight on. Then, the leading destroyer seemed to lift clear of the sea, so that Caradoc saw along the whole length of her keel. There was the flash of an explosion, and an impression of blast waves fanning outwards across the surface of the sea. More flame—this time from the destroyer herself—rose up in a frenzedly leaping tongue. Lost in a cloud of steam and smoke, she all-but disappeared completely, with her toppling mast shaping a slow parabola across the sky as it fell.

With her hull almost riven in two, the stricken destroyer began to settle. Too late, the second destroyer turned to port under full helm. This time, there was a muffled thump, and the waters under her stern seemed to boil with an inner turbulence before bursting upwards into a towering column of water. With her screws and rudder gone, yet impelled by the inertia of her great speed, the destroyer drove on for a considerable way before the drag of her shattered stern left her stopped and helpless in the water.

Nosing cautiously in towards her sisters, the third destroyer began lowering boats.

'Sir!—' Souris said, with an urgent look astern. But, if Caradoc heard his first-lieutenant, then he mistook his meaning, interpreting it as a request to be allowed to alter course and join that third destroyer in her rescue work. But Caradoc had no eyes for the sinking ships. It was *Iskaria* he was watching now.

Backwards and forwards like a Pompey whore, indeed! *Now*, he knew why she had been reaching in and out from the shore, between the shallows and the ten fathom line. A whore, maybe—but a deadly, murderous one. Caradoc's hot Welsh temper had the better of him now. He wanted nothing so much as to get his hands on the man who had laid those mines and choke the life out of him.

'But—*Sir!*'

Souris's increasingly urgent shout barely reached Caradoc through the rage pounding in his head. In his lust to run that damned schooner down, he was deaf to the howl of the squall bearing down on *Bryony*'s stern. He was blind to its purple-black pall clamping down over the waters, while the last, undershot vestiges of light drew the sinking destroyers and the fleeing *Iskaria* in lines that were harshly unremitting, and yet at the same time without substance or reality.

'*Sir!*—'

For a third time, Souris shouted. But it was a cry that was immediately torn away by the wind, leaving the first-lieutenant's mouth wide open in a vacant, soundless gape as the storm at last caught them.

A horizontal rain, solid as driven steel rods, lashed flatly across *Bryony*'s decks. It drilled agonisingly through thin shirts, flaying like some icy cat-o'-nine-tails at the bare flesh beneath. The destroyers were almost instantly blotted from sight; like some evil, flitting moth, *Iskaria* flickered briefly on the extremities of vision—and then vanished. Ankle-deep in an instant, ploughed and pocked by rain, the water sloshed across *Bryony*'s decks and gouted from her scuppers.

The rain was followed by the wind—a bawling, brawling tumult that hammered at the body and dazed the senses with its ferocity. It flattened the men crouched on *Bryony*'s deck, sending them spinning like nine-pins.

The forestay snapped the packthread; the foremast gave a long, shuddering groan and a crack that was loud enough to be heard even over the raging wind.

Caradoc at last came to his senses. He cupped his hands, and—as the foresail was ripped away like a pocket handkerchief—gave the order to get in sail. Sensing rather than hearing the command, the men on deck moved to obey.

But—too late? Even as they did so, the outer jib followed the foresail, and a green and solid wall seemed to lift itself high over the schooner's transom—a wall which broke and fell on her in a waist-deep welter that searched her out from stern to bow.

At *Bryony*'s wheel, Wells struggled to hold her. With foresail and outer jib gone, the press of wind on her huge mainsail was acting like a weather-vane and threatening to drag her round beam to wind. With the schooner's rudder already hard over, Wells knew he must soon lose his fight unless they got that mainsail off her fast. Any moment now, she would simply broach to and roll over on her beam ends.

Nor could he himself hold her much longer on his own. With the wheel kicking like a wild thing in his grip, Wells felt as though his arms were being torn from their sockets. With relief, he sensed a dim figure looming up beside him in the driving rain.

Then, through his rain and wind bleared vision, Wells saw the figure raise an arm—an arm which, *Jesus*! swung down to bring something crashing into the side of his head just above the temple. Wells staggered and flung up an arm to defend himself. A second blow fell and he lost his grip on the wheel, whose spokes—spinning with an increasingly savage speed—sent his now unconscious body sprawling away across the schooner's deck.

Freed from the restraint of her rudder, and with the press of her mainsail now in the ascendancy, *Bryony* fell beam on to the wind.

*   *   *

In the rose light of evening, *Bryony* lay in the shelter of the smallest of the group of islands making up Anafi. The island was flat and desolate-looking, with scant vegitation, and only a distant scrub of low trees to break its monotony. An oily swell was all that remained of the gale—a swell which like some sleeper's breath, rose and fell along the rocky shoreline, exposing, then submerging dark banks of swaying weed. The barometer which—unnoticed—had fallen so swiftly in the afternoon, was now rising again with an equal rapidity.

Caradoc was in no mood to notice his surroundings.

117

With Souris by his side, he went round *Bryony*'s deck surveying the damage wrought by the gale's brief but telling anger. Conscience nagged at him. Like a man probing an exposed nerve with his tongue, he reviewed the full implications of his folly. Thanks to his own stupidity, he had as near dammit lost both *Bryony* and every man-jack in her. Blind rage and a blinder ignorance had got the better of him and the little cherub-up-aloft whose job it was to save drunks and bloody fools from themselves, must have worked double-watches on his behalf.

The Luck of the Nine Blind Bastards.

Yes: *Bryony should* have been lost—he knew that without even bothering to look at Souris's closed face. His impetuousness had cost *Bryony* dearly enough as it was: foresail and outer-jib lost—and the wireless aerials, without which they were deaf to the outside world; the foremast badly sprung; the galley washed out, and the forehold half-full of water. The list was a pretty formidable one.

Worse: at some time during the gale, Able Seaman Fadger had simply vanished overboard. Nobody had seen him go—he had simply disappeared without so much as a cry. It was no good pleading with himself that Fadger had been useless both as a seaman and as a man. The inescapable fact remained that he, Ralph Caradoc, had been directly responsible for Fadger's death—thanks to that wild, insensate few minutes in which he had been deaf and blind to everything but *Iskaria*'s pursuit.

With an effort, Caradoc dragged his mind away from its morbid self-condemnation. There would be plenty of time for that later. At the moment, there was more urgent business. That badly-sprung foremast was the most pressing worry. As it looked now—and remembering how early in the gale that menacing groan and crack had come—it seemed a miracle that the towering column of cedar hadn't gone by the board within the next few minutes. Beginning a few feet above *Bryony*'s deck, the fibres of the mast were grotesquely knotted and splintered, so that it looked like a hazel-wand that had been wrung in the hands of some mad giant.

118

A small group of *Bryony*'s most experienced hands were now busily engaged in fishing the mast with spare spars, and the air round its foot was now blue with tobacco smoke, bad language, advice and technicalities delivered in half a dozen varying accents.

Souris's olive mask of a face broke into its familiar grin: 'Good, aren't they, sir? They don't need much telling.'

Self-recrimination surged up within Caradoc again, and he felt like snarling at Souris: 'Go on, man. Say it and get it off your chest. *They don't need much telling—not like your bloody-fool of a captain.*'

But, instead, he growled: 'Do you think *Iskaria* was as badly mauled by that blow as we were, Number One?'

Souris shook his head: 'I wouldn't like to say for sure, sir. They were getting sail off her fast, the last I saw.'

There was a guffaw from the men woolding the mast, and the woebegone figure of Warren appeared among them. Green-faced and unsteady on his feet, the telegraphist presented a miserable appearance. His shirtfront and chin were smeared with drying vomit, and a bruise like a bantam's egg rose out of his thinning hair. Caradoc gaped at Warren's abject figure, torn between exasperation and an unwilling sympathy. The poor devil was a sad specimen at the best of times. Now he almost looked ready to burst into tears.

'What happened to you, Warren?'

One of the group woolding the foremast made an unprintable suggestion, and Caradoc fixed the offender with a cold eye.

Warren's voice was a whisper: 'I did my best, sir.'

'I'm sure you did—but I asked "what happened"?'

'It was the storm, you see, sir.'

'Yes, I see—go on.'

'Well, sir . . . This signal came in for us. I . . . I was just going to bring it up to you, when the storm hit us. I was knocked over and hit my head against something, sir. And, when I came to, the door of the wireless-room was jammed tight, and the place was half-full of water—' Warren's eyes grew round and frightened: 'I . . . I thought I w-was going to drown, sir . . .'

119

'Has it taken you all this time to get yourself out?'

'Yes, sir. I couldn't make anyone hear me for a long time, but then Takis the cook came and forced the door . . .'

'I see—Have you got that signal safely now, Warren?'

'Y-yes, sir . . .' The telegraphist handed over a signal-pad as unpleasantly smeared as himself.

Ignoring this, Caradoc took the pad and glanced significantly at Souris: 'This might tell us a few things we'd like to know, Number One. A few whys and wherefores, maybe—and, even why those destroyers were so eager to have a word with *Iskaria* having mistaken her for us. Carry on up here, would you, Number One—but I'd like a word with you and Pembury in my cabin when I've decoded this.'

'Very good, sir.'

Caradoc turned to go below, but as he did so, another thought struck him. He seldom drank at sea, but at this moment he felt he could do with a damned stiff drink—and, doubtless, so did everyone else. He saw no good reason why they shouldn't get it. After all, there were *other* methods of issuing spirits other than strictly in accordance with article 1827 of K.R's and A.I's.

'Number One!'

'Sir?'

'If you look below, I rather imagine you'll find that one of our rum jars has been damaged.'

Souris looked puzzled: 'Will I, sir?'

'I'm *sure* of it, Number One.'

'In that case, sir,' Souris said, with his face broadening into a grin of comprehension; 'I'd better look into it right away.'

'Do that. Oh, and you'll not forget to put the jar's loss down to stress of weather, will you?'

'I won't forget, sir.'

Michael Souris looked after his captain's retreating back with a new respect. Rules were meant for bending—and little men in offices the whole world over would swallow *anything*, if only you used the right form of words.

*   *   *

120

An hour later, Souris and Pembury stood in Caradoc's cabin. Both had read Caradoc's transcription of the decoded wireless message, and their faces wore similar looks of disbelief, for *Bryony* had been ordered to cease her search forthwith and return to Malta.

Forgetting his captain's presence, Pembury had reverted to the language of the schoolroom and called the signal 'a jolly rotten shame!' The signal had been brief—but not so brief as to preclude a veiled hint of political implications. *Bryony* was being warned off—but why?

Both Caradoc and Souris were aware of hidden forces at work somewhere—persuasive voices in neutral chancellories; voices at whose sound, Greece, though willing enough to swallow the camel of a French base in Milos, became unable to strain at the gnat represented by *Bryony* . . .

That left but one question: whose voices? A question whose only logical answer must surely be that German Intelligence, as centred in Athens, had become worried as to how near *Bryony* was to solving the enigma of *Plan Atlantis* . . .

Souris looked at the decoded signal again and asked: 'What do we do now, sir?'

Caradoc didn't answer him directly, but asked a question himself: 'How soon will *Bryony* be fit for sea again?'

'Three days, sir—*two* if we really get down to it.'

Caradoc smiled: 'Crack the whip then, Number One . . . We'll—er—not be able to rig new wireless aerials, of course.'

'No, sir.'

'Good.'

There was a long pause in the cabin—a pause whose silence almost shouted that Caradoc was up to something. Souris's face wore a look of quiet expectation; Pembury looked like an eager puppy.

At last, Caradoc said: 'As I see it—and for whatever reason those destroyers were chasing her this afternoon— *Iskaria may* or may not be part of *Plan Atlantis*. Certainly, she laid those mines this afternoon—which, regardless of any other considerations, makes it our duty to stop her before she can do the same thing again. My personal view, is that she *is* part of *Plan Atlantis*—but we'll conveniently forget that for the moment. We'll just concern ourselves with finding her and bringing her to book.'

'But that signal, sir?' Pembury asked.

Caradoc smiled at the midshipman, screwed up the signal's decoded transcript and tossed it out of the open scuttle: 'So far as I'm concerned, we never received it.'

'Golly, sir. The blind eye, eh?'

'No, Mr Pembury—the deaf ear.'

* * *

The euphoria with which Caradoc made the decision to disobey his orders failed to last. As the full extent of *Bryony*'s storm-damage revealed itself and was slowly patched up the following morning, self-condemnation returned.

The plain fact of the matter was that he was unfit for command. His wanton lack of self-control had all but drowned everyone on board—just as it had been directly responsible for Fadger's loss overboard. And that Fadger had been an idle, mess-deck lawyer did not absolve him.

Guilt nagged Caradoc's footsteps like a shadow. There was more self-indictment, too, in the memory of how he had given notice of his intended disobedience to Souris and young Pembury the previous evening. The decision to ignore that signal was one thing; choosing to make a parade of it another—mere vainglory.

The *'deaf-ear'*, indeed... That should bring the house down at his next court martial.

Caradoc reached for his pipe, but even this was no anodyne now—and the Greek tobacco tasted fouler than ever. With the black dog howling balefully in his ears, Caradoc frowned as Souris's head appeared round his cabin door.

'Can you spare a few minutes, sir?'

'I suppose so, Number One. What is it?'

'Petty Officer Wells and Able Seaman Hughes have put

in a request to see you, sir. They say it's important.'

'*How* important?'

'*Very*, I'd say, sir.'

And so it must be, Caradoc decided when Souris wheeled the two men into his cabin. Both stood stiffly to attention, and Wells had gone to the formality of replacing his fez with a battered uniform cap. Caradoc looked at Wells with interest. The petty officer had done well the previous afternoon. Looking at him, Caradoc almost failed to recognise him as the same man who, as a young O.D. in *Harbinger* had spent most of his time with his name in the destroyer's Minor Punishment Book.

Hughes, on the other hand, looked miserable but determined; and his face wore the expression of a man who believed himself to have done wrongly but for the right reasons.

'Well, Petty Officer Wells?' Caradoc asked, remembering anew the awkwardness of that repeated syllable.

Wells gazed up at the deckhead as though somehow contriving to disassociate himself from his own words:

'It's Hughes here, sir. He *thinks* there's something he ought to tell you.'

Caradoc turned his attention back to the little Welshman: 'Have you, Hughes?'

'Yiss, sir . . . Indeed, sir . . .' Hughes swallowed and then went on manfully: 'I wish to tell you that I killed Able-Seaman Fadger, sir.'

'You mean, you *murdered* him?'

'Yiss, indeed, sir.'

'*No, sir!*' Wells interruption was emphatic: 'You know what Hughes's English is like, sir. The silly Welsh bugger—sorry, sir!—'ll get himself hung if he don't watch it.'

Caradoc asked sternly: 'Did *you* see Fadger go over the side, Wells?'

'No, sir. But—'

'Then how can you know whether what Hughes says is true or not?'

Wells said hotly: 'I *can*, sir—because Fadger took advantage of that squall to try braining me while I was at the wheel.'

123

'Go on.'

Wells delved into the depths of his 'crap-traps' and produced a heavy spanner: 'Fadger attacked me with this, sir. Earnshaw found it in the scuppers this morning, and McNasty—I mean, F.R.A. McNab—confirms that it's one that's been adrift from the engine-room for days.'

'I see...' Caradoc felt a small sense of reprieve growing within him—a reprieve that he quickly squashed. It was scarcely a matter for self-congratulation that in a ship under his command, one member of his crew had tried braining another.

Caradoc looked at Hughes grimly: 'And just where do *you* come into this?'

The idiom was plainly beyond the Welshman's understanding, for he looked towards Wells for guidance.

Wells explained patiently: 'The captain means: what did you do?'

'Me? Oh, sir ... I hits him then, don't I?'

'How did you-er ... hit him?'

'I puts my head down, see?' Hughes suited the gesture to the words: 'I puts my head down and I putts him in the pelly, just like my Auntie Blod's old billy-goat.'

Caradoc suppressed a grin at Hughes's graphic if ungrammatical description. Hughes was a wiry little fellow, but in normal circumstances scarcely a match for the weighty larrikin that Fadger had been. That howling torment of wind and rain had been terrifying enough in itself—but to have fought a brief and murderous little battle in its midst was something else again. But there was just one more thing that had to be made quite clear for everyone's peace of mind, and Caradoc asked: 'Hughes— when you butted Fadger, did you mean to kill him?'

Hughes looked shocked at the notion: 'Oh, no, indeet, sir. It iss not right that he should be hitting Petty Officer Wells like that—so I putts him in the pelly; and then he shouts "Hughes, you bastard!" and falls down on the deck, and when the next wave iss gone, Fadger is not on the deck anymore.'

'And *that's* the truth of it, so far as I can make out, sir.' Wells said earnestly: 'It would've been me that went over the side if Hughes hadn't put his oar in. Fadger's no great loss to anyone to my way of mind—but Hughes insists that he ought to stand trial or something. That's why I took the matter to the Jimmy—the first lootenant, sir. He said *you'd* know what best to do.'

Caradoc looked at Hughes as sternly as he could: 'Will you abide by my decision, Hughes?'

'Yiss, sir . . . Please, sir . . .'

A glimmer of an idea was coming to Caradoc as he said: 'Even if that meant not quite telling the truth?'

Ancient anarchy and noncomformist conscience fought an obvious battle within Hughes, until he conceded at last: 'If you wass to say so, sir . . .'

'I do say so . . .' Caradoc did some swift thinking: 'Fadger was married, wasn't he, Wells?'

'Yes, sir—*and* with a couple of youngsters, I believe. He boasted to Earnshaw that he'd run off and left 'em. That's one of the reasons why Earnshaw split his lip for him . . .'

Caradoc said with an air of finality: 'Well, if Fadger had a wife and children, *that* settles things. You're no murderer, Hughes—but Fadger would have been if you hadn't stepped in. If that fact were to come out, then there'd be *no* pension for Mrs Fadger and her children—*do you understand that*?'

'Yiss, sir . . .'

'So we forget the whole thing, see? So far as anyone's concerned, Fadger went over the side through stress of weather—through that only, and through no other cause . . .'

'Yiss, sir . . .'

A much-relieved Hughes and Wells were dismissed from the cabin, and, when they had gone, Caradoc found Souris inclined to be congratulatory.

'Haven't you work to do on deck, Number One?'

'Er-yes, sir . . .'

When his first-lieutenant had gone, Caradoc looked at his reflection in the cabin mirror without affection, and with a very similar capacity for the fine, Welsh conscience that had so troubled Hughes.

Failure, fraud, mountebank, *hypocrite*! Caradoc abjured

himself. Just whose bacon had he been so busy saving a few moments ago?

From where he stood, the answer to that looked obvious...

His own...

*   *   *

Caradoc's more normal good humour only slowly returned to him after ten minutes or so spent studying the chart of Santorini.

In one respect, he found himself thinking, being a modern naval officer must be very like being a lawyer. Both were every bit as much the children of precedent; a precedent that was equally guide, exemplar and bugbear and which governed his every action—yes!—even down to his own intended disobedience of orders.

Metaphorically figuratively, few captains ever sailed in altogether uncharted waters. There were precious few situations which some naval predecessor hadn't encountered before; precious few corners of the world where, at some time, some careful forerunner hadn't made a survey and taken meticulous soundings—soundings resulting in a chart such as the one he was using now, first surveyed by a Captain Graves back in 1848, and probably with a leary weather-eye open for Michael Souris's piratical ancestors at the same time.

The more Caradoc looked at this chart, then the more forcibly Santorini impressed its strangeness upon him. It was not a single island at all, but a cluster—a cluster whose ringlike, atoll-shaped exterior had been breached in three places, leaving a similar number of outer islands: Santorini itself, Thirasia, and, to the south-west, a tiny one, Aspronisi, where the atoll wall had almost completely gone.

The centre of the atoll was occupied by a second group of islands; the Kaimeni. Caradoc suddenly realised that, like an atoll, Santorini was still growing. But it was a growth prompted by nothing so innocent as the little creature whose life-cycle built up the exquisite coral banks of the

126

world.

No ... those three islands at Santorini's heart were the result of a sinister gestation in the bombing womb of the earth itself; the misshapen triplets born of volcanic activity ...

Caradoc passed the word for Souris to join him in his cabin. What he needed now was a little local knowledge. Caradoc pointed to the Kaimeni with his pipe stem:

'What does "Kaimeni" mean, Number One?'

'The Burning Islands, sir ...'

'Hmmm ... I thought it'd be something like that. Are they inhabited?'

Souris shook his head: 'They're pretty hot and dismal places, sir. Just piles of loose scoria and a nasty smell of sulphur. Caiques and small coasters quite frequently put in to Neo Kaimeni to get their bottoms cleaned by the fumes bubbling up ...'

'I see ...'

Caradoc gazed down at the chart, even more absorbed by his gradually increasing picture of Santorini. That caldera up through which the Kaimeni grew ... It was simply enormous—at least seven miles by five, and anything up to two hundred fathoms deep in places. The abrupt hachuring of the coastline surrounding the caldera hinted at some cataclysmic explosion that had all-but blown the island apart. An image shaped itself in Caradoc's mind; and, taking up a pencil, he sketched a few experimental lines on the little sketch of the island's northern profile that was appended at the foot of the chart. The result of his doodling was to give the sketch a steepening cone—a cone that must have been—

'How high would you say, Number One?'

'Ten thousand feet, sir—perhaps more.'

Caradoc was awed. Ten thousand feet was a great deal of mountain: 'And the island's supposed to have blown itself to pieces?'

Souris nodded.

'Lord! Krakatoa must have sounded like a penny-banger in comparison. When was the eruption, d'you know, Number One?'

'I've heard it put at around fifteen hundred B.C., sir...'

'Comfortably before our time then...' Caradoc paused and considered. Going off like that in the enclosed waters of the Aegean, the explosion and its effects must have been tremendous—like a grenade going off in a salmon pool. The whole of what then made up the civilised world must have been shaken to its very foundations.

He looked up at Souris and said: 'Maybe Kattschner's theory that Santorini is really Atlantis isn't so wide of the mark...'

'You could be right, sir...' The first-lieutenant conceded.

'Just *how* right, I wonder?' Caradoc mused.

Souris returned on deck to supervise the setting up of new shrouds to supplement the woolding of the sprung foremast. Alone in his cabin once more, Caradoc tapped his empty pipe against his teeth: intuition told him that Santorini was the end of *Bryony*'s long search. Was—or *had been*, he warned himself grimly. *Bryony*'s storm-damage had lost them precious time, just when they could least afford it. If he arrived in Santorini to find his bird had flown, then his disobedience of orders would be all for nothing.

Right, but too late, would be no excuse in the Navy's book...

Caradoc turned his attention back to the chart. Since that cataclysmic eruption over three millenia ago, the Kaimeni had insidiously built themselves up from the floor of the caldera until, at their highest point, on Neo Kaimeni, had reached four hundred feet above sea level.

One day, in some far distant future, the great cone of Santorini would have fully restored itself again. And then, sooner or later, history would repeat itself, and the island would blow itself apart once more.

Just how long would it be before that happened? Thousands of years? Millions? Caradoc grinned: there were *some* consolations represented by the almost unimaginable vastnesses of geological time.

They made his present worries look pretty small beer!

*　　　*　　　*

Perhaps the very extraordinariness of Max's return to Germany obscured its true importance. The security of *Plan Atlantis* had been prejudiced—yet whose duty it was to recognise the fact, failed to take Max's evidence at its face value. As a returning hero, he was listened to eagerly. But what he actually had to say was ignored, filed—and thereafter disappeared into that limbo commonly euphemised as 'the usual channels' . . .

The senior officer who should have made the matter his urgent business took himself off on leave; the file (now coffee-stained) remained unread; and the Athens agency controlling certain German naval activities in the Aegean was unalerted.

Max himself was made much of; feted; lionised. Tactfully ignoring the precise reasons why Kapitän-Leutnant Kirbschaus had come to find himself in an open boat in the middle of the North Sea, the German press gave itself over to bellicose rejoicing.

For Max, the fuss and the fanfare were all too much. Five days after his return, he became conscious of a blinding pain behind his eyes; his vision doubled; the walls of his room bulged in on him, and he became delirious . . .

The senior officer who had taken himself off on leave, returned to his desk in early August. It was another three weeks before he remembered the *Plan Atlantis* file. Guiltily he berated his subordinates, called for the file, and then, belatedly, took action.

By that time, *Bryony* was within a few miles of Santorini . . .

*　　　*　　　*

Under reduced sail, *Bryony* eased her way through the sparkling sea at a recuperative three knots. She was not making for Santorini directly. Before leaving Analfi, Caradoc and Souris had conferred over the chart a second time. The schooner was not merely low on fuel, her tanks were bone dry.

With the foremast in its present weakened state, Caradoc was disinclined to take risks. Before embarking on what might well turn into a second stern chase, he was loth to join action without the Thornycroft. Should that mast go by the board altogether, or be bedevilled by a flat calm, the ability to use the engine could well make all the difference. 'Lose not a day' was a Nelsonic imperative with which Caradoc was in the heartiest concurrence. But, with an available fuelling point only thirty miles away, caution dictated that he gave *Bryony* as much liberty of manoeuvre as possible—even at the risk of losing his quarry's scent.

But a sort of fatalistic calm held Caradoc now—a calm that was not so much a belief in his own luck, as a blunt determination that having at last prised up the blind rock of *Plan Atlantis*, he was going to take a damned good look at whatever might crawl out from beneath it . . .

Now as *Bryony* eased herself through the water, he possessed himself with the same patience that he had learnt in *Undine* during her slow patrolling in the Western Approaches.

Bryony was now making for Khristiani Island—that insignificant outcropping of the Cyclades, nine miles south-west of Santorini. Caradoc had expressed some surprise when he had examined the island on the chart. Nine-hundred feet high, and rising up from sea level in a dog's-tooth pinnacle of rock, it seemed an unlikely spot to select as a refuelling point. With no obvious anchorage, it also looked extremely inaccessible.

But Souris was more optimistic. He leaned over the chart and pointed out a little indentation on the island's southern shoreline:

'*There's* our anchorage, sir . . .'

Caradoc looked doubtful, but consulted his orders: 'You're right, Number One. But I must say that it looks a bit hazardous to me . . . *These* say that it's rock-girt, but that there are leading-marks—a timber cross with a white-painted rock fifty or so feet above it . . .' He bent down to reconsider that chart: 'Yes . . . There's our rocks all right . . . getting in there should be great fun . . .'

'Oh, it's not too bad, sir . . .'

'Have you been there?'

'A couple of times, sir. It's a safe enough anchorage in weather like this. There's usually a bit of a swell as you might expect. But it's only really unhealthy when the wind backs right round . . .'

Caradoc nodded: 'Well, we shouldn't need to be there for longer than an hour or two. We'll have all hands ashore to get that petrol on board as soon as possible . . .'

'Right, sir . . .'

But by late afternoon, Caradoc was no longer certain of a daylight landfall. The wind fell away, and *Bryony* barely ghosted through the water. With evening, the western sky became a brazen, dazzling vault—a vault in which the sharp little point of Khristiani vanished, and was blotted out.

Caradoc fumed. Every passing minute made it clearer that *Bryony* would not fetch her intended anchorage till long after nightfall. Besides: it was now late August, and in the dark of the moon. If they failed to take off their petrol to-night, then they would have lost a further eight hours.

Lose not a minute! Caradoc came to a decision and turned towards Souris:

'You say you've landed on Khristiani a couple of times before, Number One?'

'Yes, sir . . .'

'Could you find those leading-marks in the dark?'

'I could try . . .'

'Good! When we get in close enough, I want you to take the dinghy away with a couple of lanterns and show me the way in.'

Souris looked puzzled: 'But there'll be no wind at all under the lee of the island itself. How will you get *Bryony* in, sir?'

'The way your piratical ancestors and mine would have done it, Number One. If the worst comes to the worst, we'll put both boats over the side and *tow* her in. But I hope it won't come to that. Pass the word for McNab will you, Number One . . .'

'Right, sir . . .'

McNab came up on deck with the air of a dissenting

minister whose duty compelled him to visit a brothel. Caradoc came straight to the point: 'McNab—those tanks of yours . . . Just how dry is "bone-dry"?'

'What I told you, sir, neither mor-re or less . . .'

Caradoc half-closed his eyes as he gazed along *Bryony's* decks, taking note of her trim, which was slightly down by the stern. He made this point to McNab and then added:

'The tanks are set fore-and-aft, aren't they, McNab?'

'Aye, sir . . .' McNab unwillingly conceded.

'Yet their dip-rods are amidships?'

'Yes, sir . . .'

'Does the petrol outlet pipe—if that's the right name for the thing—reach right down to the bottom of the tanks?'

McNab looked scornful at this example of his captain's ignorance: 'Of course not, sir—else the carburettors awould get blocked with muck picked up fra' the bottoms o' the tanks.'

Caradoc longed to shake McNab—a longing that was reinforced by the Scot's answer to his next question.

'So in fact there could *still* be some petrol sloshing round in the after ends of the tanks?'

'Aye, sir . . .'

'Then what's to stop us either siphoning the stuff out, or boring temporary holes in the bottom of the tanks?'

'Nothing, sir—except that the petrol would be *dirrrty* petrol.'

The last thread of Caradoc's diminishing patience snapped:

'Then *filter* the bloody stuff!'

The colour drained from McNab's face and he stiffened to attention: 'Captain or nae, sir, there's nae need for language like tha' . . .'

Wells grinned and recalled old times in *Harbinger* as he heard his captain's once-familiar quarter-deck bellow: 'McNab! I don't give a fish's tit whether you think you're one of the Lord's Anointed or the fluff under the Archangel Gabriel's foreskin—but while you serve with me, you'll do as you're bloody told and look lively! Understand?'

Wells stifled his laughter as McNab shot below like a

frightened rabbit. *Taffy Caradoc was a right bastard when roused*! Still with his feathers very obviously ruffled, Caradoc jammed his pipe in his mouth.

The glow of the sunset faded into a short twilight that quickly deepened into night. A strong reek of petrol tainted the darkness as a sulky McNab milked the last of *Bryony*'s precious fuel from her tanks. Various clatterings and bangings announcing the E.R.A.'s progress came up through the open engine-room skylight.

While this was going on, the folding boat was made ready on deck, and torches and lanterns were put into the dinghy. Briefly, a small off-shore breeze, sifting down from the rocky heights of Khristiani eased *Bryony*'s progress towards the half-mile wide strait separating the island from its even smaller neighbour, Askania. But then, with the schooner only a few hundred yards from the shore, even this small zephyr died to nothing and left *Bryony* motionless in the water.

The dinghy was dropped down over the side. Together with Earnshaw and Yeo, Souris climbed down into it. The two seamen fended the dinghy away from *Bryony*'s side, dipped their oars, and the boat disappeared into the hot and sticky darkness.

While he waited, Caradoc went below to inspect McNab's work. Despite his pique, the E.R.A. had done well. He had temporarily rigged an auxiliary tank made from a small petrol drum, and was now busily filtering his salvaged petrol into this with the aid of a funnel and a wad of muslin.

Caradoc watched this process for a few moments, then returned on deck. He looked towards the shore—but all was in darkness, and there was no sign that Souris and the dinghy had reached the beach as yet. Caradoc did his best to possess himself in patience. The dinghy was a heavy little beast. Besides: not being over-familiar with *Bryony*'s intended anchorage, Souris would want to approach it with caution.

The minutes ticked away. McNab came up on deck to report that the little auxiliary tank was now ready for use. The E.R.A. turned away in the darkness, tripped over

133

some unseen obstruction and fell heavily. McNab said something.

Wells's voice insinuated itself into the silence that followed: 'McNab—'

'Yes?'

The reply was softly delivered, but in a fair approximation of the Scot's own tones: 'E.R.A. or no, there's nae need for language like tha'...'

A ripple of smothered laughter ran round the shadowy figures on *Bryony's* deck, and Caradoc sharply called for silence. Another quarter of an hour followed.

'Sir!' Pembury's voice called out of the darkness: 'The dinghy's coming back...'

Caradoc stared towards Khristiani. He heard the groan of an oar in its crutch, and then caught the momentary bloom of luminescence as the oar blades bit at the water. The boat came alongside, and someone shone a torch down into it.

'Dowse that light!'

The torch went out immediately, but not before Caradoc had seen that only Earnshaw and Yeo were now in the dinghy, and that Souris was missing.

Earnshaw came up on deck, and Caradoc took him down to his cabin to explain. The Yorkshireman came straight to the point:

'We got in among them rocks all reet, sir, and then t'Jimmy tells us to hold water wi' t' oars, and whispers that thears a schooner in't anchorage already...'

'A schooner?'

'Aye, sir. T'same one as we chased the other day...'

'Is she, by God! So where's the first-lieutenant now?'

'Ah were coomin' t' that,' Earnshaw said in a tone that reproved his captain's impatience: 'Mr Souris got Yeo t'put an oar over t'stern and scull to the t'other side of t'bay. Then we found a place to land him wi' t'lanterns...'

'What's his idea?'

'He said t'tell thee, sir, that at thi signal, he'd light t'lamps as were originally intended, and that they'd be directly behind and above t'*Iskaria*...'

'What was the signal to be?'

'He said Yeo and me was t'put well clear o' *Bryony*, and then I were t'keep on flashing "Z" every half-minute till t'lanterns were lit . . .'

'Did the first-lieutenant think the schooner had already spotted us, Earnshaw?'

'Aye! He reckoned they must ha' doon, sir . . . after all, we spent most of the afternoon coomin' up to the island . . . Besides, sir—they must have bin able t'hear thee on board t'*Iskaria*. We could from where we were all reet . . .'

'Damn!' Caradoc did some furious thinking. The *Iskaria* had intended an ambush. Now, both schooners knew of the other's presence—though if Souris succeeded in lighting his lanterns, then *Bryony* would have a momentary advantage. Just how heavily armed would the *Iskaria* be, Caradoc wondered. At least as heavily as *Bryony* seemed the likeliest guess . . .

Still: his duty was to bring *Iskaria* to book. There was a score to be settled there for those men whom the enemy's mines had drowned.

Caradoc and Earnshaw returned to the deck—the Yorkshireman back to the dinghy, and Caradoc to close up the guns' crews with a brisk flurry of urgently whispered orders. Wells moved to the wheel, and the dinghy pulled away from *Bryony*'s side. Caradoc positioned himself by the engine-room's open skylight.

'McNab! Stand-by!'

'Aye, aye, sir . . .'

Ten minutes passed with mouth-drying slowness, until a couple of cableslengths away northwards, Earnshaw's torch briefly split the darkness with the dah-dah, dit-dit of the letter 'Z' . . .

The thirty seconds following Earnshaw's signal seemed endless, so that as they ticked away, it felt as though that brief wink of torchlight had been a trick of memory; an optical illusion. Caradoc sensed the tension of the men round him on the deck.

Just when even Caradoc was beginning to doubt that he had ever seen Earnshaw's signal, the Yorkshireman's torch flashed again, faint but unmistakable. Two things happened at once: a machine-gun began chattering from the unseen enemy's deck, its muzzle-flash spitting angrily in the direction of *Bryony*'s dinghy; in the same instant, too, a match flared high up on the darkened mountainside, and then a lamp bloomed into life.

Caradoc yelled at the waiting guns' crews: 'Wait for the second lamp, and your target'll be directly below and in line with the lamps! Fire as you bear!'

His heel stamped on the deck. Beneath him, the Thornycroft grumbled into life, and a shudder ran through *Bryony*'s hull as her screw began turning. The water boiled under her transom, and she surged forward.

'Work up to half-revs . . .'

Even now, the E.R.A. seemed inclined to protest. His voice came up through the skylight: 'Sir! The petr– '

'Damn the petrol! Half-revs!'

Caradoc's helm orders were as lacking in complication as those to the guns: 'Wells! When that second lamp is lit, get the two lined up, and take her straight in without any nonsense!'

'Aye, aye, sir . . .'

A second machine-gun had begun its rattling by now, its muzzle-flash probing uncertainly towards *Bryony*. Somewhere away to port came a curious pocking sound which Caradoc identified as the sound of its bullets smacking into the still surface of the sea.

Heavier metal . . . A shell ripped through the air with a high pitched tearing sound. Caradoc instinctively ducked and then straightened up sheepishly, glad that the darkness had hidden his futile gesture. The enemy was firing blind—but just how long before the bugger got his eye in? An impatient anger rose in Caradoc.

Just where the hell was that second lantern? And what the devil did Michael Souris think he was playing at over there?

*   *   *

So far as the first-lieutenant was concerned, it seemed he was playing a game not so very far removed from that very

136

dangerous one he had played three months back on Tourko Vouno. Once the dinghy had disappeared, Souris found himself on a slab of still slightly sun-warmed rock, and worrying how best to carry his jingling storm-lanterns. He moved inland, finding himself on a rapidly steepening slope. The lanterns swung on their wire handles, chinking and chattering companionably.

Souris cussed under his breath. In the hot stillness of the night, sound seemed to be carrying for miles. In the dinghy, he had been able to hear the murmuration of voices echoing across the water from *Bryony*'s deck.

On the contrary, there was no sound at all to be heard from *Iskaria*. Presumably, she must have been aware of *Bryony*'s approach for hours, and was now waiting in the knowledge that *Bryony* was bound to do one of two things: sail past the island—or straight into a trap...

Thanks to *Bryony*'s lack of fuel, things hadn't quite worked out like that...

Souris moved on up the slope—but the glass bowls of the lamps chittered in their seatings, and he froze to a halt. Surely *someone* must have heard him by now? But, no... his progress remained unchallenged, and after a few moments in which to regain his breath, he moved on again.

He willed himself to take his time and climb slowly up the uneven and precipitous hillside. Almost by accident he found what he was looking for—a crag of grey rock, carved by wind and weather into the shape of a grotesque head. It jutted high above the slope, but Souris knew that there was a way up its back. Hampered by his lanterns, it was a good five minutes before he reached the crown of the rock, and lay down to wait for Earnshaw's signal.

An age seemed to pass. *Where had Earnshaw got to? Surely he couldn't have misunderstood his orders?*

Five more minutes passed ... ten ... fifteen ... The sudden, and now-unexpected blink of the torch took Souris by surprise. He groped for his matches, and then, reaching for one of his lamps, pushed down the little lever that raised the lamp-glass so that he could reach the wick.

Absurdly, it was only now that he at last realised the dangers that would come with his lighting of the lamp.

Once he struck the match and put it to the lamp, he would be clearly visible for miles—a perfect target for any sentry with a rifle . . .

Souris steeled himself to act. To be all thumbs at a time like this would only double his danger. Earnshaw's torch flashed again, and in the same instant almost, Souris heard the chatter of a machine-gun from *Iskaria* below him. He ripped his match along the side of its box, his night-vision instantly dying as the match flared. He gave it a second to burn up, and applied it to the lamp. The wick hung fire for a tantalising moment, then burst into light. Souris jammed the lamp-glass back down onto its seating. The whole top of the rock was now bathed in a brilliant yellow glow, and Souris felt like a rabbit caught in the beam of a headlight.

There was a crack of a shot from somewhere close at hand. Souris flung himself headlong from his perch. In his efforts to save the glass of his precious second lamp, he fell awkwardly and felt something give in his knee.

'Halte!'

But Souris was off down the slope, trying to ignore the yelping agony in his knee and frantically zig-zagging to put the unseen marksman off his aim. Nightblind now, he almost crashed straight into the second leading-mark—an old spar with a cross-piece of timber nailed a few feet from its top.

Souris thought he had shaken his pursuer off, but knew that he couldn't be so very far away. Once again, he struggled to keep calm as he lit his second lamp. Seventy yards away came the report of a second shot, and something kicked the stones at his feet into a momentary spurt of sharp little splinters. He reached up and hung his lamp on the cross-piece of the spar, then leapt out of its aureole of light into the surrounding sanctuary of darkness. His injured knee collapsed beneath him, and faster and faster, he found himself rolling down the rocky scarp of the hill.

He crashed to a halt against a boulder, listening to the clatter of pursuing boots above him and to the distant growl of *Bryony*'s Thorneycroft booming across the bay. The snarl of weaponry below him, reminded him of the angry

138

bickering of a pair of farm dogs.

Souris looked back up the hillside towards his lamps. Both were shining bright and clear. A figure moved into the circle of light thrown by the lamp on the spar. Again the rifle snapped, and the figure crumpled and fell. God! Souris exulted, one of the sentries had mistaken his opposite number for the lighter of those Judas-beacons . . .

Souris knew that it was up to him to keep this second man preoccupied and away from those vulnerable lights. If one was to be put out now, then *Bryony* would be left blind in amongst the bay's guardian rocks. Standing painfully, he hurled stone after stone into the darkness, shouting like a madman as he did so, and then limping away along the slope. More shots followed, with the eery whicker of ricochets ululating across the open hillside.

A perverse sort of frenzy seized him, and Souris hopped up and down on his uninjured leg, taunting the unseen marksman above him: 'Missed me, you bastard! Missed me!'

It was a mistake that should have proved fatal. With his night-vision now almost recovered from the flare of lighting those lamps, Souris was suddenly aware of a shadowy figure poised against the sky-line a mere dozen yards away—the derided sentry with the rifle at his shoulder and with its barrel pointing straight towards him. The madness drained from Souris as he waited the inevitable shot.

When it came, it was so much louder than he expected. The whole world seemed to burst in one great convulsive explosion that flung his body feet into the air, and briefly lit the island as though it had been struck by lightning. As his body crashed to the ground, one last inconsequential thought shot through his mind.

Ya t'onomatou Theou! Nobody had told him that being shot felt like *this*!

*   *   *

Souris's second lantern sprang into flame, Wells fed the spokes of the wheel through his hands, and *Bryony* swung on her heel in answer to her rudder. The three-pounder barked out for'ard and was answered by its heavier opponent on *Iskaria*. Neither shell found its mark. They would all know about it when one did, Caradoc told himself: a few hits from either gun would be enough . . .

Now that action had been joined, he felt a return of that same fatalistic detachment he had experienced in *Undine* when she had at last cornered her U-boat. He had done everything he could, and had got his ship into the right place. The outcome was now largely out of his hands and dependent on the skill and coolness of the men around him: of the three-pounder's crew for'ard; of Wells; and of Hughes, who chattering angrily to himself in Welsh because the pom-pom's field of fire was masked, waited impatiently for his chance to shoot.

'Rocks to port, sir!'

Grey against the darkness, a mass of weed-covered rock slipped by, loud with the suck and slap of the schooner's wash.

'Rocks to starboard!'

A second slab of stone shone spectre-like against the shadow. There was a muffled thump from below as *Bryony* lightly touched some small underwater outcrop, and a delicate shudder ran through the whole length of her hull. They were damned close in now. A cables-length—no more . . . The two heavy guns seemed to be snarling at each other, muzzle to muzzle. But still, in the darkness, neither had as yet scored a hit.

But now, there was a splash of flame and smoke right beneath *Bryony*'s bow. For'ard, someone yelped out in pain, and the schooner's head payed off to port.

'Hold her, Wells!'

Now that his gun was no longer masked, Hughes took the most of his opportunity and the pom-pom began an angry fulmination into the darkness, pumping out its little shells with the jabbing accuracy of a boxer. Each separate shell made its mark in the barely-seen *Iskaria* as a brief splash of flame. Then, even as Wells managed to bring *Bryony* back on course, and the pom-pom was again masked, the battle was over . . .

A sharp little tongue of light leapt upwards from *Iskaria*, momentarily showing her against the backdrop of the island behind her. Then, she seemed to burst apart in a great gout of flame. Mercifully, the worst blast of the explosion went upwards. Debris rained down, pattering on *Bryony*'s decks and splashing into the sea.

The one moment, *Iskaria* had been there, the next she was gone. Her end was as simple and final as that . . .

*   *   *

All afternoon, an illogical yet pervasive sense of anticipation had slowly stolen over Max Kirbschaus—a feeling that, at any minute, something momentous and little short of miraculous was bound to happen. It was an odd sort of mood to be in, and Max put it down to a slight touch of the sun, coupled with the view at which he was looking—a distant backcloth of wooded slopes, with here and there a warm grouping of roof-tops, each clustered round schloss or church tower. Nearer at hand, the valley became a green patchwork of tumbled meadows, and the hospital grounds themselves stretched down to a willow-lined river.

Here, a hundred or so pyjama'd and dressing-gowned figures took their ease in the afternoon sun. In wheelchairs, on crutches, or with bandages binding eyes that would never see again, each broken figure was mute testimony to the frailty of man's body when pitted against modern explosives.

Max closed his eyes, letting the bright sun set the insides of his eyelids a-dance with a myriad gleaming, changing patterns. His illogical sense of expectation returned . . .

'Kapitän-Leutnant Kirbschaus! *You-are-not-wearing-your-dressing-gown!*'

The voice—feminine—just—spoke in the horror of someone seeing one of the world's larger imperatives wantonly disregarded. Max stifled an irritated urge to giggle. Severally or altogether, the voice implied, he could break as many of the Ten Commandments as he liked—but with a proper regard for hospital rules *and* wearing his dressing-gown . . .

Max opened his eyes and found himself staring up at Nurse Muller. Stiffly carapaced in starched white linen, Frieda Muller's homely face was now marred by angry heat blotches which, together with her incipient moustache, gave her the look of a dyspeptic sergeant-major.

'But I'm going home tomorrow, Frieda . . .' Max answered her reasonably.

'It's the chill that you might get to-day, and what Sister Kohner would say if *she* saw you without your dressing-gown that worries me, Käpitan-Leutnant. Now do sit up!'

Recognising the dreaded words 'Sister Kohner' used as the ultimate threat and sanction, Max obeyed. Nurse Muller picked up the dressing-gown that Max had folded into a comfortable pillow. Grass-stained and creased, the dressing-gown was a sorry object. Nurse Muller banged and thumped at its crumped folds.

'What Sister will have to say when *she* sees this, I don't know . . .

'I'll tell her I fell over,' Max said equably.

'And *whose* fault do you suppose that will be?' Nurse Muller countered: 'Mine, you silly man! So far as Sister Kohner's concerned, everything is *always* my fault!'

Max looked at her with sympathy. Clumsy to a fault, she was still a damned good nurse. With wounded and frightened men, she was tenderness itself. To distract Nurse Muller's mind from the grubby dressing-gown, Max pointed down the slope towards the figure of a man seated on a distant bench. Even at a hundred and fifty metres, there was something faintly familiar about the figure which nudged something in Max's memory.

'Who's that fellow?'

Nurse Muller shook her head, and her cow-like eyes grew round with compassion: 'Nobody knows, Kapitän-Leutnant . . .'

'What do you mean "Nobody knows"?'

'What I say. All his papers and identity discs were lost in transit on his way from the front . . .'

'Was he badly knocked about?'

'Pretty badly. See his bandage? He was shot through the

142

head.'

'Good God!'

'Oh, he's recovering. He's not been made an imbecile or anything like that. It's just that he's still so very badly shocked. Nobody has heard him say a word beyond "Please" and "Thank you".'

'In German?'

'But, of *course*! Why on earth do you ask such a silly question?'

Max was unsure—except that his sense of familiarity with that distant figure was growing within him. At a hundred and fifty metres, he could be mistaken of course. But, at the same time, there was something about the unknown man which conjured up a half-forgotten memory of rolling downland and cool hop-avenues, brindled with sunlight and shadow.

Max brushed some grass-cuttings from his trousers: 'Let's take a look at this chap . . .'

Together with Nurse Muller, he strolled slowly down the hillside. Max knew he would be mistaken, of course—the same as when, embarrassingly, one hailed a perfect stranger as an old friend.

But, the closer he got, the less Max was sure. The set of a head, the line of a back were often quite as identifiable as a man's face. Hearing the sound of Max's footsteps as he came across the grass, the seated man turned and looked straight at him. The stare was entirely without recognition, but Max was now certain of the stranger's identity. He sat down beside him on the bench and took out his cigarette case.

'Cigarette?'

'*Danke schon . . .*'

Max smiled. Nobody had listened to the stranger with an intent enough ear. The pronunciation of that umlauted 'O' had been good—but not quite good enough. Max recalled a now long-ago summer afternoon when he had spent half an hour teaching the man now seated beside him how to say *schon . . .*

Max lit the other's cigarette and said in English: 'How are you feeling, Aidan?'

'Very well, thank you...' Aidan's eyes took on a puzzled look and he said: 'How do you know my name?'

'Don't you remember me?'

Aidan considered and worriedly rubbed at his forehead. He looked, Max found himself thinking, very much as Lazarus must have looked waking from the dead.

At last Aidan said: 'You're a friend of Ralph's. You stayed with us at Ragged Robin Farm...'

'That's right, old chap...'

Nurse Muller was breathing down Max's neck: 'What is he *saying*, Kapitän-Leutnant? And who is he?'

'He's a British Officer, Frieda—and a very old friend of mine. I used to stay—'

But Max was wasting his time. Regardless of the hospital rule that nurses should not run, Frieda Muller was off down the hill in a flurry of skirts and petticoats to spread the news.

His voice, uncertain with lack of use, Aidan said: 'My wife... Barbara...'

Max laid a comforting hand on his shoulder: 'Don't worry, old fellow. We'll find a way of letting her know...'

* * *

With her cable shackled to one of the steamer buoys below Phira, *Bryony* lay at last in the great caldera of Santorini. Yesterday, as she sailed in through the caldera's south-west entrance, Caradoc had refused to allow himself to be impressed. He had seen cliffs before—cliffs that were higher, grimmer; cliffs whose broken striations glowered with an equally threatening menace. But, the further *Bryony* had penetrated into the caldera, then the less easy had he found it to maintain his pose of determined indifference. Nor, he noted, did anyone else on board judge it necessary to copy his assumed detachment. For'ard, all pretence at work ceased as the schooner's hardbitten crew stared about them—something they had rarely bothered to do after *Bryony*'s first few landfalls.

Santorini *was* different... As *Bryony* swung to her buoy, Caradoc found the island increasingly working its dark spell on him. Striped like some huge, fantastic blancmange—except that its colours were sombrely red, ochre, purplish-brown and black—the cliffs rose sheer to starboard in towering and sometimes overhanging buttresses and columns; buttresses which, long since, blasted upwards by titanic forces, had frozen into these convulsive and agonised rigidities of shape.

Caradoc put his binoculars up to his eyes and looked towards the shore. A cableslength away was a stone quayside, a few untidy-looking buildings and a pocket-handkerchief of a harbour. Behind the quay, a vertiginous zig-zag path weaved its dizzy way to the cliff-top summit on which Phira itself was perched—a line of houses which, gleaming whitely in the morning sun, were poised on the lip of the thousand-foot abyss. In defiance of gravity and the island's not infrequent earthquakes, a number of barrel-shaped houses clung to the sheer slopes beside the cliff-path, precarious-looking as swallows' nests.

Caradoc lowered his binoculars to where on the quayside, a flurry of activity told of someone's arrival down from Phira. Mules and men milled about, and a babble of voices echoed out across the two hundred yards of water separating *Bryony* from the shore. Caradoc grinned as he spotted Michael Souris in amongst the crowd on the quay, his hands and arms shaping gestures that, in his role of an R.N.V.R. officer, he conscientiously denied himself. Even at this distance, Souris's splendid black eye gleamed like a dark patch on the olive skin of his face—a legacy of the blast which had ripped *Iskaria* apart and had flattened him into the hillside of Khristiani.

Apart from a couple of minor splinter wounds, the first lieutenant had been the schooner's only casualty. They had been damned lucky . . . There had been no survivors at all from *Iskaria*—only the unfortunate sentry who had been about to shoot Souris when the explosion had occurred. And even he was in pretty bad shape. He was now lying on the deck for'ard under an awning, too badly injured to get down *Bryony*'s narrow companion-ways. He was unconscious now and passing blood. Quite what was wrong with the poor devil was anyone's guess—a ruptured spleen or kidneys seemed the likeliest thing.

Pembury called out eagerly: 'There's a boat pulling off from the quay, sir!'

'I can see her, thank you...'

Caradoc focussed his binoculars on the boat. She was bigger than *Bryony*'s own dinghy—a local caique with a figure carrying a black bag and wearing a floppy felt hat sitting beside Michael Souris amidships. The boat came alongside, and Souris helped the floppy-hatted man over *Bryony*'s rail.

'Dr Katsoulakos, sir...'

The doctor bowed, shook Caradoc's hand, and was then led for'ard to examine the patient. A rapid fire of question and answer was exchanged between Souris and the doctor. Then Katsoulakos examined his patient, his expression becoming graver as he palpated the unconscious man's distended abdomen and lifted his closed eyelids to peer beneath.

'Po-po-po-po-po-po!'

'Dr Katsoulakos says that the patient is very seriously injured, sir, and will certainly die unless we can get him ashore so that he can be operated on at once...'

Caradoc felt himself placed neatly in a cleft stick. Sending the prisoner ashore would put an end to secrecy. Yet, letting that poor devil die on board, would be to break the unwritten law of the sea—the law that said you did your damnedest to sink your enemy, but that you succoured him afterwards. It was no choice at all really, Caradoc knew, and he barely wasted a moment considering it.

'We'd better get the prisoner ashore, Number One...'

Gently—but with some confusion because of the necessity for Souris to translate Dr Katsoulakos's instructions—the wounded man was strapped to a makeshift stretcher and lowered into the caique.

Caradoc snapped: 'Mr Pembury—you'll take command. I'm going ashore with the first-lieutenant...'

'Very good, sir...'

'Don't say "very good"—you sound like some bloody butter-slapper in Lipton's...'

'Very—Aye, aye, sir...' Pembury looked startled at his

146

captain's sudden ill-temper.

Caradoc followed Souris down over *Bryony*'s rail and the caique made for the shore. As they moved across the sparkling wavelets of the caldera, Caradoc found the Greek doctor staring at him with dark, intelligent eyes, before turning to Souris then asking what was obviously a question.

The first-lieutenant shot a warning look in Caradoc's direction, and then sought his advice.

'Dr Katsoulakos says did we hear that explosion on Khristiani the other night?'

'Tell him . . . Tell him it was probably a mine washing up on shore and that we heard it from the sea . . .'

Souris spoke eloquently in Greek and with much waving of his hands, but it was obvious that Dr Katsoulakos did not believe a word. The doctor looked at Caradoc for a moment or two with quizzically raised eyebrows before turning to ask Souris a second question. Caradoc felt a premonition of what that question was about, even though he only understood one word: '*Anglia*' . . .

'The doctor says your answer was very interesting—but how is it that you and your crew are English, and yet the man on the stretcher is German?'

Caradoc sat up with a jerk. He had been certain that they had removed every identifiable shred of the injured man's clothing.

'Ask Dr Katsoulakos *why* he should think that?'

Souris obeyed, and without a word, the doctor merely lifted the blanket covering the prisoner's arm.

'Damn!' Caradoc glowered. It was such a little thing that had been overlooked—a tattoo's anchor on the seaman's forearm with the words '*Gott Mit Uns*' on a scroll beneath it.

That just about put the tin lid on things, Caradoc decided as the caique came within fifty yards of the quay. The cat was now well and truly out of the bag. *Bryony* might as well shut up shop, obey her recall, and go home now with her work half-done.

But, before the caique reached the quayside, two things happened. Still deeply unconscious, the wounded man struggled against his blankets and began muttering the same phrases over and over again, just loudly enough for Caradoc to be able to catch his words as he bent forward to listen. Then, the muttering ceased abruptly, and Caradoc only realised the prisoner was dead as he saw Dr Katsoulakos make a triple crossing motion against his waistcoat buttons and remove his floppy hat.

Ashamed and angry with himself, Caradoc found himself inwardly cursing: if only that damned prisoner had said what he'd had to and had got his dying over earlier . . .

But it was too late now . . . Unless he dropped Katsoulakos over the side, the whole of Santorini would know *Bryony*'s purpose in the next hour . . .

* * *

But would they? . . . Caradoc watched as *Bryony*'s dinghy returned just after noon. Souris looked tired and was limping badly from his twisted knee as Caradoc led him below.

'How did you get on, Number One?'

'Pretty well, sir . . . Greek red-tape is pretty formidable stuff—but Dr Katsoulakos helped me find my way through the tangle . . .'

Caradoc handed Souris a glass: 'The whole island must know what we are by now . . .'

Souris shook his head: 'I don't think so, sir. Dr Katsoulakos is a fervent admirer of Venizelos—which means he's pro-Allied. So far as the authorities are concerned, the body that will be buried will be that of a Christian Arab. I've sailed with one or two of those in my crews before now . . .'

'But that damned tattoo?'

'Dr Katsoulakos will make sure that no one else sees it, sir . . .'

'You seem to have handled things very well . . .'

'Thank you, sir. But it was the doctor really . . .'

Caradoc felt his mood of flat depression giving way to one of renewed optimism; a growing certainty that despite everything, *Bryony* was back in the hunt. The feeling grew

148

as Souris said:

'Would you be able to come ashore with me in the first dog, sir? Dr Katsoulakos and I both think there's someone that you should meet . . .'

*   *   *

Shortly after four o'clock, Caradoc found himself seated on the back of a mule as it picked its uncertain way up that zig-zag pathway climbing from behind the quay. The saddle was mediaeval in appearance, and every bit as hard-arsed as it looked.

As his mule struggled up the cliff, Caradoc looked down at the mule driver trudging up the path beside him. The fellow didn't exactly excite confidence. Once, he cruelly jabbed his goad so hard into the rectum of Caradoc's mule that the wretched beast almost flung Caradoc over its head.

For a nasty second, he had a bird's-eye perspective of the now toy-sized quay, far, far below him. Vertigo threatened, and Caradoc closed his eyes. He opened them with relief when the pathway at last flattened out into a small plateau. Souris paid-off the mule driver who wandered away without a word of thanks.

Hobbling badly, the first-lieutenant led the way down a narrow wend that was little more than a convoluted gut, too narrow for wheeled traffic. Walls of white-washed stone hemmed them in—walls whose shuttered windows and iron-squinted doors smacked more of the near-East than anything European. But, in the near-East, Caradoc told himself, there would have been noise and babel; the busy comings and goings of colourfully robed figures. Here, there was only a dusty, sunlit silence, and a brooding sense of enclosure.

Caradoc began to feel the watchful noiselessness unnerving. Even the usually ebullient Michael Souris appeared in a low-keyed mood.

Caradoc knew just enough about architecture to recognise something of the styles surrounding him; Turkish secrecy, Venetian grace—the heavy hand of those Norman barons who, returning from the Crusades, had regarded the Aegean Islands as so many consolation prizes.

Yes, for all its beauty, Phira's mood was withdrawn and defensive. The key to this sense was revealed as the wall beside Caradoc dropped away, and he found himself staring out over the tumbled roof-tops of Phira and across the caldera. Breathtaking as this panorama was, he found that his eye was always inevitably drawn to the low hummocks of the Kaimeni. Wherever one looked, the burning islands seemed to insinuate their presence like a sly and insidious threat . . .

Souris tugged at his captain's elbow: 'This way, sir . . .'

They struck off down an even narrower ally—one whose high walls were bridged by several arches. Souris knocked at a little round-topped door. An iron-grille was opened; a face peered at them, and they were permitted to enter.

Caradoc found himself in a shaded courtyard, surrounded on three sides by low, white buildings; at the fourth, a chapel with the inevitable dome hung above the caldera like a lighthouse.

A sense of incongruity siezed Caradoc. Wherever he had been expecting to be taken, it was hardly here, into what was obviously a nunnery judging by the swathing black robes of the tiny woman who escorted himself and Souris across the courtyard. But there was no time for questions as the little nun led them through a series of bare, lime-washed passages. Sombre ikons punctuated the bareness—ikons from which Byzantine saints stared down with costive disapproval.

At last, Caradoc and Souris found themselves in what were obviously the convent guest rooms. One last door opened out onto a farther terrace. In the centre of this was a day-bed where, half-sitting, half-lying, and with one heavily bandaged leg sticking out from his voluminous black cassock, was the figure of a priest.

'Michaeli!' he boomed.

'Father Iannis!'

Father Iannis and the first-lieutenant clasped each other in a joyous bear-hug that gave Caradoc time to take a long look at the bed-bound man. Oddly (and despite the fact

150

that the priest gave Souris a smacking kiss on each cheek), Caradoc was reminded of Rear-Admiral Auberon who had been instrumental in getting him appointed to *Undine*. The eyes of both old men shared a similar look of shrewd appraisal; the same expression of experience and paradoxical innocence. Both looked like Old Testament patriachs.

Yet, Old Testament appearance or not, there was nothing sacerdotal about the impatient bellow with which the old man called for wine. It was a heave-away-God-damn-and-blast-yer-bloody-eyes sort of roar such as a Whale Island Gunnery Instructor might have envied—and it served much the same purpose. The little nun scuttled away at the double and returned with a bottle and glasses.

To Caradoc's surprise, the old priest began speaking in English: 'Po-po-po-po-po:-Michael! Look where I am come to . . . An old crock in a cage of cackling little black hens . . .' Sharp little eyes were turned in Caradoc's direction: 'And you, my son. Who might *you* be?'

* * *

An hour later, Caradoc found himself on mule back again, returning down that precipitous path from Phira to the quayside, his head singing with Father Iannis's powerful wine. *Nictere*, the old man had called it, Caradoc vaguely seemed to remember.

As he struggled to focus his wandering vision, Caradoc found himself doubting Father Iannis's existence. Surely with English every bit as fractured as that of Hughes Pom-Pom, and given to blasphemies that would have been considered extreme in the fo'c'sle of a Liverpool tramp, and good *papas must* have been a figment of his imagination, what with those black-habited little nuns hopping around at his word of command like so many newly-joined boy seamen?

But, *no* . . . The priest had been real enough, as had his wine. And he had talked good sense, too—seaman's sense—sense which had filled in several gaps in the enigma of *Plan Atlantis*. Caradoc struggled to disperse the

wine-fumes in his brain as he remembered what Father
Iannis had told him. The eruptions on Neo Kaimeni had
been going on for two months now. They had stayed
uninvestigated after three local fishermen going to clean
the weeds from the bottoms of their boats in the usual way
above the volcano's vent-holes, had simply disappeared.
Only the remains of one boat had been found, its timbers
ominously charred. The matter had been reported to
Athens, but the accident had discouraged any further local
investigation . . .

Mysterious lights had been seen at night. Father Iannis
had left his bed at this point and hopped over to the terrace
wall to show Caradoc some marks scratched into the
stonework.

'I take bearing . . .'

Caradoc squinted his eye along the marks and over the
caldera beneath: 'These point to the entrance between
Thirasia and Aspronisis . . .'

'Ne . . . and somes nearer . . .'

'As if from Neo Kaimeni itself, perhaps?'

'Ne . . .'

'What sort of lights?'

'In-outs, in-outs . . . Like dirty mans winking at pretty
girl . . .'

'Morse?'

'Ne . . .'

The old priest claimed to have seen a submarine too—
had seen it clearly one morning through the big, old-
fashioned telescope that he kept by him on his day-bed.

Caradoc invited Father Iannis to make a sketch of this
submarine—a sketch that, for all its clumsiness, confirmed
what Panos's description had told them about the U-boat;
that it was a small coastal minelayer. One small
discrepancy troubled Caradoc. He took Father Iannis's
pencil and drew a circle round the gun drawn in on the
whaleback of the submarine's forecasing. It looked far too
big . . .

'Machine-gun?' he queried; and then, seeing the priest's
look of puzzlement, added: 'Tacatacatacat-atacatacacac!'

'Oui!' Father Iannis discouragingly replied, with an

upward jerk of his head: 'Big gun! *BOOM!*'

Big gun! *BOOM!*—that sounded very definite to Caradoc as his mule negotiated a particularly tricky part of the path. Still, on a submarine that small, it probably couldn't be anything bigger than a fifty-five millimetre, say . . . Hardly in the BOOM class at all, he comforted himself.

Caradoc brought his mule to a halt and stared out across the caldera. The smoke from Neo Kaimeni lay in the low pall across the southern half of the island. Inwardly, he damned himself for a fool. What was it that smoke had reminded him of, the day they'd sailed past the North Entrance of the caldera? *A smokescreen laid by a destroyer?* That was neither more nor less than what that greasy cloud was. A smokescreen . . .

Souris reined in by Caradoc's side and said: 'Sir—why did you ask those particular questions of Father Iannis? And why didn't you seem very surprised by his answers?'

'Because I've known them ever since this morning, Michael—ever since I heard what the German sailor said just before he died . . .'

'*What* did he say, sir?'

'He said *de feurige insel* . . . *de feurige insel*—The Burning Island . . .'

*   *   *

Half an hour after Caradoc and Souris had returned on board, *Bryony* was under way again, with the wind broad abeam, reaching out through the caldera's south-west entrance between Aspronisi and Cape Akrotiri. By way of a diversion, Caradoc would have preferred leaving by the North Entrance, but this would have meant a great deal of time consuming backing and filling or using the Thornycroft.

Caradoc was loth to reveal the existence of *Bryony's* powerful auxiliary to any prying eye. The longer they could keep that secret to themselves the better. In order to gain distance from Santorini (and careless of the tooth-sucking that this caused for'ard), Caradoc even risked using the foresail on the woolded foremast. The wind was steady, and looked likely to remain so; and, beyond a few protesting groans, the mast seemed to be holding up well.

Once under way, Souris sent the watches to supper in turn, and early. Until now, supper—in *Bryony* the day's most substantial meal—had been taken after nightfall when appetites had returned after the heat of the day. This break from routine, and the abruptness of the schooner's departure, sent a buzz of speculation through the fo'c'sle. The suggestions as to the reasons for *Bryony*'s sudden leave-taking ranged from the probable through to the ribald.

'Happen t'Jimmy's got anoother fancy piece tooked away somewhear . . .'

'Just so long as this one's daddy hasn't got a shotgun . . .'

Aft, Caradoc tapped at the chart with his knuckle: 'We're dependent on your local knowledge again, Michael. Where would you suggest? Here?'

'In Port Megalo, sir? No-o . . .'

'Then *where*?'

'Judging by what Father Iannis said about those missing fishermen, and what I know about Neo Kaimeni, I should say here . . .'

Caradoc followed Souris's finger to where it indicated a deep indentation, not unlike an opened cat's paw in shape on the western side of Neo Kaimeni.

'—That's just below the volcano's main crater, and there's that right-angled elbow half-way in to protect you from prying eyes from the caldera . . .'

Caradoc considered the chart: 'It's a pity this is on such a damned small scale . . .'

'With your permission, sir—' Souris rummaged in the chart drawer beneath his captain's desk, and then triumphantly held up what he'd been searching for: 'I found this in a Ruad flea-market years ago . . .'

Caradoc looked at the thing in astonishment. It was a more or less detailed chart of the western side of Neo Kaimeni, and drawn to a generous scale. It was obviously the rough for some unfinished survey, and the Lord alone knew how it had ever found its way into a Ruad market.

Captain and first-lieutenant studied the chart in detail. Now, they could see how small the inlet actually was. It ran in for perhaps two hundred and fifty yards before a dog-leg turn north-eastwards. A further two hundred yards in, it ended in the four, fanned-out knuckles of a cat's paw. At its turn, the creek narrowed to a mere fifty yards in width, and, judging by the hachuring with which its northern shoreline had been represented, there were steepish cliffs on that side.

'Very snug . . .'

'*If* you don't mind living in a permanent reek of sulphur.'

'Hmm . . .' Caradoc studied the chart more closely and mused aloud: 'There's plenty of water all the way in . . . Fifteen fathoms at the entrance . . . Fourteen at the narrows—and seven in the paw itself . . .'

'Enough water to hide the sort of U-boat that Father Iannis described to us . . .'

'Exactly . . . We may be jumping to conclusions, Number One—but I don't think so. We'll have a look-see anyway— and we'll go in prepared for trouble . . .'

Conscious that he had sent the men to supper early, Souris asked: 'To-night, sir?'

Caradoc shook his head: 'Too chancy . . . No, Michael, dawn's our time, I think. And we'd better pray that our friend with the gun that goes BOOM isn't there to greet us . . .'

*   *   *

As he finally explained it to Souris—and with young Pembury and Petty Officer Wells in attendance—Caradoc's eventual plan was simple in the extreme. To get as far as possible into the creek, and then, if there was any sign of the enemy, to cause as much damage as possible before getting out again.

'Will we go in under power, sir?' Wells asked.

'Not unless there's a flat calm in the morning. My guess is, that like us, *Iskaria* probably had an auxiliary engine, but we didn't find enough of her to be sure . . .'

Light dawned on Pembury: 'So our aim is to look as

155

much like *Iskaria* as possible, sir?'

'That's the general idea. She got herself up to look as much like us as possible—so now, I think we'll return the compliment. If we go in at dawn, the small differences shouldn't be too noticeable. Besides, Number One, you'll know those differences better than I do. Can you get a party onto ironing them out in the night?'

'Yes, sir . . .'

'There's another thing . . . We'll go in as if we're confident of our welcome. Wells—we've got a musician or two for'ard, haven't we?'

The petty-officer looked doubtful: 'Well, sir—Yeo plays the mouth organ, Duffy's got a squeeze-box, and Ferris fancies himself on the banjo. But I wouldn't say they was *musicians* . . .'

'Well, they bloody-well better had be by morning. I want to be able to hear a good rousing performance of *Deutschland Uber Alles* as we go in . . .'

Pembury asked naively: 'Then what do we do, sir?'

'We take a look round—and if there's anyone at home, we hit 'em for six . . .'

Yes, that was roughly the score, Caradoc told himself ten minutes later when he was once again alone in his cabin. But *only* roughly . . . A fine damned fool he was going to look if he sailed into that nameless inlet with a fou-fou band going at full blast merely for the delectation of the local seagulls . . .

Yet, intuition told him that the inlet would *not* be empty. In his own mind, he was quite sure that the enemy was using it as a temporary base. But in what strength? Caradoc shook his head: *that* was anyone's guess . . .

He moved across to his desk and re-examined Souris's chart. If *Bryony* could get as far as those narrows unchallenged, then surprise would be on their side. After this, in waters as constricting as a goldfish bowl, the range would be nil, and any shooting that would be done would be over open sights. Even as *Bryony* broke through the narrows, she would have to begin turning to get out again. With her over-long jib-boom, the schooner would only have three or four times her own length in which to manoeuvre. Please God, he didn't run her slap into that cliff-face, or wipe her screw off on an outlying tongue of rock.

For a few moments an alien pessimism settled on Caradoc, until through the open skylight above his head, he heard an experimental plinketty-plonk from Ferris's banjo. Scouse Duffy's squeeze-box and Yeo's mouth-organ tentatively joined it. The music made by the trio was nervous and unsure. But then, a far from uncertain voice—Earnshaw's—called for silence, snapped a few pointed directions, and then with a brisk 'a-one, a-two, three, fower!' set *Deutschland Uber Alles* going again. This time, banjo, squeeze-box and harmonica were joined by a new sound—the high, sweet, belling tone of a cornet played by someone who obviously knew what he was about.

Caradoc listened. Led by Earnshaw's cornet, the quartet was now making a very fair fist of things. The sound must be carrying for miles in the hot night air. It would be too ironic for words, Caradoc told himself, if some prowling destroyer of the Aegean Squadron were to hear the quartet and heave a couple of four-inch bricks in *Bryony*'s direction . . .

Up on deck, and while the quartet practised, Souris and Wells set about eliminating those remaining differences distinguishing *Bryony* from the schooner she had destroyed. The enemy had made a thorough job of his disguise, so that *Bryony*'s task was now largely one of paintwork—the suppression of the exquisitely gilded gingerbread work at her bow, and the blacking out of her varnished rail.

Below decks, a small party led by Hughes Pom-Pom, worked with sailmaker's needle and palm to sew an oddly-shaped patch of darker canvas into *Bryony*'s forestaysail. Shaped like a large letter H, this had been conspicuous the day they had chased the *Iskaria* off Cape Kolomvos, and it occurred to Souris, that such a patch might well have been let into the enemy's sail as an instant recognition signal. The first-lieutenant mentioned this to Caradoc when he came on deck, and Caradoc was quick to agree.

'You could well be right, Number One. That patch *was*

noticeable—but not too obviously so, if you know what I mean. I've been doing a bit of thinking, too. That line of cliffs to the north as we go in . . . If *I* were running things there, then I'd have a look-out on those cliffs twenty-four hours of the day . . .'

'So should I, sir . . .'

'Hmm . . . If there is one, we'll have to foozle the blighter somehow. Send Earnshaw to me when he's finished frightening the fishes, will you?'

'Aye, aye, sir . . .'

Mr Pembury heard Caradoc's voice in the darkness and went on dabbing at his section of rail with an unthinking brush. For once, the apparent calmness in his captain's voice failed to give Pembury confidence and he was afraid.

It was odd, he thought, but when he had won his D.S.C. at Gallipoli, fear had failed to touch him. Ignorant of what the landings would be like, he had merely been a little nervy in the hours before—but no more so than before a particularly important race in his father's yacht, *Moonshine*. His only *real* apprehension had been that of making a spectacular ass of himself—the sort of thing that, in deference to his father's brewing interests, had earned him the nickname 'Bottled-Stout' at Dartmouth.

But he *hadn't* made an ass of himself in those blood-dyed shallows of Cape Helles. Nor had he been the least afraid, even when the Turkish machine-gun bullets had begun pecking at his boat and two of the sailors with him had been killed. Afterwards, and in the Navy's understated way, he had even been led to believe he had done tolerably well.

But this hard-won beginning of self-assurance had been whittled away from him in *Devastation*—thanks to the unremitting efforts of Sub-Lieutenant Rixon. In *Bryony*, that confidence had begun to return. But the plant was still a very tender one. Besides, Pembury told himself, since Cape Helles, he now knew what to expect . . .

As he half-heartedly daubed at the unseen rail beside him, fear knotted itself into a tight little lump beneath his ribs. And, with this fear, came the increasing certainty that in the morning, he would be killed. The knowledge shaped itself with a bleak inevitability. Pembury shivered. He had heard of people having such premonitions. They were seldom wrong . . .

Suddenly, to his complete surprise, Pembury felt much better. If he was as good as dead already, then why worry about it? The tight little lump beneath his ribs dissolved, leaving Pembury blissfully relaxed. Petty Officer Wells materialised out of the darkness beside him:

'Come on, Mr Pembury, sir—smack it about there!'

'Right-ho, Wells!' Pembury was able to answer with a cheerfulness that surprised himself.

But, thank God for the darkness, he thought as the petty officer disappeared again. No one had witnessed his craven moments of weakness and self-doubt . . .

*   *   *

At midnight, Caradoc brought *Bryony* about on a north-easterly course and heading back in the direction of Santorini. It was his aim to lie off Neo Kaimeni for the remainder of the night, and wait till he judged the light just good enough to enter that inlet.

Earlier, when the quartet had finished practising, Souris had sent Earnshaw below to Caradoc's cabin. Caradoc had wasted no time, but had come straight to the point: 'How good a signalman are you, Earnshaw?'

'Ah'm nowt t'write home about, sir . . . Ah'm middlin' wi' t'little hand-lamp though . . .'

Caradoc nodded: 'Good. Now look, Earnshaw, when we get into that inlet, it's likely we'll be challenged. The codes and challenges I've been given were only ever provisional, so we'll have to play things by ear. As far as I can make out, our correct reply to a challenge *ought* to be the one word *Kalliste*. Have you got that?'

'*Kalliste* . . . Aye, sir . . .'

'But I could well be wrong . . . In which case, ask for a repeat. Do it slowly—fluff it—take up as much time as you can. If there's still *trouble*, I want you to slam this out as fast as possible—' Caradoc handed Earnshaw a slip of paper, and watched as with lips moving, the Yorkshireman deciphered his flamboyant handwriting.

159

'Ee! What's *this*, sir?'

'"Mary had a little lamb"—in German . . .'

'Tha-at should confuse t'booger . . .'

'*Then*, if there's still doubt, just add *Hau Ab*?'

'How-what? Sir?'

'*Hau Ab* . . . In German, it's about as polite as what you invited Duffy to do to himself when he played a few wrong notes earlier . . .'

A wide, embarrassed grin split Earnshaw's face: 'Ah gets thee, sir . . .'

As Earnshaw turned to leave the cabin, Caradoc asked: 'By the by, Earnshaw—where did you learn to play the cornet like that?'

The seaman looked warily up at the open skylight above his head and whispered: 'Ah were in't Sally Bash as a little lad, sir . . .'

Caradoc gaped at Earnshaw's retreating back in astonishment.

Earnshaw, foul of mouth and dealing with a bottle of *raki* as though it were lemonade was one thing.

Earnshaw in a red jersey emblazoned with the words 'Blood and Fire' defied belief . . .

*　　*　　*

An hour before dawn, found *Bryony* lying hove-to, three miles north of the inlet, with the southward set of the current gently pulling her back. Disguised now, with its newly-sewn H of greying canvas, the forestaysail was dragged up on deck and reset.

Caradoc flashed a torch at his watch, rapidly went over his calculations of distance, speed and the coming light one last time, then made his decision.

'Right! Let's bring her round, Number One!'

For'ard, the clew of the forestaysail was hauled out to starboard, and, under the gentle pressure exerted on it by the wind, *Bryony*'s head slowly payed off to port until she was pointing southwards again with her canvas filling, and Wells feeling her come alive again under his hands as she regained steerage way and answered the bite of her rudder.

The pre-dawn darkness seemed to solidify, pressing down on eyes that were already short of sleep. Even though Caradoc was looking for it, the dawn—as ever—took him by surprise. Starlight or not, surely five seconds ago he hadn't been able to see Souris standing a yard or so away? Slowly and reluctantly, the light crept back into the world.

Away to port, and exactly where dead reckoning had said it should be, a hump of tenebrous blackness against the brightening eastern sky, lay the low hummock of Neo Kaimeni.

Caradoc allowed himself a brief moment of self-congratulation. So, he'd got his sums right, had he? Well ... nearly all of them. The critical one was still in the balance. Just how far were they now from the mouth of that bloody inlet—and just how strong would the light be by the time they reached it?

But, even as he asked himself this question, Souris spoke: 'There's that little cape sticking out, sir—*and* the spur of cliff above it ...'

Caradoc relaxed: 'The old girl must be moving on rails, Number One ...'

The schooner moved on until the mouth of the inlet was abeam. Surprisingly, there was no obscuring cloud of smoke.

Caradoc turned to Wells: 'Steer south-east, Wells ...'

'Sou'-east it is, sir ...'

There was an urgent flurry of activity round the sheets, and the great boom rolled across in a controlled, majestic gybe. Tension became a tangible *frisson* in the air.

This was it ...

Caradoc looked about him. For a few moments more at least, the dawn light gave one the feeling of being imprisoned with a pearl. It would be a minute or two yet before colour and confusion came back into the day.

Grey and grainy as something seen in a film, the sea parted round *Bryony*'s flanks. Three cables—two—and then there was that steep bluff of the inlet's protecting cliff

161

rising up to port—crumbling, grey and primordial-looking. Caradoc stared at it through his binoculars. Neo Kaimeni had a lunar look; an alien and inimical deadness.

Mustering his little band on the hatch-covers, Earnshaw glanced briefly shorewards:

'Eh! You looks about as welcomin' as Old Trafford on a wet Bank Holiday . . .'

In the dim light, Caradoc noted that the quartet—now surprisingly joined by Mr Pembury with mess-fanny and a pair of wooden spoons as drumsticks—were wearing pusser's flannels and their service caps; caps from which every last trace of stiffening had been beaten, and decorated with the hanging black ribbons of the German Navy. Caradoc grinned his approval. Earnshaw had imagination; a touch of the impresario . . .

But now, the southern entrance of the inlet was abeam to starboard; a hummocked dune of grey scoria. Caradoc looked along *Bryony*'s still shadowy deck. It was still a surprise to him how, in a ship as small as *Bryony*, so few formal orders ever needed to be given. Just before dawn, the crews of three-pounder and pom-pom had closed up round their hidden weapons without a word from either Souris or himself. Snub-nosed Lee-Enfields had been strategically placed round the deck, and a tripoded Lewis gun set up, discreetly shrouded for the moment beneath a length of old canvas.

A *Lewis*? Caradoc suddenly thought. Now where the devil—and when—had they managed to acquire *that*?

But there was no time left for such questions now. Already, the inlet was beginning to narrow, and *Bryony*'s progress was perceptibly slowing as she came into the lee of those looming grey cliffs.

Caradoc searched every crevice of these through his binoculars. Somewhere up there *must* be a look-out—a look-out who any moment would flash his challenge . . .

*   *   *

Perched on a ledge right in Caradoc's line of vision, yet for the moment unseen, Matrose Ernst Doppel was a grey, disgruntled man. He was disgruntled because Metz, his

162

relief, was all of a long quarter of an hour adrift. He was grey, because sweating through the hot, Aegean night, he had gradually become coated with layer on unpleasant, irritating layer of grey volcanic dust. So thick was this coating that, perfectly camouflaged against his surroundings in the oyster light of dawn, Doppel had become indistinguishable from the cliff-face on which he was perched.

He *felt* indistinguishable from it too. A stupid man at the best of times, Doppel now had room in his head for only two things; his anger at Metz and the refreshing swim he would take after his long walk back to camp along the cliff-face.

With his mind thus occupied, Doppel almost failed to see *Bryony* until she was right below him. His eye automatically took in the H of darkened canvas on her forestaysail, and it never so much as crossed Doppel's mind that the slowly moving schooner below him was not the *Iskaria*. Doppel groped in the dust for his signal-lamp. He'd better hurry with his challenge. *Iskaria*'s captain, Bulow, Leutnänt was a notoriously taut officer at the best of times.

A right bastard . . .

*   *   *

The blink of Doppel's signal-lamp sent a stir of movement round *Bryony*'s deck. So: they weren't here on a fool's errand after all . . .

'It's a challenge, ah think, sir . . .'

'Make the reply . . .'

'Aye, aye, sir . . .'

The shutter of Earnshaw's lamp chattered as he made the word *Kalliste*. There was a moment's pause, and then the lamp on the cliff-side winked again.

Out of the side of his mouth, Earnshaw muttered: 'Trooble, sir . . .'

'What's that signalman like?'

'Lousy . . .'

'Blind him with science then . . .'

'Reet, sir . . .'

Suddenly Earnshaw found he was enjoying himself: he could clearly sense the growing indecision and confusion in the man opposite him. The blink of his signal-lamp took on a stuttering, uncertain quality. Earnshaw gave him 'Mary had a little lamb' at breakneck speed. Doubt seemed to hang like a palpable cloud over the cliff-face opposite—and then, slowly, falteringly came the request for a repetition of the signal.

Earnshaw produced his Ace of Trumps: '*Hau Ab!*'

The doubtful cloud seethed with indignation; a fretful snicker of light was aimed in *Bryony*'s direction. Earnshaw turned to Caradoc: 'Did th-at mean what ah thowt it meant, sir?'

'Yes . . .'

Earnshaw glowered at the cliff-face: 'Cheeky booger!'

'It means we've passed muster anyway . . . Now! Band!'

Earnshaw laid down his signal-lamp and picked up his cornet: 'Mr Pembury, sir . . .'

Pembury's spoons rattled professionally on the mess-fanny; then he gave it the authentic thump! tump! tump! of a brass band's big drum—and cornet, squeeze-box, mouth-organ and cornet burst into tune: '*Deutschland, Deutschland Uber Alles!*'

*   *   *

Up on the cliff-face, Matrose Doppel was almost in tears. He had been a fool to let *Iskaria*'s signalman rile him into making that stupid signal back. If Leutnänt Bulow had seen it—and the Leutnänt had the sort of eye that saw *everything*—there would be the devil to pay when he got back to camp . . . Why, oh why hadn't that idle fool Metz turned up on time . . . ?

Shaking with anger—and apprehension—Doppel laid down his signal-lamp next to his eyrie's only other piece of equipment—an unused field-telephone.

Metz chose that moment to turn up, cool—and, as yet—clean, and seemingly in no particular hurry. Metz took in *Iskaria*'s slowly receding shape—and Doppel's almost-tearful anger.

164

'Hallow, Ernst—what's biting you?'

'*Hau Ab*!' Doppel snarled and began making his way back along the cliff-face.

*   *   *

With his little band now happily thumping out *Deutschland Uber Alles*, Caradoc began barking orders in German—a German that had been adequate once in the days of his close friendship with Max Kirbschaus, but which was now sketchy in the extreme. He still had a few technical phrases at his command, and eked these out with frequent yelps of '*Raus! Raus!*' which was the nearest German equivalent he could recall to '*smack it about there*!'

Yet Caradoc's staccato bark was enough to convince the relief look-out, Metz. Complacently aware that he was beyond censure, Metz sketched an obscene gesture in the direction of *Iskaria*'s receding stern. That pusser so-and-so Bulow was in good voice this morning. Trust him to bring the schooner into the inlet under sail when she had a perfectly good Maybach diesel beneath her hatches. The way her canvas was beginning to shiver, it looked as though *Iskaria* might not have wind enough to negotiate the narrows. Metz looked down from his godlike perch with interest: it would be fun if Bulow made a mess of things. That Maybach was a tricky beggar to start . . .

Down on *Bryony*'s deck, Caradoc, too, was beginning to have his doubts about passing the narrows without recourse to the Thornycroft. What little wind was finding its way into the inlet was fluky and uncertain, and *Bryony* now barely had steerage way. Caradoc leant over the engine-room skylight: 'Start her up, McNab . . .'

A muffled shout answered him from below, and the clonk-clonk of the engine turning over—but no familiar tiger-purr as the Thornycroft growled into life. A reek of petrol filled the air.

'What the deuce is wrong down there?'

'She's flooded, sir—'

'Then damned-well unflood her . . .'

Bryony was still moving—just—the waters parting

165

reluctantly round her sharp bow, then sliding past her hull with barely a murmuration or a ripple to mark her progress. Only the smallest of stirrings in her canvas showed that there was still any life in the wind.

Caradoc nodded towards Souris: 'You know her better than I do, Number One . . .'

Minute adjustments were made to the sheets, but any improvement was compounded of imagination and hope. At *Bryony*'s wheel, Wells stood, legs a-straddle and on the balls of his feet as he tried to urge the schooner on by sheer will-power. With his hands loose on the spokes of the wheel, he could feel the life dying out of *Bryony* in a series of lessening tremors.

Yet *Bryony* still had way on her. The tormented line of cliffs slid reluctantly past, till there were only fifty yards separating the schooner from the closing teeth of the narrows. Slowly, almost imperceptibly, the two ugly little croppings of jumbled rock drew nearer. Another long minute—two—and *Bryony* was drifting between them.

'Steerage-way lost, sir!'

Even as Wells shouted—and so unexpectedly that Caradoc almost jumped—the Thornycroft burped uneasily into action. Its beat was uneven and uncertain at first. A fog of blue smoke burst from its exhaust. Then with the unevaporated petrol purged from its system, the engine throbbed out with its old familiar power.

'Quarter speed!'

Wells felt the schooner come alive under his hands again. It was a *different* sort of life to that she possessed under sail—but, for the moment at least, Wells was too preoccupied for such niceties. Others, more pressing, called for his consideration: the fact that there was precious little room to port, and the knowledge that with her right-handed screw set assymetrically through her quarter, *Bryony* was the very devil to turn in that direction at the best of times . . .

Wells breathed a sigh of relief as Caradoc pushed on as far as he could across the inner anchorage before ordering that necessary turn to port. With her long bowsprit almost hanging over the dunes of the inlet's eastern flank, the schooner turned slowly and reluctantly.

Up on the cliff-top three hundred yards behind, Metz almost hugged himself. So! That stiff-necked donkey, Bulow, had all-but piled *Iskaria* up, had he—band and all! Metz shook his head in amazement. A band! *And Deutschland Uber Alles* . . . There was nothing anyone could teach Leutnänt Bulow about *bullshit* . . .

Down on *Bryony*, Caradoc grinned at Wells: 'Just like the old days in *Harbinger*, eh, Wells?'

'We wouldn't have got away with *that* with her steerin', sir . . .'

'No-o . . .'

Caradoc turned to face for'ard again, just in time to see a great billow of dark cloud rise from the far end of the inlet. It lifted into the air for a hundred feet or so, and then subsided into a sluggishly drifting blanket that flattened itself across the island.

Caradoc sniffed. There was sulphur in that smoke all right, but other oilier and more chemical smells as well. The enemy obviously had smoke-making apparatus of some kind—apparatus which was switched off at night, presumably for his own comfort and to conserve fuel . . .

'Stop engine . . . slow astern . . . Rudder hard-a-starboard . . .'

Slowly *Bryony* gathered sternway, turning broadside on to the inner end of the anchorage.

'Stop engine . . .'

McNab let out the clutch and, idling, the Thornycroft rumbled softly to itself while *Bryony* lay motionless in the still water. With Souris beside him, Caradoc looked shorewards. It seemed absurd that no one had as yet twigged them. The shore lay no more than two hundred and fifty yards away, four separate inlets just as the old chart had told him, and each just big and deep enough to hold a couple of vessels the size of *Bryony*. One *did* hold a vessel—a stumpy, black-painted three-masted schooner.

'D'you know her, Number One?'

'She's another one of the Koritsases, sir . . . The *Manolis* . . .'

'Hmm . . .'

Seen through Caradoc's binoculars, the nearby shore-line seemed brought to within arm's length. There, unmistakably, was a naval base. Caradoc took in its details: the grey-brown tents pitched in tidy rows; the open-sided wooden hut that looked as though it was fitted out as a workshop; the separate dumps of oil-drums and other equipment, protected from the sun under swags of sagging canvas.

It all looked so peaceful and innocuous. Men went about their duties only bothering to spare *Bryony* the briefest of glances; a fat sailor shared a forbidden cigarette with a gangling friend; the off-duty part of the watch, near-naked and brown of body, wandered up from the beach, and its morning ablutions, easy and relaxed.

Caradoc felt an unwelcome stirring of compunction. He was about to tear this pacific scene in shreds. In the next few moments, those naked, relaxed bodies would be riven by bullets and splinters of shrieking steel...

And so might his *own* be if that second schooner carried the same lethal cargo as *Iskaria*, he told himself.

Souris glanced round at his captain: 'At least there's no submarine, sir...'

Caradoc swept his binoculars round each of the four inlets in turn, unsure whether to feel disappointed or relieved:

'No...'

Compunction made him hollow with distaste for what he was about to do. He had achieved total surprise—yet, now, the necessity of using that surprise to *Bryony*'s advantage smacked of cold-blooded murder. For Christ's sake, get on with it, man! Caradoc urged himself. Any minute now someone on shore must look towards *Bryony* and wake up to the fact that she was not what she seemed.

The first rays of the sun decided him. Five more minutes, and the undershot brilliance of the coming day would spotlight *Bryony* while dazzling her own gunners. He must give the order to fire now, while the schooner's targets were sharply defined against the bank of oily smoke. As Caradoc took one last look shorewards, he saw an officer come out of his tent, turn towards them, then wave his hand in languid, unofficial greeting.

Caradoc hardened his heart: 'Stand by! Three-pounder—take that schooner! Hughes—concentrate on the shore targets! The Lewis, and those of you with rifles—'

But somehow, Caradoc found that he couldn't force himself to shape that part of his order into words. He jerked his head in the direction of the German Ensign flying above him.

'Right . . . Get that down . . . Colours!'

A twitch of the signal halyards broke out the White Ensign waiting hoisted above his head.

'*Shoot!*—'

The sides of the false deckhouse crashed down to reveal the gun beneath; the canvas screen was whipped from the pom-pom. The three-pounder barked flatly, and its shell reached the shore almost in the same instant, with an abrupt cut-off screech, ending in a muffled explosion and a grey gout of dust from the cliff-face above the three-masted schooner. From her decks, startled yet still-uncomprehending faces were turned in *Bryony*'s direction.

The second shell settled their doubts for them. It hit the schooner squarely amidships in a welter of flame and splintering timbers. A returning pang of his earlier compunction gnawed at Caradoc. A three-inch shell was capable of puncturing two inches of wrought iron at a hundred yards. What chance did that wretched schooner have at only double that range?

Having found their target, the three-pounder's crew wasted no time. Firing with a rapidity and an accuracy they had never been able to achieve in practice, shell after shell was hammered into the already stricken schooner.

The pom-pom, too, was in lethal form. With his usual accuracy, Hughes was finding his target with the precision of a cobbler banging tingles into the sole of a shoe. The rapid hammer of the pom-pom beat out with a monotonous and deadly rhythm, whilst Hughes urged on himself and his loading-number with a stream of unintelligible Welsh. The air was full of the reek of cordite smoke. Empty shell cases gleamed wickedly in the growing sunlight as they flew from pom-pom and three-pounder and clattered across the deck.

The open-sided hut that was the workshop, was methodically pulverised into oblivion. Its roof collapsed; the bed of a large lathe flew through the air, then went cartwheeling into the volcanic dunes behind. Two figures, barely recognisable as men, tottered from the wreckage of the hut and collapsed onto the ground.

Hughes Pom-Pom coolly shifted his aim to the first of those supply dumps under its improvised tentage. Oil-drums danced in elephantine fashion, then rolled slowly down the beach, their punctured sides whirling dark streams of oil as they went. A subdued 'Woooo-OOF!'—and a sheet of smoky flame rolled across the shoreline.

Caradoc looked round *Bryony*'s deck. Crouched by the schooner's rail, a dozen sailors were keeping up a persistent spatter of rifle fire. Caradoc noticed Ferris, Earnshaw, Duffy and Yeo amongst them. *Bryony*'s makeshift band was playing a very different tune now . . . Behind the Lewis, Michael Souris picked his targets along the shoreline, treating them to abrupt and devastating little bursts of fire.

Unwillingly, Caradoc let his eye take in the slaughter on the beach. Those peaceful, unhurried moving little groups of men were gone. Only huddled and motionless figures lying on the beach remained to show where these had been caught by the murderous suddenness of *Bryony*'s attack.

Beneath the outcrop of rock where they had been sharing their surreptitious cigarette, the fat sailor and his lanky mate lay side by side, their bodies twisted into a parody of restful abandonment. Caradoc felt sick . . .

The three-masted schooner was by now ablaze. Flames leapt from her hold and licked up her masts. Her topsides were punched with ugly, gaping holes through which showed the roaring fury of the holocaust within. Well, if the *Manolis* was carrying the same cargo as *Iskaria*, they would all know about it any second now, Caradoc told himself grimly.

Something like a spatter of hail swept across *Bryony*'s deck, kicking wicked little slivers of timber from its planking. Pembury went down, clutching a hand to his

170

chest, his white-shirt front one great blotch of blood. Duffy clapped a hand to his behind as though stung by a gigantic bee.

But the machine-gunner's part in the battle was short-lived. A sharp-eyed seaman had spotted the enemy's hiding-place, and with a 'There away!' was pointing to a ledge half-way up the cliff-side. Hughes swung the pom-pom through its arcs, found—lost—and then refound the spot amongst that grey tumble of scoria opposite, and began firing with all of his usual precision. The sharp-nosed little-rounds painted the distant bluff with sudden little puffs and blisterings of dust. A small avalanche of rock began to crumble away from the cliff-side. Looking like rag dolls that had been tipped from their box, a pair of miniscule figures tumbled from their perch with loosely flailing arms and legs. The parabellum itself was clearly visible for a moment or so before a last shell from the pom-pom hit it fair and square on the muzzle and turned it into scrap metal.

'Every one a coconut!'

A ragged cheer rose from *Bryony*'s deck— a cheer that Caradoc barely heard, for a new hazard presented itself a bare ten yards away.

'Rocks to starboard!'

Caradoc moved across to *Bryony*'s rail. Was he delirious or something? The rocks seemed to be tumbling over themselves in their anxiety to reach the schooner's side: and though she no longer had any way on her, or even appeared to be drifting, the ugly little lumps were getting closer every second. There was something uncanny and apparently outside all natural laws in the phenomenon. Caradoc watched the rocks in disbelief.

For'ard a voice called out: 'Christ! Them rocks is *floatin'*!'

The answer still didn't hit Caradoc. Then, he heard Souris's voice say quietly:

'That stuff's pummice . . .'

Rationality seemed to return to the world. Feeling foolish, Caradoc heard himself say: 'And bearing down on us? That means the wind has veered round then . . .'

As if in confirmation of this, the flat banks of smoke

ashore coiled round on themselves like dark, malignant snakes. Flattening out, the murk oozed across the face of the inlet, bringing with itself a pungent reek of burning oil and sulphur. With a hiss, audible even over the banging of the three-pounder and the malevolent yapping of the pom-pom, the shattered wreck of the three-masted schooner slid beneath the waters of the inlet.

Little was visible along the shoreline now, through the writhing veils of smoke. Intermittent tongues of flame stabbed through the darkness for brief moments before being quenched by fresh clouds of convulsive, stinking smoke. A Chinese-cracker popping behind this swirling screen suggested some new danger—but it was a danger more illusory than real; the creaking of a floorboard in a darkened room. The fires in those supply dumps so systematically shot to pieces by the pom-pom, had by now reached the enemy's ammunition. The crackling behind the smoke continued, punctuated by the thud and grumble of flames finding their way to heavier stuff. The dark womb of the smoke bank was pierced by darting streaks of light.

'Check! Check! Check!'

Caradoc called a halt, and unwillingly, the guns'-crews ceased firing. Unnoticed above their heads, the rising sun lost its brilliance, became a dull disc, then disappeared behind the rising smoke.

Awed at their handiwork, *Bryony*'s sailors stared towards the shoreline.

'Proper little November the Fifth, isn't it?'

But the danger from that ammunition exploding along the shoreline was becoming real now. Something splashed heavily into the water twenty or so yards astern of *Bryony*; a rain of smaller debris pattered across her decks and puckered the flat surface of the inlet.

Caradoc looked towards the beach without pleasure and without triumph. He had been given a job to do, and so far as he could see, had done it. If this last five minutes had put paid to the mystery that had been code-named *Plan Atlantis*, then—and whatever his prospective courtmartial might find to the contrary—he could regard his disobedience of orders as having been worthwhile. His work was over now; finished. All that remained now, were the reports, the inevitable post-mortems, the disapproval and the censure.

For the moment, at least, all that was left for him to do now was to get *Bryony* safely out of this hellish little inlet before the changing wind brought down those swirling banks of smoke to blot out invisibility altogether.

'Slow astern . . .'

The Thornycroft's subdued note changed and became its familiar growl again as McNab increased revolutions and re-engaged the clutch. The screw sent a sudden flurry of water chasing for'ard along *Bryony's* sides and she gathered sternway.

'Hard a-starboard!'

With a shudder, the schooner obeyed her rudder, coming round till she was stern on to the carnage she had caused. Moment by moment now, the smoke was thickening—still pungent with burning oil, but now with that choking and mephitic sulphur-stench its predominant ingredient. Breathing was becoming difficult now; men were coughing, drawing down lungfuls of the yellow filth that now served for air, and then choking as the blast furnace exhalation rasped and tore at the lining of throat and lung.

The explosions along the shoreline had a deeper, more sinister note now; an inward growl as though dragged up from the bowels of Neo Kaimeni itself—the throbbing growls of some primordial beast disturbed and angered out of its long, uneasy hibernation.

In those few places along the shoreline still unobscured by smoke, the rocks took on a hazy, uncertain look, as though the earth itself was subject to some profound inner tremulation. The island was like a glass, Caradoc found himself feverishly thinking—a glass poised waiting the titanic note that would shiver it to fragments . . .

The pungent reek of sulphur thickened; steam mingled with the smoke. Cutting through the mounting din, a low susurration began, like the sound of steam escaping from the safety-valves of a boiler that had been kept too long pent. The sound hissed across the inlet as though a line-squall was bearing down on *Bryony*. But there was no squall . . .

A glance round the schooner's deck showed Caradoc that everyone sensed that they were in the midst of something quite beyond normal experience: a something so profound in its potential terror that, for the moment at least, curiosity rather than fear paradoxically held the upper hand.

All Caradoc's instincts now were to get out of this damnable inlet, and get out fast, before it became a trap, a grave . . . The violence of the enemy was no longer to be feared. Something altogether more formidable threatened *Bryony* now—the violence of the untamed earth itself.

'Stop engine! Half-ahead! Wheel 'midships . . .'

Reassuringly, and with only the barest traces of anxiety in it, Wells' voice answered: 'Midships it is, sir . . .'

Unheard in the din about them, the Thornycroft pushed *Bryony* back towards the narrows.

High-pitched and disbelieving, Hughes's voice screamed a blasphemy, and his urgent finger stabbed in the direction of the little bay on their port beam. Faces were turned in that direction, staring in disbelief. Here, in a near-tideless sea, where what passed for a spring tide barely made the difference of a foot of water, the sea had drawn back down the steep beach for perhaps a dozen yards, leaving a weed-covered foreshore on which surprised fishes flapped and leapt.

And, where the inlet's lowered waters began again, the sea stirred within itself as if in echo of that tremulation they had earlier noticed along the shoreline. A thin, uneasy miasma hung above it, as though the inlet was a cauldron whose waters were about to boil—which, all Caradoc's instincts suddenly screamed at him, *was precisely what they were about to do* . . .

From behind the wheel, Wells suddenly shouted:

'Submarine to starboard!'

Though a bare fifty yards from *Bryony*, the U-boat was glimpsed only as a silhouette through the swirling smoke. Though small for her kind, the coastal minelayer looked gigantic in the enclosed waters of the inlet. There were grey figures on her conning-tower; others crouched round the gun below it. Confused shouts—a jag of flame—a crash, rip and howl—and something seared low across *Bryony*'s decks and exploded in the dunes beyond her.

Hughes was the only man on board with quick enough reflexes to respond. The Pom! Pom! Pom! of his gun echoed flatly in the enveloping fog like three abrupt and rhythmic full stops. A screech of torn metal and a cry of pain came thinly back from the submarine—and then it was swallowed up by the stinking vapour.

Caradoc concentrated on finding a way out between the closing jaws of the narrows. With the sea withdrawing like that, the gap between those two rugged little capes would be little more than thirty yards wide. A second shell howled at *Bryony* out of the murk—a shell which hitting the water flatly, skidded across the surface of the sea as though some devilish giant was playing ducks and drakes.

The little U-boat itself made a brief appearance out of the smoke-bank astern. Again Hughes engaged it with his pom-pom. Caradoc found himself staring almost straight down its muzzle as it fired. His ears seemed to implode with the pressure, and when Hughes ceased firing as the submarine again disappeared, Caradoc found himself stone deaf. A tingling silence engulfed him.

Wells too, it seemed, was in the same plight. He gaped vacantly as Caradoc shouted a change of course at him, cupped a significant hand to his ear, then angled his hand to show the course he intended taking. Caradoc nodded and mouthed:

'Get her out!'

Wells nodded his acquiescence, then grimaced; a look that said quite clearly:

'If there still is a way out . . .'

Trapped in silence, Caradoc experienced a moment of detached awe. The very earth now it seemed was blasting itself apart as though in contempt for the creatures its surface cooling had spawned. Look! It seemed to be saying: I can draw you, suffocate you, destroy you with the same insolent ease that *you* wipe out a troublesome ants' nest with a kettle of boiling water . . .

Schooner and submarine sighted each other again briefly—fired—and, this time, kept on firing even when the sulphurous pall had again swallowed them both. Yet, improbably, neither hit the other. At a range where a schoolboy with his catapult might have taken his tithe of damage, their shells screamed harmlessly wide to add to the crashing tumult of the eruption ashore. Blindly, the guns'-crews of both ships continued to hammer at each other. In their urgency to encompass the other's destruction, it was as though Englishman and German had become possessed by an unreasoning madness that ignored the greater danger threatening from the shore. What was happening, was frenzied, farcical—and yet not without a sort of bizarre magnificence. Wagner with the stops out; *Gotterdammerung* with a pair of knockabout comedians in its leading roles . . .

Caradoc's sense of detachment grew. For the moment, at least, he was an observer, an indifferent eye recording the disintegration of the world about him.

His left ear popped and cleared—and detachment vanished as sound returned to fill the silent vacuum within his head. A rumble along the line of the shore made him look back. The murk of fumes and vapour was briefly shredded away, revealing a sight that Caradoc had difficulty in believing he was really seeing. The beach itself seemed to be on the move, curling up and rolling onwards like a wave—a wave whose breaking crest was a wild surf of candescent magma.

Moving swiftly, this surging wave sucked into itself the few terrified figures that ran before it. A blast of heat fanned out across the water, searing most of the remaining oxygen from the atmosphere. Men retched and choked in the effort to get their breath. For'ard, first one man and then another collapsed on the deck, totally overcome by the sulphur-laden blast. The new black paint along *Bryony*'s rail bubbled up in cancerous-looking blisters. An increasing rain of hot grey ash fell on the schooner, covering her decks like a sinister snow and scorching at exposed flesh.

A boat with frantically windmilling oars appeared out of

the fog and thumped into the schooner's side. A rifle cracked, and one of the men in the boat fell headlong into the sea, his body threshing for a few moments in the near-boiling water before disappearing.

Caradoc was appalled. Those sailors down there were no longer 'the enemy' but fellow creatures desperately seeking escape from a hideous death. Someone for'ard—Yeo—was evidently of the same opinion. A line was heaved down from *Bryony*'s side, and figures so grey that they might have been made of moving stone, tumbled over the rail. The line parted, and the boat fell away.

Briefly, the submarine again appeared astern. There were no men crouched round its gun now, and its topsides were so blistered and ash-covered that the vessel might have been a half-tide rock. Even as Caradoc watched, the U-boat blundered beam on across the surface of the inlet.

But, *Bryony* herself was in the very teeth of the inlet now—a strait which, as Caradoc had guessed, was little more than half the width it had been when they had entered. A submerged cropping of rock ground along the schooner's starboard side and grated under her chine. Caradoc waited for the ugly crash of metal that must come as the blades of her screw struck that unseen fang of rock. But no sound came, and he thanked God that when the Thorneycroft had been fitted, the dockyard shipwrights had been forced to place the propeller shaft through *Bryony*'s port quarter.

Beyond the narrows, the air was clearer, cooler. The smoke was still thick, but breathing was no longer an agony. Three hundred yards lay between the schooner and the open waters of the caldera. With an effort of will, Caradoc fought down the temptation to bellow for all the revs McNab could give her. Those remaining three hundred yards were themselves hazardous enough in all conscience.

It was as well Caradoc resisted the temptation. A gust of wind blotted out the surface in the inlet beneath a swirling cloud of sulphurous steam. Light-headed and tired beyond measure, Caradoc was momentarily disorientated.

But now, *Bryony* was out into the calder again. Blue

water glistened about them. The sun broke free of the overcast above them, shining with its usual intensity. Regardless of its sting on scorched and blistering faces, men peered up at it as though seeking reassurance in its familiar heat.

Caradoc looked aft. There was no sign of the enemy. Astern of *Bryony*, Neo Kaimeni was obscured beneath a shroud of mingled smoke and steam. Ahead, the long white ridge of Thirasia lay on the purple water. With his voice cracked and hollow, Caradoc called to Wells:

'Steer west-sou'-west . . .'

Wells, it seemed, had also regained some measure of hearing, though his voice was barely recognisable as he croaked in acknowledgement:

'West-sou'-west it is, sir . . .'

A shower of clinging grey ash fell from *Bryony*'s sails as their sheets were trimmed. Caradoc looked along the deck. Grey figures hobbled about their duties, their faces masks of the all-pervading greyness. It was impossible to recognise in either men or schooner the trim tautness that had existed only a short hour before. Only Hughes seemed to have any remaining spark left in him; the muzzle of his pom-pom still searched along the line of that receding smokebank.

Bryony heeled to the press of the north wind. With screw and sail working together, the schooner was headed towards the caldera's south-west entrance.

Two minutes . . . Three . . . And there was still no sign of that bloody U-boat . . .

A flat and triumphless sense of victory stole over Caradoc. One way or another, they had dished the blighter after all. The submarine must have been trapped in that inlet as its entrance had closed. Without compassion, he thought of the men trapped in the U-boat's hull. In the steaming waters of the inlet, they must have been broiled like fish in a kettle. A hideous death . . . But just at the moment, Caradoc found that he didn't care. There would be time for a return of finer feelings later . . .

Hughes's urgent voice cut across his abstraction:

'Oh, God!—*Get down sir*, please, isn't it!'

178

The pom-pom swung round and Caradoc found himself down in the grey dust on the deck. As he dropped, he caught a glimpse of the submarine emerging slowly from the smoke-pall, and turning southwards to creep along its rolling flank.

Caradoc swore. Evidently the U-boat captain, whoever he was, was endeavouring to escape through the narrow channel that lay between Palaia Kaimeni and Neo Kaimeni. With his mouth half-full of ash, Caradoc yelled at Wells, similarly crouched by the schooner's wheel. The petty-officer brought *Bryony*'s head round to the south, the pom-pom was swung away from its dangerous sternward line, and Caradoc stood as it resumed its emphatic stammer.

In the same instant, Souris's voice sang out warningly: 'She's by the lee, sir! . . .'

Caradoc was nonplussed—but not so others. The stone figures that had seemed so drained of strength or will a few moments before, came pounding aft through clouds of kicked up dust. Only then did Caradoc belatedly understand what was happening as the lee runner was set up, the main sheet hauled in, and *Bryony*'s fifty feet of main-boom rolled wildly across. The backstay parted with a crack that could be heard even above the thudding of the pom-pom.

'Je-sus!—' This, long-drawn and despairing from Wells—but no worse disaster followed. With the boom now safely out to starboard, *Bryony* was headed back towards the land and in pursuit of that U-boat slinking away to the safety represented by that narrow strait between the two volcanic islands.

Now, the three-pounder could again be brought to bear. Without wasting time, its crew siezed their opportunity and fired. Over—or so Caradoc could only assume. There was neither a splash nor the brief sparkle of a hit.

But now the pom-pom was silent, and with Hughes, desperately seeking to clear the jam. Sweat made dark runnels through the grey coating on his face; his high, clear voice let fly a stream of liquid, labial Welsh in which only a few words of English were oddly contrasted:

'*Pluddy* preach-plock! . . . *Pluddy* dust!'

The three-pounder barked out again. Another miss . . .

Caradoc watched through his binoculars as the enemy's gun was swung towards *Bryony*. About 50mm calibre he had guessed in the inlet, and probably as quickfiring as the pom-pom. For all of the three or four hits that Hughes had earlier inflicted on it, the U-boat now had the upper hand. The submarine fired, with a sound that eventually arrived across the water as a flat and unemphatic 'Blap-blap-blap . . .' Thirty yards ahead of *Bryony*, the *Bryony* was churned into three brief waterspouts.

With the pom-pom's stoppage now apparently cleared, Hughes fired again—but, as he did so, *Bryony* was hit for the first time. There was a crash under her bows. At the second shot, six feet of rail and bulwark dissolved into a shower of flying splinters; and the third shell, hitting the foremast above that so-painstaking achieved woolding, brought the great cedar spar crashing down over the side in a welter of canvas and cordage. The three-pounder was buried: beneath the heavy swathes of the foresail; men struggled to escape from the stifling folds of canvas.

'Axes!' Caradoc despaired. With the three-pounder buried, and the pom-pom once more jammed, there was nothing now to stop that U-boat systematically knocking them to pieces. He struggled to keep a clear head.

'Stop engine! . . .'

The last thing they could afford now was to get one of those trailing rope-ends frapped round the propeller . . . Almost unnoticed, another shell smashed into *Bryony* between wind and water. Axes gleamed and fell in the sunlight. Another burst of fire—mercifully short this time—but sending fountains of water skittering across the deck.

Suddenly, above the plunk of axes and the thud of the U-boat's gun, there was a new sound—a ripping-calico and express train howl that ceased with an immense column of water raising itself fifty yards beyond *Bryony*'s bow. The column seemed to hang in the air for an age before collapsing inwards on itself and crashing back down into the sea in a widening circle of cordite-stained water.

With every eye in the schooner firmly fixed on the U-boat, no one so much as glanced towards the entrance of the caldera.

'*Ker-BANG-er!*' A second time came that tearing hurroosh of sound. Everyone on *Bryony*'s deck instinctively ducked. But the shell went over the schooner and splashed down ahead of the retreating enemy.

'We've got company, sir!'

Caradoc followed the line of Wells's pointing finger to where between Aspronisi and Cape Akrotiri came the vessel that had fired those warning shots.

Yes, Caradoc told himself, taking in the approaching ship's four tall, archaic funnels and the muzzles of her six-inch guns gaping in *Bryony*'s direction—they had company all right. A cruiser, and possibly the oldest still this side of a breaker's yard. But the meaning of those two shots had been unequivocal enough:

'Behave yourselves—or I'll blow you both out of the water . . .'

The only real question was the cruiser's identity. *Whose* was she? Not one of the belligerent powers, that seemed certain—not with those buff funnels and white-painted hull. Caradoc stared at her through his binoculars. The flutter of blue and white above her stern told their own story. The cruiser was Greek, and therefore neutral, but with her pride very obviously affronted by this violation of her territorial waters.

The cruiser's captain sought to re-emphasise the argument of his warning guns. Two flags broke out at the yardarm—triangulated red-and-yellow above chequered black-and-yellow.

OL: HEAVE TO, OR I WILL OPEN FIRE ON YOU.

With its promised escape hole now looming so near, the U-boat chose to ignore the signal, and crept on towards the difficult Palaia channel. Once again, the muzzle of one of the cruiser's guns belched flame and smoke, and there was that tearing convulsion as the shell ripped its way through the air. This time, the shot fell very close to the submarine, and a brief tower of water climbed high above it before crashing down to leave the U-boat bobbing like a child's toy in a bath.

The effect was immediate. The figures on the submarine's conning-tower and crouched round its gun, began waving urgently. A signal-lamp began blinking, and the waters churned past her side as the U-boat went astern. The cruiser seemed satisfied, for no further shots followed. Boats were lowered from her side, and handflags wig-wagged peremptorily from her bridge.

'*My boats are being sent to you. Captains to repair on board immediately.*'

Caradoc took off his cap and scrubbed at its filthy cover with an even grimier forearm. The coming interview would be embarrassing to say the least. Caught where they had been, neither he nor the U-boat's captain had a leg to stand on. Caradoc was sharply reminded of a time when, at prep school, he and another fellow had been caught scrapping right outside the door of the Head's study...

Caradoc turned to Souris who had just succeeded in getting the last of *Bryony*'s people out from underneath the foresail, wilted but otherwise undamaged.

'D'you know that cruiser, Michael?'

'Yes, sir. She's the *Karteria* ... Captain Giorgos Soteriades.' The first-lieutenant pulled a face: 'He's ... um ... a cousin of mine ...'

'He would be. What's he like?'

'Very *pusser*, sir ... I-er shouldn't trouble yourself giving him my compliments ...'

Pusser ... Yes, Caradoc could see that as he watched the cruiser's approaching boats. The sailor's uniforms and the boat's paintwork were gleaming; the oars dipped and rose from the water in perfect unison. Mmmm ... Captain Soteriades was going to be a very sticky proposition indeed ...

The leading cutter went straight on towards the U-boat, and Caradoc, and he lifted his binoculars to his eyes as it rounded to against the submarine's side. Something very strange appeared to be happening ... All the U-boat's small crew were out on her casing—a dozen men, with the still figures of two more. Weighted bags, obviously holding the submarine's Confidential Books were flung into the sea, and then the two injured men were gently passed

182

down into the waiting boat. With an increasing urgency, the other dozen scrambled down after them.

What the devil? . . . Caradoc only began to understand at last as the U-boat's stern sank slowly beneath the surface. Its bows were cocked high for a moment, showing streaked and rusted undersides. There was a sign of vented air, and then, sliding down into the water stern-first, the submarine was gone, leaving the heavily-laden cutter rising and falling on the resultant popple of water.

As the second cutter came alongside *Bryony* and he dropped down into it, Caradoc found that he was now every bit as unrepentant as he'd been all those years ago while being led into the Head's study, and with his opponent's nose dripping all over the carpet. He grinned up at Souris and shook a triumphant fist: 'The bugger's scuttled himself, Michael! We've dished him! We've done him!'

But Caradoc's triumph was shortlived. Returning to its normal level, the sea rolled back in towards Neo Kaimeni, lifting the cutter high above *Bryony*'s rail for a moment. Caradoc found himself tipped from his thwart and headfirst down onto the boat's bottom-boards.

Unchecked, the wave rolled on into the hidden inlet with a hiss and a sigh, and a great column of white steam burst upwards over the grey moonscape of Neo Kaimeni.

*   *   *

Marvelling at the fact of his own survival, Pembury allowed Michael Souris to strap his chest. Although long and ugly-looking, the wound went little deeper than a scratch. Earnshaw shook the grey dust from his bullet-riven cornet: 'Eh! Look what t'boogers ha' done to ma fookin' troompet!' he said disconsolately.

Wells was inclined to be philosophical: 'Ah, well, Yorkie—the Jerries always was a musical people . . .'

Earnshaw glowered.

Part Seven

September 3rd 1916. A King Sat on a Rocky Brow . . .

Below the glittering wolf-fang of Lycabettos, its tree-clad lower slopes dropped away to mingle with the red and white jumble of Athens stretching towards the distant sparkle of Phaleron Bay, Piraeus and the empurpled shimmer of the Gulf of Athens.

Apart from the fact that he again had some decent tobacco in his pipe, there was much in the view to give Caradoc satisfaction. Strung across the sea from Piraeus and into the Gulf of Salamis, a long grey line of ships told him that he had done his job well. The grey line seemed potent and unchallengeable; and, though the white streaks of bow waves told of destroyers watchfully circling their powerful charges, the underwater threat posed by mine or torpedo had been eliminated.

The fact that these ships were here at all was a diplomatic triumph; a reassertion of Allied power and authority in these waters. What if Hershing *had* sunk *Theseus* and *Majestic*? What if the Allies *had* lost three battleships in a vain attempt to force the Dardanelles? Here was proof-positive that those losses had been a fleabite—propaganda victories, and nothing more—for the Central Powers. To unversed eyes watching those passing ships, their great steel bulwarks looked inviolable and indestructible.

All the same . . . Caradoc felt uneasy in the presence of the man sitting across the table from him. Urbane in Tussore-silk suit, Panama, and freshly pipe-clayed shoes, Mr Casserlly sat with his hands primly folded over the knob of a silver-mounted cane. Untouched on the table-top, and cloudy with water, were glasses of *ouzo*.

Caradoc lifted his glass and sipped at it. Despite the informality of the setting, he knew the next ten minutes would be every bit as sticky as that other interview—the one he had faced in the Captain's cabin on board that Greek cruiser. He looked back on that half-hour without pleasure.

184

Michael Souris's cousin had been every inch the captain, and quite without trace of the younger man's impudent humour. Yes: he had been a pusser so-and-so all right...

Now, with that unpleasant scene behind him, Caradoc braced himself to ride out another with Casserlly. He felt angry and rebellious. He had been set an impossible job—and, against all odds, had pulled it off.

Casserlly lit a cigarette, then said: 'You've set us a pretty problem, you know...'

'Have I?' Caradoc only kept the mutiny out of his tones by the greatest effort of will.

'Indeed you have. The Greeks ... um ... are very annoyed with you...'

'*And* with our German chums, too, I hope...'

'It's you we're concerned with now. You violated Greek waters: you were within an ace of touching off a major eruption on Santorini—and *both* were done after ignoring the signal recalling you to Malta...'

'I finished what I'd been sent to do...'

Surprisingly now, it was Casserlly's turn to look out of countenance: 'We thought you already had—hence the recall. The notion was never anything more than to let the enemy know that we were fully aware of what he was up to—and warn him off...'

'No one ever told me *that*, sir...'

'N-no, they didn't...'

'And, besides—the enemy *didn't* take the hint...'

'No...' Casserlly failed to meet Caradoc's eye as he went on: 'That aside, we're still left with the problem of what's to be done with you—'

'And with that U-boat commander, too, I hope. It *was* Kattschner himself you know!' Caradoc insisted.

Casserlly ignored this, and went on: 'After much diplomatic coming and going, it has been decided that *nothing will* be done...'

'Why?...'

Casserlly twitched embarrassedly at the knife-sharp crease in one trouser leg: 'Because *nothing* ever happened...'

Caradoc gaped at him in disbelief: '*Nothing*? D'you mean

there was *no* violation of neutral waters? *No* battle? *No* eruption? *No* sinking of those two schooners and that submarine?'

'*Nothing!*' Casserlly insisted: 'Besides: you didn't sink that submarine. She scuttled...'

'The *same* thing... We'd checkmated her... Kattschner was without fuel, supplies or mines—and his other submarine had already foundered off Cape Matapan. He admitted as much on the *Karteria*.'

'He admitted *nothing*. Neither of you was ever on board the *Karteria*...'

Caradoc sipped at his glass, and took a long look towards the Gulf of Athens and its line of distant warships.

'I wonder just what *might* have happened to those if I had obeyed that recall of yours, sir...'

Casserlly threw back his *ouzo* in one, uncharacteristic gulp: 'I shouldn't overrate your own efforts, Caradoc...' He stood and laid an envelope on the table: 'Diplomacy *does* have its uses, you know. This, for example. Read it when I've gone. It's good news, I promise you...'

Caradoc rose while Casserlly took his leave and sauntered off down the steep pathway, an immaculate white-clad figure, dappled with the striated shadow of the pines beneath which he trod.

When he was lost to sight, Caradoc sat down again. He ripped open the envelope and read and re-read the single sheet of typewritten flimsy that this contained:

BRITISH HOSPITALITY OVERWHELMING SO REPATRIATED SELF. AIDAN REPEAT AIDAN. PRISONER WOUNDED BUT RECOVERING. MAX.

It was several moments before the meaning of this got through to Caradoc. His hand trembled as he struck a match and tried to relight his pipe. Thank God Aidan was safe. Thank God he hadn't made a fool of himself with Barbara... In an Alice-in-Wonderland sort of a way, things hadn't turned out at all badly really... Those ships down there; Kattschner scotched; *Bryony* and all her people more or less in one piece—and now, Max safely back home again with his Lotte ...

It was all really the most tremendous luck: *the luck of the Nine Blind Bastards*—whoever they were ...

Limping slightly, Michael Souris joined him at the table: 'Is everything all right, sir ...'

Caradoc put another match to his pipe: 'I suppose you *could* say that, Michael. But no medals for anyone, I'm afraid ...'

'The whole thing never happened?'

'How the devil did you know that?'

'Because I've a Byzantine mind, too ... What do we do now, sir ...'

'Speaking for myself, I'm going to get rather drunk—slowly ...'

'May I join you, sir?'

'I wasn't proposing to do it on my own ...'

Two hours later, they watched the sun drop down over Piraeus. The shadows lying across the hillside beneath them were already deep and crepuscular. The Allied Fleet was invisible now, lost on the lake of burning gold that the Gulf of Athens had become.

'*Sas paracalo!*' Souris called, pointing out an empty bottle to a passing waiter.

Surely it must be imagination, Caradoc told himself; but from somewhere, impossibly far away beyond Piraeus, he thought he could hear the faint, sweet echo of a bugle sounding *Sunset* ...